Elizabeth's Refuge

Timothy Underwood

ACKNOWLEDGMENTS

As always I want to thank my beta readers,. Betty Jo, mandieschwaderer and Brooke Till looked at the book and DJ Hendrickson did the copy edit. I also want to thank my wife, who always supports me and encourages me to celebrate my successes.

Chapter One

The delicate blue and white decorative Chinese vase splintered into shards as Elizabeth Bennet smashed it over Lord Lachglass's head.

He collapsed to the ground, like a dropped sack of manure.

Elizabeth panted desperately as she stared him. Her heart raced with pain and fear.

What now?

Half a minute earlier, when Elizabeth's employer, the Earl of Lachglass, hurled her through the ornate doorway into his bedroom, the terror she'd felt dissolved as she stumbled painfully into the heavy oak of his bed frame.

Her sudden calmness had surprised Elizabeth greatly.

She would fight, she determined. She would fight, whether she lost or won. She would fight whether he killed her or not, and she would fight whether he succeeded in his aim or not. She would fight Lachglass with everything in her being.

Elizabeth had only been in the employ of Lord Lachglass for three months. He was a handsome man of an average height and age, with a modest paunch and cruel thick lips.

Her meetings with him had been infrequent. He had only once sat with them for a quarter of an hour to observe how his daughter's studies progressed with her. Lord Lachglass was a widower with one unwanted and generally uncared for daughter. This daughter was an unpleasant and spoiled child, and mostly unremarkable.

After Papa's death, Elizabeth had lived as a dependent on her uncle Mr. Gardiner's generosity, until reverses suffered during the economic crisis following the most recent peace with the French obliged her uncle to dismiss half the servants and take lodgers at his own house. It became preferable that the number of gentlewomen dependents upon his now slender income be reduced as far as possible.

Had the Earl interviewed her in person for the position as governess, rather than his kindly and ineffectual old housekeeper, Elizabeth would have known to refuse the offer of employment immediately, good as the wages were.

Mr. Blight, Lord Lachglass's man of business, had sat in the room with Mrs. Peterson. His manners should have provided warning enough to Elizabeth of what sort of a house she was agreeing to enter.

Mr. Blight was a thin, short man with a wicked scar across his cheek that he claimed had been received in service in a war, leering eyes that watched her uncomfortably close, and a greasy goatee he stroked endlessly.

During the course of the interview Mr. Blight had not spoken once. But his eyes. It surprised Elizabeth not at all to learn all of the servants lived in terror of him.

After he had thrown her into the room, Lord Lachglass followed Elizabeth into his bedroom on softly stalking shoes that made barely a sound on the thick fur rugs. Wildly, a phrase from *Macbeth* crossed Elizabeth's mind, "With Tarquin's ravishing strides, towards his design he moves like a ghost."

Lord Lachglass laughed as he shut the door behind him. "I've waited for this," he said with a leering smirk on his sensual lips, spreading his arms out wide so he might grab her if she ran towards the door. "At last, just us, Miss Bennet."

The way he used her name made Elizabeth's skin crawl, as if his voice slimed "Bennet" with rot.

No point in screaming. When Elizabeth returned from her half day holiday, she found all the other servants gone from the house, and soon as she entered, Mr. Blight grabbed her arm, pulled her up the stairs, and explained the master wished a special interview with her.

She had been brought up to the sitting room between the master's suite and the empty mistress's suite, and Mr. Blight stepped out of the room as soon as she entered it. Behind her she heard the click of the door locking.

The room felt too warm, stuffy, and hazy, as though it were filled with smoke from the fire.

Lord Lachglass demanded she disrobe, and slapped her when she refused and attempted to leave, despite knowing it was pointless to leave the room by the door.

Elizabeth's heart raced thumpingly in her chest as Lord Lachglass stepped towards her in the bedroom. Her heart beat so fast it nearly exploded with each pattering painful beat. The hair on the back of her arms and neck stood straight. She trembled. Part of her wanted to freeze and let the Earl do whatever he wished to her body, while she stared at the wall or ceiling silently begging the world for it to be over.

But there was a voice in her mind.

It was the voice of Elizabeth's best self. It combined the sound of Jane's voice, her long dead father's voice, and the voice of her uncle, Mr. Gardiner. This voice told her to pretend to be helpless and entirely under control of the fear, and to be ready to strike like a cobra when the moment came.

As a child many years before, Elizabeth pestered a professional pugilist who gave lessons on the noble art of bare fisticuffs to the interested gentlemen of the neighborhood to teach her something as well.

The muscled pugilist refused at first, and in the end he did refuse to teach her how to *properly* box. Instead he at last observed that even though she was a gentlewoman, gentlemen sometimes didn't notice such things when they decided to become handsy, and it was best she know how to crush a man's unmentionables and knock him silly, just like he'd taught both his nieces.

Elizabeth had since never thought upon those lessons more than once or twice with a laugh.

She had always deep down seen herself, despite the death of her father and her precipitous decline in consequence over the past five years, as a fortunate creature who could expect matters in life to turn out generally for the best if she put forward a fair effort and waited patiently for her work to bear some fruit.

Really bad things, such as being the victim of a serious attempt by a titled gentleman to ravish and rape his governess, occurred mostly in novels and the fictive stories worried women passed amongst themselves.

She had always seen the chance of such a thing happening to her in actual, vivid life as a matter so remote as to not be worth worrying about.

The moment was surreal, almost dreamlike. This unreality allowed Elizabeth, despite the grip of adrenaline and the sweat gathering in her armpits, to wait patiently to strike the earl at the first moment she thought his guard was let down.

Movements that had been practiced to perfection for a few days with that pugilist flickered half remembered through her brain.

The earl laughed as he shut the door behind him. His piercing, handsome, evil blue eyes looked through her. The sneer was one of command.

He'd already slapped a purpling bruise onto her face. But Elizabeth could not feel any pain.

Elizabeth pulled her elbows tighter against herself, in a way that made her feel helpless. She trembled, and made a pretense of looking every direction. The fireplace was next across from the bed, with red embers glowing. Iron poker and scoop. A Chinese style vase with delicate blue veins and accents sat on the marble ledge above the fire, glowing in thin light through the windows. There was a vivid painting of a naked woman with impossibly large breasts sitting atop the waist of an unrobed gentleman, her eyes rolled back in ecstasy as he grabbed her hips.

Her mouth was dry.

Silk hangings surrounded the bed, with its dense pillowed red silk coverlets.

An absent part of Elizabeth's brain thought this was all very cliché for a rake's den.

Lachglass leered at her, smiling softly, making his thick lips thicker, and his paunch a bit more prominent. He stepped forward to grab her arms. He squeezed them so tight they hurt. In the moment that he grabbed her, Elizabeth realized she could not drive her knee into his crotch. The angle was wrong, and he was seemingly tensed and ready for her to do that.

The head.

The pugilist's voice snapped through her mind, in what was a long speech that seemed to take just an instant for her to relive. She felt again the warm summer breeze on her face, the scent of freshly mown hay, the callused hands of the pugilist, the coltish feel of her long legs and arms that the rest of her body had not grown into. The slow speaking voice of the pugilist, as he paused with every few words to make sure she had heard, and the way he repeated himself.

"The head. That skull bone. Thick it is." He had made her nod. "The skull is thick. You can bang a fellow up neatly if you hit a soft spot with it. The skull. There is power in the neck. Crack it forward, and you can break a man's nose, or jaw. Just don't hit him on *his* skull. 'Cause it's hard, the skull is. Hit them with your hard parts on their squishy parts."

Lachglass laughingly pulled her towards him, planning to force his gross mouth against her.

Crack.

A loud crack, and a soft crumpling sound as the nose collapsed.

Elizabeth's eyes swam as the top of her head cracked against the earl's face. He released her arms with an inarticulate moan of pain.

Now grabbing his shoulders for leverage, Elizabeth kneed his groin.

He *oof*ed again, his eyes went wide in pain and then started to water as blood flowed freely from his nose.

Elizabeth stepped back away from the earl. Her eyes flickered to the door.

With an inarticulate grunt, Lachglass snarled at her, and unevenly spread one arm to catch her if she ran past him, as he continued to grotesquely grip his wounded groin with the other.

Her heart pounded. The outside door was still locked. She could run past him.

Elizabeth turned towards the mantelpiece, but because she was frightened in that instant that it would take too long to grab and draw the poker from out of the iron holding rack, she grabbed the out-of-placedly pretty vase from the mantelpiece with one hand. It was heavier than the delicate blue tracery made it look.

Lord Lachglass stumbled towards her.

Driven by all her terror and all her determination to not lose to this horrible creature, she brought it down on his head.

Amidst shards of shattered fine china, Lachglass dropped like a sack of manure.

Elizabeth's eyes swam. She could not see anything. She panted hard. He wasn't moving. She was dizzy.

Not moving at all.

What now?

A new fear took her, and Elizabeth knelt down to the earl's body. She couldn't see him breathing. There was no sound of air moving in and out, his chest was still.

Elizabeth tremblingly moved her hand to hold over his still mouth, to feel if there was any breath.

A hard knock on the bedroom door startled her up.

"Milord, Milord, are you well?" Mr. Blight's nasal voice called out.

Lachglass's still and silent body made no reply.

They'd hang her for this.

And Elizabeth had no liking for the notion of being hung.

She had to escape. Now. The apartment suite door must be unlocked again if Mr. Blight was at the bedroom door.

Elizabeth silently stepped on the balls of her feet next to the door. Mr. Blight cautiously opened the door, saying, "Milord, apologies, sir," again as he did so. And as the gentleman's gentleman blinked at the earl's still body, Elizabeth struck him in the jaw, just below an ugly scar on his face, with a hurled elbow, the force in it gained by twisting her body as hard and fast as she could. She'd kept her palm open, as taught, so that the bones in her arm pounded into him. The sharp point of the elbow gashed open his skin.

The pugilist had told her that if she was ever in any serious danger, she must hit far harder than she even thought she could. She could not leave any shred of muscle power unused if she wished to protect herself. And he'd taught her that the elbow was a vastly better weapon than her soft and easily breakable hands.

Elizabeth ran past Mr. Blight, not giving him a chance to recover, and she didn't want to attack him with another weapon and kill a second man. The door was open, as she'd hoped, and she ran through it, and stumbling, hurled herself down the stairs.

She tripped at the bottom and fell down the last four steps, but though she thought her foot should have been twisted from the fall, she peculiarly felt no pain.

And then she was up, to the main door. Thrown open. The world seemed to appear in moments caught in portraiture or pencil sketches rather than as a smooth reality.

She ran.

The earl's house was on a fashionable square, with an oval gated park in the middle surrounded by quiet cobblestoned streets shaded by tall elms and oaks. The buildings were made of a handsome grey and brown stone. The day had a grey sleety February sky. Elizabeth did not pause as she dashed out the house and down the staircase to the building's entrance. She took the first street that turned away from the garden in the middle of the square.

Elizabeth ran.

Mr. Blight would recover, and come after her with anger and blood.

And she ran from the dead sack of manure of a body she'd left behind in the room. Elizabeth took another turn, at random, except she was confident this alleyway kept her running *away* from the house. Then yet another turn. She barely had a sense of where she was.

Without meaning to she hit a major road. Bond Street, emptier than in summer, but still full of carriages, and fashionable ladies and gentlemen strolling up and down and stopping in the expensive shops.

Tall white plastered buildings, and handsome red brick façades on either side.

She must appear so strange. The people she saw from the corners of her eyes stared at her. She full of fright ran across the road, without properly looking to both sides, or waiting.

A careening carriage carrying two ladies gripping their ostrich feather hats tightly to keep them from flying away, and a laughing gentleman in a beaver hat missed her by bare inches. The extra thrill of coming close to death only made her run faster once more.

Elizabeth had always been athletic, and she liked to run when she was in a park and not observed, but it had been years since she had run very much. In the cold air her lungs ached. They felt like they would collapse. They hurt so much, but she was still terrified, and she needed to get as far from the house as possible. As far away. Just get away.

Her legs were rubbery and they wanted to give up with every hurtling step.

She ran.

She ran down a thin street lined on both sides with handsome buildings, and reached Grosvenor square, with its tall palatial buildings and townhouses, and the large garden square with many benches. She ran past the fronts of the expensive houses, a blue streak conscious of the curious who may be observing her. Her footsteps were strangely soft for how fast she ran, as she was wearing house slippers instead of proper boots.

Out of the square.

Her chest ached hideously with each and every gasping difficult breath.

Elizabeth's brain still dwelled on the sensation as the vase cracked over his head, splintering and leaving the top in her hands, pieces turning around in her palms and nearly cutting her. The thud of his body hitting the ground. Blood from his crumpled nose and head. So much blood.

Elizabeth burst into a giant park.

Gravel pathways and tree-lined boulevards were almost empty due to the cold of the day. A thin frozen drizzle wisped from the skies. In shady spots under grey, denuded trees patches of snow remained from a snowfall a week before. The cold sweat stuck to Elizabeth's body and dress.

Despite its dourness, nature, even nature trimmed to its best effect, was to Elizabeth an old, comforting friend.

Gasping breaths.

Elizabeth collapsed onto a wrought iron bench hidden by two trees overlooking the Serpentine lake in the middle of Hyde Park, where royal swans swam, and where in December the pregnant wife of Byron's atheist friend Percy Shelley, abandoned by her new lover, had thrown herself in the lake and been found water logged and very dead the next day.

Her lungs ached.

Her fingers tingled. Her legs shook and screamed with pain. The twisted foot, after supporting her for the entire run, ached deep inside.

Elizabeth was cold.

Drizzles of rain mixed with ice and the occasional flurry of snow attacked her. The frozen water melted instantly on the ground or her soaked through cotton dress.

The light crinkling sound of a breaking vase. The vase striking his head. Was that crack she now clearly remembered his head breaking, or the ceramic of the vase breaking?

The earl's mobile, lively, self-indulgent face. Still and bloody.

Elizabeth vomited, leaving acid and food on the brown winter ground. Her vomit steamed in the cold for a moment. Her throat burned. She looked around her sightlessly.

Still seeing the still earl. Still trying to know if she had killed him.

She probably had.

The pugilist master that had told her how easy it was to accidentally kill a man with a blow to the head.

She'd had no choice.

Her head was sore. Elizabeth touched for a moment the top of her unbonneted hair, and flinched her hand away. The top of her head felt bruised and sore where she had struck his face. This brought a smirk to her face for a moment. If her forehead hurt this much, he would hurt far more.

Except he couldn't.

Elizabeth forced herself to stand.

Cold grey sleety day. She had neither coat, nor gloves, nor boots. Her indoor slippers had been mutilated by her run. No purse, no reticule, no money, no anything that would do as a substitute. The day was not cold enough that she would freeze to death — perhaps not even after night fell — but she was miserably cold and shivering.

Elizabeth could barely stand. The injured foot twisted under her, and the other leg felt rubbery and shook under the weight of her body.

Elizabeth collapsed back onto the weathered wooden slats of the bench.

She closed her eyes, and tears started to prickle in her eyes. She should just sit here for a while.

Too cold to sit still; too hurt to move.

She would go numb and stiff if she stayed long. Bizarrely, given the weather, she and her dress had become soaked in sweat during her run, and she smelled like an untidy barn now.

The Gardiners. They were a long walk away, and she needed to start now.

A few overcoated walkers took advantage of the beauty of the park, giving her strange glances from across their sideburns.

Less than a mile to the south-east was St. James's Park, with the Queen's House in the old Buckingham House on one side of the park, and St. James's Palace on the other side. To the south of that were the houses of parliament, and to the east were the slums around Convent Garden, and past that the old city of London, with Gracechurch Street right in the center, a few hundred feet from the Thames and the old London Bridge.

She would walk there as fast as she could. Perhaps it was already too late, but she thought if she hurried to Gracechurch Street she would be able to get there before anyone raised a proper alarm and soldiers or Bow Street Runners were directed by the servants and Mr. Blight to wait for her at her aunt and uncle's house. She would be able to gain from them some ready cash, a coat, and some food before she had to figure out how to disappear from the chase that would seek to find and hang the murderer of an earl.

Elizabeth stood once again on her unsteady feet.

She would not be able to walk the entire distance this way, but a branch on one of the overhanging oaks was thin enough for her to snap off in the cold that made the branch brittle and dry.

Elizabeth hobbled to the tree, and gripped her chosen staff.

It was illegal she knew, to disturb the trees in a royal park, trespassing, a crime, a fine and perhaps a period of jail. The value of the tree branch was certainly far below the hanging sum.

She tried to pull the branch off the tree with a thin little laugh. Better to laugh. Assault, murder, and *wanton and premeditated destruction of a tree*. They'd have plenty of reason to punish her when they caught her.

The branch bent, but did not snap off.

The tree was still too healthy for a clean crack. Pulling it put pressure on her now swelling ankle, and the stab of pain made her close her eyes and breathe shallowly.

She needed this stick.

Elizabeth gripped the branch firmly, one hand next to where she'd already created a bend, and the other halfway down to the tapering, bare end.

She started twisting the branch around and around, though her ungloved hands squealed in pain at the rough grip on the bark.

Each time around more of the fiber holding the wood to the tree stretched and then snapped, and then the branch twisted around and around easily, with just a strand holding the tree together, and patiently, knowing that in such tasks a hurry always made things worse, Elizabeth twisted and twisted till it came free.

Elizabeth's hands were now scraped, though not bleeding, and they smelled of the tree's juices and sap.

The stick also was not a steady cane, it bent and shivered under her weight, but it was better than nothing. Elizabeth carefully hobbled towards the fashionable houses of the British monarchs, trying to not put too much weight either on her injured foot or on her makeshift cane.

One step after another. One after another.

When she reached the streets between the houses, she gratefully used her other arm to support herself on the gates and building walls as she stumbled forward. She faced a lengthy walk, a full three miles, straight across the city. Elizabeth's frozen hobbling pace was slow, and exquisitely painful. At one time the sky burst into a full rain, soaking her till her underclothes clung around her, entirely immodestly.

She really, really wished she'd chosen to run from the Lachglass House in the opposite direction, *towards* her uncle instead of away from him.

The freezing wind blew through her. She was colder by far than she had ever been before. Step after step.

When she went through the slums around Convent Gardens, the men there sneered at her, and one grabbed her arm, before he saw the bruises on her face and decided to go elsewhere. Perhaps it was something in her eyes. She had been prepared to strike him with her head or to twist her body to hit him with her elbow that had also purpled with bruises.

It would be a silly irony if she killed an earl to protect her virtue, and then was raped by a beggar or a common ruffian. But the prospect did not scare her. She was always told to be frightened of this part of the city, and to never, ever wander there, ideally not even with footmen to protect her.

Despite her hobbling weakness, she had killed one more man than most of the unwashed ruffians who ganged in this poor area.

As she walked Elizabeth used the walls or fences that she passed for additional support beyond that provided by her impromptu staff. It took three hours for her to hobble the three miles. She knew that after it had taken so much time her hope that it would be safe for her to ask her relatives for help before running again was no longer sound.

Whatever authorities would be sent out to apprehend her could have easily been already dispatched.

She refused to think about that, and by now Elizabeth was so cold and so sore that she began not to have a care if they hung her in the morning, so long as they gave her a hot drink and let her sleep in front of a nice fire tonight.

Finally.

At last, as it was becoming dark, Elizabeth shiveringly reached Leadenhall market, where beneath sodden tents a few remaining desultory butchers and greengrocers hawked their wares to the last late evening shoppers, mostly the poorer sort, clerks or workmen for the banks and merchants who clustered in this area. The wealthier sort sent their servants early in the morning to get the freshest of the foods and meats from the markets. Her aunt and uncle still did so, as despite the reversals in fortune they had faced since the collapse of prices following the victory at Waterloo, they could easily afford two or three servants, and they still owned outright the house in which they lived.

Across the street from her, safety.

The three story house the Gardiners lived in sat on the opposite side of the street from the market. The attic and half the rooms were now rented out to lodgers, one of them Mr. Gardiner's clerk, and all of them employed in business here in the city.

A cheery light burned from the windows, and from half behind a banked pile of coals that a street vendor roasted chestnuts on, Elizabeth watched. Something stiff and sore in her kept her from crying out in greeting, as her uncle strode up the street, his beaver top hat keeping *his* head and ears warm.

The door opened, he smiled at someone within, and the door quickly closed.

Elizabeth closed her eyes and breathed deeply several times.

Safe and home.

The pursuit could not yet have arrived at the Gardiners, as Mr. Gardiner would have been called from his warehouses to see to the matter if it had, rather than walking home calmly at the end of the business day. And there would have been *something* less domestic in how he was greeted if the house was on fire with the news that she'd murdered an earl.

Elizabeth put a hand on a cold lamp post. The weather was freezing, and getting colder by the minute as evening fell. Time to be warm at last.

And then, just as Elizabeth was about to start across the street, a hackney cab, driven at the unsafe, hurtling pace that all cab drivers used, pulled up in front of the Gardiners' house.

Two men stepped out.

One a uniformed constable from the parish association funded to protect the rich district that Lachglass lived in. The other's face was wrapped up in bandages, Elizabeth could easily recognize him from his size and posture as Mr. Blight, the earl's man of business.

They walked up to the door and pounded for entry.

*****

Elizabeth hurried away, back the direction she had come. And then she went south, to the waterfront of the Thames.

She reached the waterfront near the flat top of the old London Bridge. Old people still talked about how the bridge used to be packed four stories tall with houses. Boats with lamps swinging side to side floated up and down the river, barely visible in the dim foggy evening. In the distance the last reddish hints of sunlight faded by the second. The eternal bustle of commerce, barges, stevedores, cats, dogs, and all manner of people and creatures continued doing their business along the dockside at night.

There was a barrel with a fire burning in it for warmth that dockworkers taking a break and chewing tobacco gathered around. Elizabeth cautiously stood next to them, warming her hands.

"Eh, lady! Watcha doin out so late in that dress with no coat? Sick you'll be."

"Apologies." Elizabeth shivered and flinched away from the barrel and the workmen. The man looked after her with a head-shaking frown as she fled along the riverfront away from him.

Cold wind blew off the river, freezing Elizabeth's face.

She was alone, helpless.

There was nowhere she could go in London. No one she could turn to. Anyone who she stood upon close enough terms with that they would give her shelter without any money, was someone whose connection to her would be easily discovered by the investigators.

And even if a friend hid her, their servants would talk, and turn her in for a reward. There would certainly be a great reward. She had, after all, killed an earl.

She would freeze to death, in the wet and cold.

Was there anyone she could trust to help her at this time?

The name of one gentleman crossed her mind. He had been named as the inhabitant of a particular house on a square a few blocks from Lachglass's house. She had been told that this man was present in the town after the spectacular society marriage of his sister a few weeks ago by a gossiping footman while Elizabeth walked her ward around the streets.

It was a slender hope.

But this man whose name occurred to her had once, in a more fortunate time for her, many years before, told Elizabeth with dark passionate eyes that he ardently admired and loved her. And then she refused his suit out of misplaced spite and misapprehensions.

Wind blew through Elizabeth's dress, and a proper soaking rain now entertained her. Elizabeth started back towards where she had started, going towards the scene of her crime once more. The night was full of cold sleety rains, caught halfway between hail and plain rain, with little flutters of snowflakes melting in the lamplight.

One step after another. That was all it would take. One step after another.

Elizabeth wanted to lie down and cry, and let darkness take her. Her stomach hurt with hunger, and her foot ached and twinged with every step.

But Elizabeth kept walking.

Chapter Two

The moment Darcy entered the door to his finely appointed townhouse, his housekeeper Mrs. North greeted him in an unusual agitation. She flapped her hands and tugged at her bracelet. "Sir, sir, I've been waiting for you to return for the past hour. A strange gentlewoman is asking after you."

Darcy blinked. "A strange gentlewoman? Did she leave her card?"

"In the drawing room. Told her to wait for you. Couldn't send her off. Not in the cold. Not at all. I gave her a toddy, and told her to just sit there and keep warm. It's all so irregular. I think she is in some trouble, but a very sweet and good natured young gentlewoman. I can tell, you know. I can tell. Someone did wrong by her."

With a small smile Darcy shook his head. "Mrs. North, this is most unlike you. I can hardly make out the direction of your communication. Who is the woman seated in my drawing room who saw fit to call at," Darcy frowned in thought, "ten o'clock in the evening, since you said she has been waiting for me for an hour now. This is *most* irregular."

The thought crossed his mind that the entire situation might be some bizarre attempt to entrap him in marriage by entangling his reputation with that of the strange girl who had called. But that made no more sense to him than anything else that Mrs. North had said. Besides now that Georgiana was happily married to Mr. Tillman, Darcy had rather less reason to concern himself with the possibility of scandal.

"Um. Yes. Um. Let me explain." Mrs. North's head bobbed up and down as she stammered. "Nothing like this ever happened before. But I am sure she is a good sort, even though I don't know her. I'm worried she'll be quite sick from all that cold, walking around all day she said, in just a thin dress — no coat. It's been raining all day, off and on, and with that wind. She'll be fortunate if she doesn't catch her death of the cold."

"I begin to think that I will need to see this woman myself to gain any sense of the matter."

"Yes sir, that is likely best. I am sure the matter is not her fault, but I expect someone imposed on her. Miss Bennet's face is bruised. And her forehead and arms too, I dare say that—"

"Miss Bennet!" Darcy exclaimed, all hint of sleepiness and amusement at the situation suddenly gone. "Miss Elizabeth Bennet?"

"She did not say her Christian name, but—"

"Around this height, dimpled cheeks, and eyes which are roughly the color of the Thames at twilight—"

"No smiles to see any dimples on the girl tonight." Mrs. North tilted her head and smiled a little. "But her eyes are like that."

"Good God." Deep breath. And then Darcy took another deep breath. "I shall speak to her."

Perhaps it was one of her sisters.

Perhaps it was a completely unrelated Miss Bennet.

In the brief moment before he entered his drawing room Darcy wondered why Elizabeth would reenter his life at such a time. When he had finally entirely put that old affection behind him, and he at last was seriously looking for a prospect for wife, since he had reached the age when a man *ought* to marry if he had not already.

Besides he thought he would be decidedly lonely in a few weeks with Georgiana gone to her husband's estate in the north, and General Fitzwilliam soon to return to the division he commanded in the occupying army in France.

Darcy stepped briskly into the room.

She was Elizabeth.

His heart leapt in his chest and pattered fast.

Elizabeth clutched a blanket around her next to the fire and she seemed to not realize he was there. A small house kitten from the kitchen had climbed into her lap and was pushing its paws into her leg again and again, while she absently petted him and stared into the fire.

Her hair hung loosely around her ears and eyes, and she looked small and young, as if she had not aged a day in the four years since she refused his request for marriage. His heart went out to her, wanting to protect and comfort her. She looked like a wrung out rat, and she looked beautiful.

And then she looked at him, and as Mrs. North had said, her forehead had a big bruise, black and blue. And there was another softer bruise, shaped like a handprint, on her face.

Elizabeth.

What happened to you?

She stood up, the cat in her lap squealing as she absently put it on the arm of her chair.

"Mr. Darcy!"

He bowed. Darcy tried to speak but his voice would not come.

She was beautiful.

She shivered despite the warmth of the well heated room. And she was so bruised.

"What happened?" He forced himself to speak slowly and quietly, as though he was trying to comfort an injured and skittish horse.

But Darcy felt a roar of rage that screamed behind his ears. He added when she swallowed before answering, "Elizabeth, I am glad you came to me in whatever trouble you have found yourself."

"I was…" Something flashed in her eyes, and she did not speak for a moment.

"You need not speak," Darcy said, with the terror that she had been assaulted and defiled by some vicious man, "not if it is painful for you to recall. I trust you. Inform me how I might aid you."

"No, I must tell you. You may not wish to help me when you understand."

"I shall always wish to help you."

Elizabeth smiled humorlessly. "I must also ask you to withhold any promise until you have heard what I have done." She tottered forward, limping terribly on one foot that looked swelled in her stockings to twice its size. He caught her arm to steady her as she tripped on the flat surface and nearly fell. Her closeness brought with it a strong scent of sweat that was somehow pleasant.

She flinched, but then smiled up at him. "Thank you."

Darcy looked down at his hand on her soft yet strong arm. Beneath his fingers was a mottled blue and black handprint.

He let her go with a hard breath. Despite the rage that flooded him, Darcy kept his voice quiet and soft. "Who did this to you? I swear I shall call him out and kill him."

"That shall be impossible."

"I care not who the man is. The king himself, I would call out — do you wish to protect this man? I care not who he is."

Elizabeth smiled in her humorless manner again. "The trouble is, that I believe I have already placed this gentleman on my credit, and so he cannot go onto yours."

"What do you mean?" Darcy stepped closer to her. Her cheeks were flushed, her hand felt hot. "What happened? Tell me everything, and above all, tell me how I might help you."

"May I sit?" Without waiting for his reply, Elizabeth hobbled back with his arm supporting her to the chair by the crackling fire piled high at Mrs. North's command, and she collapsed into it. "I believe — had no chance for me to confirm — I believe I killed the Earl of Lachglass when he tried to… to…"

"You need not say it."

"He did not succeed." Her wide eyes looked at him beseechingly.

Lord Lechery — that was how Lachglass was known amongst the men of the *ton*. And Elizabeth had killed him. Lachglass was almost a relation, as he was the cousin of his Fitzwilliam cousins, on their mother's side.

"It would not have made a whit of difference to me, not in the slightest, if he had succeeded in his vile design against you."

Elizabeth smiled at him, with something of the generous sparkle he remembered better and better from the time of their acquaintance those many years before. "I am glad to hear that you are so minded. For my part, I am glad that since I did kill him, I did so *before* he achieved his aim. Better to be hung a maiden."

"I shall not let them hang you. I swear to that." Of course Elizabeth, brave and strong Elizabeth, had defended herself. "Is there any chance they do not know it was you?"

"None at all. I met his man of business, and smashed his cheek in as I fled the house."

"You did!" Darcy looked at her admiringly. "Shall I need to fear for myself in your presence?"

Elizabeth smiled back at him almost mischievously, though it did not reach her eyes. He could see that she wished to maintain as light a mood in her distress as she could. "You perhaps ought."

"Mr. Blight." Darcy blinked at this detail. He'd met Lechery's servant several times, and thought he was as thoroughly distasteful as his master. "Tell me all details — is there any chance they know you are come here?"

"I doubt there is. We seem to be entirely unconnected. In a way we are entirely unconnected—"

"Nay, say it not. Madam, we always have been connected, even when we did not feel the binding."

Elizabeth replied with a weak watery smile. She forced that smile. "I am glad… glad you do not despise my face. I always, always hated to think that you though ill of me, even though I deserved for you to think terribly of me."

"Never — there was nothing you said to me then that I did not deserve, and the memory of the reproof you gave me has been most valuable to me over the years, in reminding me to show less of arrogance and more of kindness to those around me."

"I *am* glad to see you once more," Elizabeth replied with a pale smile, "and I am also glad you do not despise me for breaking all notions of propriety to renew the acquaintance in such a manner as I have, I am—" Elizabeth paused, and she seemed to pant. She shivered, though it was almost too warm in the room, and sweat stood upon her forehead.

She added, her hand trembling slightly, "It would have been greatly to my preference to not have obliged a peer of the realm to take up permanent residence in a much smaller plot of land than he is used to. On account of the fear that *they* shall oblige me likewise to take up a similar residence."

"I tell you, I shall not let you be hung."

"If I must, I'll walk the gallows walk, and I'll walk that walk brave as any man. He was such a man, such a man as deserved such a fate."

"How did you end up in a position of vulnerability to Lechery? I mean Lachglass."

"Lechery?" Elizabeth laughed with real humor. "Had I known his true title, I may have exercised more caution in accepting the post of governess in his house. But I had never even met the gentleman till I was one week into dealing with his unenthusiastic daughter."

"I understand," Darcy replied, not greatly surprised. He had known that the resources of her family were slender, and a fall from gentility of this sort was hardly unexpected or unusual. "I am sorry for your loss."

"How do you know my father has not thrown me off for some strange reason?"

"It would have been a difficult matter in such a case to find respectable employment."

"As the matter turned out," Elizabeth laughed, "I did not find respectable employment."

When Darcy smiled back at her, she touched her forehead.

Her face and forehead was flushed, and it had become redder, he realized in the past minutes as they talked. "I feel queer, of a sudden," she said in a tinny voice. "And quite dizzy."

And then before Darcy's terrified gaze, her eyes rolled up into her forehead, and she slumped into the chair in a dead faint.

Darcy anxiously jumped forward and felt her forehead.

She was burning up with fever, but at least he felt her thin reedy pulse pumping blood through her precious body.

With a leap, Darcy rang for his servants, pulling the bell rope connected to the servant's quarters again and again until Mrs. North followed by a maid and a footman bustled into the room. "A doctor, for Miss Bennet. Immediately. Immediately. The physician immediately."

Chapter Three

The first time Elizabeth awoke was from the sharp sting as the surgeon's knife cut open the vein above her wrist so that he could let her blood. She blearily looked towards her arm and tried to pull it away. But the steady and experienced hand of the surgeon held her arm in place, as her blood burbled purply with each pulse into the wavering cup held against her arm.

"Shhhh. Shhhh. You will be all right. You will be well soon." Darcy's deep comforting voice sounded from her side.

She was lying on a soft bed. Her throat felt raw with flame. She tried to swallow, but she could not because it hurt so much.

The doctor finished his work and tied a strip of white gauze around her arm tightly. "Rich colored blood. I think the young miss will recover," he said looking at the cup.

Elizabeth tried to swallow again, but a droplet of saliva caught in her throat and she started desperately coughing. Mr. Darcy and the doctor helped her sit up higher as she coughed, each cough causing a spasm of achy pain to go through her chest. Everything hurt.

"Keep her seated up. I have made the observation that when a patient is made to keep their chest upright when their tonsils are swollen, or they are otherwise ill, it reduces the frequency of pleurisy of the lungs. There is no authority or experiment to support this belief, but I suspect an upright posture permits the patient to cough more productively when oral secretions make inroads into the breathing passageway, instead of down the esophagus. Keep Mrs. Benoit—" Elizabeth blearily blinked at this name. Everything swam before her eyes, and she could not think clearly, but she was fairly certain her name was *not* Mrs. Benoit. "—with her head and chest elevated. Enough cushions so she can comfortably sleep. Sleep will do more for her than my ministrations can. I'll visit again tomorrow at this time, and bleed her once more depending on the progression of the illness."

Darcy stood, and shook the doctor's extended hand with his fine hand. Darcy had such a fine muscular hand. Elizabeth stared at the hand. The light from the candle was painfully bright in her eyes. Her throat hurt so much.

The servant in the room stuffed cushions behind her on the surgeon's orders, pillows that cradled her head. She wasn't as comfortable this way at first, but when her head lolled to the side backwards, she began to drift off again, though the afterimage of the candle burned into her sleep, and ate into her delirious dreams.

Elizabeth did not remember later any moments of distinct consciousness for the next three days. What she did remember, always, till the day she died, was the sense of Darcy's presence next to her, warm, comforting and helping her to sleep and know all would be good. Her hand would search out his, and he would let her hold his.

Quite improper, but she was happy for this.

Each evening the doctor would come, frown and tap his nose, take Elizabeth's pulse and temperature, and leave with a cup of her blood to drink. For she presumed, in this strange state of mind that her fever had given her, that that must be what doctors did with the blood, and that perhaps the bleeding did nothing beneficial — it had certainly done little to help Papa after his stroke — but the doctors had perpetrated bleeding as a scam upon all of society so that they could satisfy their endless desire to drink blood.

Elizabeth also had memories — she was not quite sure if they were memories or fragments of a dream — of vomiting, throwing up over Darcy's fine wool clothes. Of throwing the covers to the side feverishly because she was too hot. And other memories that she was sure were dreams.

Jane and her sneaking into the same bed, whispering as little girls. A seven-headed hydra, each head that of Lord Lachglass, that though she smashed with her skull every head, there was always another sneering head, leering forward to bite her. A swinging gibbet, they led her up to be hung, but when the lever was pulled, instead of her hanging, she saw in impossibly vivid color Mr. Blight, his tongue sticking out and his face blue and black.

And then she was back in the bed.

Dark. No candle burning, but a dim red glow from the fireplace.

Elizabeth felt sick with shuddering aches, and she suspected she yet burned with a little fever, but she knew she was healthier than she had been for the past days, however many they had been. And at last she could appreciate that she was lying in the softest, comfiest bed she had ever slept in, including the one she'd possessed when she was one of the more blessed Miss Bennets of Longbourn.

She looked to her side. Darcy sat up in the winged armchair, lightly snoring.

Elizabeth felt a powerful wave of affection for him that went up and down her achy limbs and filled her soul. Her true hero, Fitzwilliam Darcy.

She looked at him, her eyes still bleary from illness and fatigue. His features and clothes were barely visible in the dim firelight. But she felt a deep thankfulness to him.

After so many years, when he had every right to despise her, he immediately, and without question, gave her sanctuary, paid for her care, and then sat by her bed to keep her company as she was sick.

He must love you still.

The thought came to Elizabeth, and while a female modesty suggested such thoughts should always be discouraged, rationality interposed between modesty and her mind: A man did not sit by the bedside of a woman in such a way unless he cared very deeply for her.

Elizabeth was glad of it. She did not yet know what to make of her sentiments towards Darcy, and her life was so strange. That she had murdered her employer the earl should make it impossible for her to ever marry anyone, let alone Mr. Darcy.

They could never marry.

The impossibility did not change anything. She was happy, deeply and desperately happy to believe he still loved her.

There was breathing on the other side, and Elizabeth rolled her head over to look. There was a woman wearing the clothes that marked her as a fine lady's maid. No doubt Darcy had always kept one of his servants present in the room with them when he was in her room to maintain a frail semblance of propriety.

Elizabeth grinned.

The woman stirred and stood. She placed her hand on Elizabeth's forehead.

"Water," Elizabeth whispered hoarsely. But though her throat was dry and rough, it did not feel painful and inflamed the way she remembered from the past days.

The woman smiled at her and poured water from a pitcher by the bedside into her cup, very quietly. Elizabeth took the cup in her shaking hands, but needed the maid's aid to hold it steady so that she could drink slowly.

Elizabeth then closed her eyes.

She felt quite terrible still. Much worse than she could ever remember feeling. Achy and weak. But she also felt surprisingly clean. "How long?" Elizabeth whispered without opening her eyes again.

"Three days, ma'am, since the evening you came to us." The maid spoke very quietly, clearly hoping like Elizabeth to not wake Mr. Darcy from his snores. "Do you feel better?"

"Horrendous. Like I'd been tied to the ground with stakes and left to bake for a long summer day." Elizabeth opened her eyes and looked at the maid, whose profile was barely visible in the light. "But I no longer have any delirium that I can detect in my mind."

"I am very glad. The physician said the critical point would be yesterday. There was a fear you would die once or twice, Mrs. Benoit."

Elizabeth quirked a smile. She whispered, "So that is my name now?"

"I had a suspicion it may not be your true name. The maid who let you into the house swore until Mrs. North properly talked to her that you *had* introduced yourself as a Miss Bennet," the maid replied with a quirk of her lips that made Elizabeth suspect she had a fine sense of humor. "But it seems a simple mistake to make as the two sound similar. And as you and the master are old friends, *he* would certainly know about your marriage."

"Oh yes… my marriage. Poor Mr. Benoit, he never cut a memorable figure."

The maid snorted with humor.

At the sound Mr. Darcy started and woke up. His eyes gleamed at her in the dim reddish glow. "Elizabeth, I mean Miss Bennet. I mean Mrs. Benoit." Darcy looked at the servant.

"*Mrs. Benoit,*" the maid replied with a smile in her voice, "says she is much improved."

Elizabeth smiled at Darcy, though her lips felt cracked and painful. "I think the fever is gone."

He quickly touched her forehead and then pulled back. "I worried."

She smiled at him. "I know. You have saved my life."

"Nothing, nothing."

Elizabeth's eyes were starting to blink closed. "I am yet very sleepy," she yawned. "And rather sick. But I am not likely to die in the night. Mr. Darcy, you should go to your own bed and sleep properly."

He did not move. Elizabeth opened her eyes again and saw a mulish look on his face. She smiled sleepily at him. "I am sure that…" Elizabeth glanced to the other side of the bed, "What is your name?"

"Becky, ma'am."

"I am certain Becky can ensure I do not die in the night and am provided water and the like. You must sleep properly, though. I'll be easier if I know you are caring for yourself now that I am well." Elizabeth felt her aches returning, and she then closed her eyes, waiting with her ears to see if Darcy would leave the room.

But she fell back to sleep before she could decide if he'd left.

*****

When Elizabeth woke again, light seeped around the edges of her curtains, and the fire still burned. She looked around and the same maid from the last night was still sitting in the chair, but Mr. Darcy was gone.

There was the repeated soft clicking of needles together as the maid worked on a matter of knitting, which she put down when Elizabeth stirred. "Awake again, Mrs. Benoit?"

"Awake." She glanced back at Mr. Darcy's seat.

"Took a while to convince him to leave. But when he felt your forehead again and decided there was no returning fever, I was able to convince the sweet master to get his needed sleep. He's exhausted himself caring for you. Quite a fine gentleman. I had no notion since I came back to the house that he was attached."

Elizabeth had had no notion that he was still so attached either. But she was happy that he was.

She tried to sit up with her legs hanging off the bed. And she managed to sit up, with difficulty, though she was still achy and weak.

"Now do be careful," the maid cautioned worriedly, putting her cool hands on Elizabeth's shoulders. "Ought to have the physician back to tell you that you can stand up before you try to."

Elizabeth shook her head and ignored Becky to place her feet on the ground. Her head swam around and around in circles, and her stomach yet felt quite tender. "More water, please."

She gratefully drank the water and closed her eyes after she had finished the cup.

She just concentrated on the feel of thick rug beneath her bare feet. She sat for a minute, quietly with the maid, and then putting her hands under her, Elizabeth stood. Her legs were wobbly, and the only reason she did not collapse was Becky's help.

"You don't want to stay in bed longer than you have to," Becky stated.

"Never in bed. Never been bedridden."

"Fortunate you are in that. After my child was born, I had a fever that nearly carried me off. I was sick for three weeks."

Elizabeth took several deep breaths. The longer she stood the steadier she felt. That was a good sign. "Please help me to the chamber pot. I would rather not continue to use the bedpan."

"I'd surely prefer you to use the pot as well." The maid laughed. "Not my normal duties, but Mr. Darcy did not wish to hire a nurse from outside the household. And while I can leave *matters* for the maid to dispose of, Mr. Darcy put me in charge of keeping you clean and dressed."

"No, he would not want to hire someone from out of the house." The thought of what she had done arose again. Elizabeth refused to consider that thought.

The maid helped Elizabeth walk to one of the closet doors, through which was a tiny room with a fine painted wooden box, whose top lifted to reveal a hole underneath which sat the chamber pot. Elizabeth approved of setting the chamber pot in a closet instead of right in the bedroom itself. One of the luxuries of the wealthy. A further luxury was that there was a small iron box in the cabinet for the chamber pot where hot coals had been placed that made the wooden seat pleasantly warm when Elizabeth sat on it.

It was good to be rich.

She shivered on the seat, despite the warm air of the enclosed room, for several minutes before she relieved herself and stood, holding her hands to either wall. Her wrists with the mostly healed scars from the where the doctor bled her caught her eyes.

She had nearly died.

It would have been novelistically appropriate if she had died as a balancing retribution for killing the earl, but Elizabeth was rather decidedly happy she had not.

When she came out into the main room, a maid of all work had joined Becky. From her dress and her manner Becky was clearly of a higher order of servant than the maid who under Becky's inspection changed all of the sheets and covers on the bed.

"Just another minute, ma'am, and you'll feel ever so much more comfortable in an entirely clean bed."

Elizabeth smiled her acceptance and sat down gratefully in an armchair Becky pulled out for her and let her sit in. It was the same velvet winged chair Mr. Darcy had snored in the previous night. She fancied that she could still smell a remainder of his scent.

"We'll change your clothes too. I've changed your night dresses every day. Soon as Susy is done, I'll get you fixed up proper to sleep. And cook has sent up some broth. Mr. Darcy is yet asleep, and we've decided to leave him to sleep till he wakes naturally."

"Yes." Elizabeth swallowed. "He has been very kind."

She was suddenly terribly hungry. "Please, bring the soup."

A hot bottle and a tray was produced, and set in front of Elizabeth on the chair, and she made an effort to eat, but she only managed half before she felt too tired and weak to continue sitting up.

Becky helped her to sit on the bed, pulled off her night shirt, expertly pulled on another one, and helped her to lie back in the bed, far more comfortable than before. She then clucked and said, "Your hair will be a right horror to manage when you are well. All sorts of tangles and snarls. But *sleep* now. Do not worry about that at all *now*. I've managed worse in my day, I have. I'll have your hair set well and pretty as can be, soon as you are recovered enough to sit up long enough."

Elizabeth almost laughed. The last thing she worried about was her hair.

When she woke again the light outside was dim and fading. Occasional carriages still rolled along the street outside the window outside her door. A different servant than Becky sat by her bed, boredly waving a ribbon in front of her own nose and watching it flutter. The young woman blushed and put the silk piece away as soon as she saw Elizabeth's eyes open and on her.

"Good evening, ma'am." The servant stood and curtsied. "Do you need anything?"

This time Elizabeth could sit up easily, though she still felt achy and weak. "A glass of water, if you please."

The servant poured and handed her the cup, and she drank it down quickly. She felt much better than she had even this morning, though she was still dizzy if she tried to stand up. She realized she was very hungry, and asked the servant if some food might be sent up for her. Perhaps gruel, since she felt steady enough to take that in addition to the meat broth of this morning.

The servant bowed and left her, after opening the curtains at Elizabeth's direction.

Elizabeth stood up and managed to walk to the window. She stared out, shivering.

There was a flurry of snow outside, and the garden square Darcy's house sat around was decked in five or six inches of a white blanket.

With a knock the door opened and Becky and Mr. Darcy came in. Mr. Darcy blushed at seeing her standing in the voluminous wool nightgown that was a little too big for Elizabeth, and he stepped back muttering apologies.

Becky carried a tray up with the requested porridge and another hot bottle of soup. "Well, ma'am. You look better."

Elizabeth laughed and gestured to the door Darcy had escaped through. "The poor dear. Were my clothes cleaned, and is there any chance I can change into something with which I might properly accept a visitor?"

"Yes, certainly. From something Mr. Darcy said, I believe he has a matter of some importance to speak to you upon."

"I can imagine." Elizabeth shivered. She remembered a hanging she once saw.

No such anxiety until it was absolutely necessary. That would not be helpful. "But first dinner. Porridge, my... well not my *favorite*."

"Was the doctor's order." Becky laughed. "You are a fine lady, ma'am. Expect you eat ragout, and white soup for every dinner."

"For dinner? For breakfast I say."

Elizabeth sat back in the armchair, and fed herself first from the gruel, and then from the soup. But again she was only able to eat a surprisingly small amount before she felt quite full and unable to consume another bite.

Becky had busied herself pulling several articles of clothing that were definitely *not* the dress Elizabeth had arrived at Darcy house in from the closet, and laying them on the bed as Elizabeth ate.

Elizabeth asked her as she did so, "So are you married?"

"Was, my poor dear, he died, and with something of a debt. Left just me and my daughter alone. Just three months ago he died, he did. Still cry about him every day. I'd left service with Lady Monroe to marry him. Brought him a tidy sum of my savings as a dowry too. Poor man could not stop from gambling. Don't blame him for it — he was the sweetest man in the world. But just goes to show. A woman should not trust her money to a man." Becky laughed. "Wish we'd had one of those settlements you quality always use. But God I loved him. Loved him heart and soul. The Darcys were kind enough to give me a place, with no significant responsibilities in my mourning period. My mother was the lady's maid of Lady Anne. The master's mother. She was a fine lady. A fine, fine lady. Most aristocratic featured beauty in the *ton*, but always a kind word to a child like me. And she doted on our present Mr. Darcy. He's a fine man too."

"The very best."

"Don't forget that, Mrs. Benoit. We all care for him."

Elizabeth smiled. "Even to the point of being suspicious of strangers who do not remember their own marriages."

"Not too suspicious!" Becky laughed. "So don't go telling the master any of that. Besides Joseph, that is Mr. Darcy's gentleman, he says he remembers you from when Mr. Darcy met you, and that he always believed you were good quality and better than just a decent sort. Won't say the slightest more of course, and none of us would expect him to, but that settled some nerves. That it did. It is strange doings."

Elizabeth finished the food and pushed it away. "I'd imagined I'd be much hungrier."

"It's the illness. You'll be hungry again in an hour or two, I suspect, if you haven't eaten much for a few days your stomach forgets a bit how to eat a large meal. Let me help you to dress and ready, ma'am."

"Miss Bennet."

"What?" Becky tilted her head as she helped Elizabeth to stand.

"Miss Bennet is my name. A secret shared too far is no good, but you already know enough to sell me out. And… I'd prefer to trust those who Mr. Darcy trusts."

"Well that's touching, *Mrs. Benoit*. I am touched." The woman smiled at her. "But I am quite sure you have only forgotten your marriage, some damage from your illness, I dare say, though it is clear all your *other* faculties are intact, because else Mr. Darcy would not have told us all that you are Mrs. Benoit."

Elizabeth decided that was that, and she grinned at the maid. "A right strange illness, to take the memory of a husband."

"I dare say, he must not have been a very good one, though I have suspicion you will do right better with your next."

Elizabeth blushed at *that* remark.

It was easy and quick for Becky to slip the dress over Elizabeth's shoulders, and fasten everything that was to be fastened — though she wasn't tightened into a corset — but the harder matter to manage was her hair.

"Needs to be brushed all of the way out and worked with. Sleeping on it and tangling it for three days straight." Becky looked mournfully at it. "I suppose you don't want to be sitting up for so long yet, do you."

"I *have* been ill," Elizabeth replied, amused.

"Such beautiful hair! I love this shade. You have far better hair than Mrs. Monroe had — though my former mistress's hair was quite fine. But yours has a perfect clarity and color, and once the sweat and grease is out of it—"

"You know," Elizabeth said, laughingly, "how to mix a fine compliment together with a crushing blow to a lady's self-importance."

"It is my duty to ensure you look your best. You would not wish Mr. Darcy to see you with your hair all a mess, would you?"

Elizabeth flushed again, and though she had to laugh at herself on the inside, she confessed both to herself and Becky that she in fact did *not* want Mr. Darcy to see her with her hair a mess.

As it happened it took twenty minutes for Becky to carefully pull some of the largest tangles apart, and she worked gently enough that Elizabeth's scalp only *half* felt like it had just had nails pulled out of it. She wrapped Elizabeth's hair into a simple braid and bun that she said should protect it from further damage until she had the chance to *properly* clean and brush her hair.

Then clucking her tongue, Becky used some white creams to hide and smooth away the remaining black and blue bruise on her forehead.

Elizabeth was already quite tired at this point, but she wanted very much to talk to Mr. Darcy, and so she settled into the bed again, but this time dressed in a semblance of normality, and she was seated almost upright against the giant pile of pillows carefully collected behind her. So prepared she sent Becky off to tell Mr. Darcy that she was now prepared to receive a visitor.

As it happened, and not to Elizabeth's surprise, he was still standing in the hallway right outside her door.

Chapter Four

For a moment Darcy could not say anything when he stepped into the room and saw Elizabeth smilingly seated up, her hair lit like a halo by the last rays of the dying sunlight.

His breath caught, and she looked at him and smiled, and there was something in her eyes that made Darcy think that Elizabeth knew how he saw her when he looked at her, and that she liked it.

He swallowed, and he walked forward.

She stretched her delicate hands out to him. "Mr. Darcy. I must thank you again, and again, and again."

Her voice was rough and had a nasal burr. But it was also strong.

"No thanks. No thanks are needed." Darcy took and kissed her hand and then pulled the chair that he'd been sitting in to care for her close again and looked at her closely.

She looked clean and neat now, and the scent of sickness that had been in the room for the past days only lingered at the edges.

"You had Becky to dress me, and not in my own clothes. I at least must thank you for *that*." Elizabeth winked at the maid. "I should not say this in front of her, but she is quite capable and determined."

The lady's maid blushed when Darcy looked at her and looked down and mumbled something.

Elizabeth laughed and that sound made Darcy's heart soar. "I forget that we are only to speak freely with each other when the master is not present. Propriety and decorum in front of the servants."

Darcy peered at Elizabeth carefully and studied her. She was pale now rather than flushed. But while she looked somewhat thinner than she had when she arrived before her fever, there was a clearness to her skin that was different from the dried, almost parchment tone of her skin in the depths of her illness.

The fear that had entered his heart the moment he saw her collapse in a faint in his drawing room now at last left.

Elizabeth, he hoped, would not too long from now be recovered fully in health.

"Becky, I must have a few words with Mrs. Benoit alone. Might you stand in the corridor, and I will leave the door unlocked, enter again in two minutes, and I think that shall be enough to ensure some propriety is observed."

"Yes, sir." The woman bobbed her head and stepped outside.

The room was overly warm; the fire had been kept high to ensure the invalid was not bothered with a draft from the window.

29

Darcy could not keep from remembering how he'd kept company with Elizabeth during her thrashing fever. He stared for a moment at her hand, lying white and small on the coverlet. He wanted to grip it again, like he'd dared to when she'd called his name during her illness.

But now she was not in a dream, and he now was well rested, not with his judgement and sense of normality drained by two nights of fear and waiting for the doctor, and hanging on every change of Elizabeth's breathing or complexion to determine how she fared.

This was now a normal evening in a normal room where he was attending a gentlewoman who he respected in the highest way a man could respect a woman. He must behave himself.

"The news. I presume they hunt me for his murder."

"Lord Lachglass is not dead, nor permanently injured beyond a scar on his forehead and the likelihood that his nose will heal bent."

Elizabeth's eyes wavered from side to side, and her head tilted confusedly, as though the notion of him yet living completely shocked her. "But… I know I could not tell… but I had convinced myself."

Darcy touched her soft arm covered by the pretty yellow wool dress Becky had adjusted to fit her. "Does it disappoint you to not be a murderess?"

"A little, perhaps?" She laughed weakly, but shook her head. "Alive. And Mr. Blight?"

"A bribed servant claims he walks around with a bandage around his face, and has eaten only soup for the past days, but otherwise is well."

Elizabeth nibbled adorably on one of her knuckles. "Truly, so easily resolved. Not dead. Almost as though all was a bad dream."

"No." Darcy shook his head. "I am afraid matters are not over yet. He wants revenge. He has men throughout the city asking for you. I sent a letter to your aunt and uncle through means that I am certain cannot be tracked that you were with friends, to relieve their worry, once I learned that Lord Lachglass was yet alive. But until you are healthy, I think we should refrain from going to them."

"What can he do to me at this point?"

Darcy could imagine many things a vengeful and vicious man could do to Elizabeth. At present he had asked his man of business to hire his own investigators to look into Lord Lachglass's affairs, political, business and otherwise. There were enough rumors around Lord Lechery that it would not surprise Darcy at all if he could shake from the trees some proof of serious wrong action to hang over the aristocrat's head, even if Darcy understood the privileges of titled gentlemen well enough to know that he would never see Lachglass hung, as he ought to be.

Or have his head chopped off if he insisted, as he no doubt would, on the aristocratic right to not be executed like a commoner. Darcy's thirst for vengeance upon the man who imposed himself on Elizabeth would be satisfied by a chopped off head entirely as well as by a hanging.

Darcy feared what Lord Lachglass might attempt to do to Elizabeth if he knew where she was.

She still waited for a reply, and he did not want to scare her with the imaginations that haunted his mind: Assassins, frivolous accusations, kidnapping — especially kidnapping.

Darcy shrugged. "I do not know, but I would prefer not to find out before his temper has had a chance to cool."

"I still want to add to your note to my Aunt and Uncle one of my own."

Becky knocked on the door, and Darcy called for her to come in.

With a bob of her head, the servant walked to the far side of the room and pulled a dainty chair next to the window, so they could pretend she could not hear their conversation if they spoke quietly. She settled on her lap some blue piece work, and with a barely audible clicking of her needles against each other, she became, for Darcy at least, almost part of the furniture.

Except he was very aware that she still had ears.

"Ah, Mrs. Benoit," Darcy began, unsure and awkward suddenly, and needing to use the false name to both remind himself not to call her either Miss Bennet, or his dear, sweet, Elizabeth.

Elizabeth laughed, "I confessed only a half hour past to Becky there that I have no memory of my marriage — now do not feel you need to answer a word, Becky. I know how stern Mr. Darcy is. I'd not break propriety in the slightest if *I* served him, which fortunately I do not."

"You do not want to serve me?" Darcy replied, with an amused voice.

"No, not at all. I have had enough of *service* for a life. And if it comes to it, that I shall enter service again, I like *you* far too much to lose the right to tweak your nose — as a metaphor — whenever the urge comes to take me."

Darcy grinned, and he replied with his straightest face, "I am much too respectable a gentleman for my nose to ever be tweaked."

"A pity." Mirth played around the edge of her pale lips. "I do dearly love to tweak noses." Then she flushed. "Ah, I have perhaps done enough business with noses of late though."

Darcy winced. "So I have heard. But precisely how did you cause that…" He glanced again at Becky. It really was inconvenient both maintaining propriety and not speaking anything in front of the servants. He *did* trust Becky, and he wanted to find a place for the woman in his house, as it was the proper thing to do for the daughter of a woman his mother had remembered in her will.

He would not have placed her in the position of being in charge of Elizabeth's care if he had not trusted her, and known who her people were. And for that matter, they had both known each other as children, though the separation between a gentleman and a person from the lower orders had already been there.

Despite that, discretion in front of servants had been drilled into Darcy's mind by his father and mother. It was always a simple notion: Never trust one who must earn a day's wage with information of true importance. There were ample stories of men betrayed in some important way by a servant. Mr. Darcy always maintained a distant but courteous manner with his servants, even maintaining his dignity around those such as Mrs. Reynolds who had helped to raise him as a child, and who was related to the family.

Elizabeth's convivial manner with Becky felt strange to Darcy to watch. Once he would have seen it as a sign of her poor breeding — in a way he still thought that, but the insult was now turned around and pointed towards himself: Elizabeth did not have an overly rarified breeding and an overly refined sense of her own self-importance.

Both features of Elizabeth that showed her superiority.

"Mr. Darcy," Elizabeth said archly, "we must have some conversation. Only a little may do — you were quite verbose when it was only the two of us. As for what I did to the nose of that personification of at least two of the seven sins — though he certainly does not personify sloth, so he cannot manage for all seven — I used my head, like every clever and sensible young woman ought."

"So *that's* how your forehead was bruised." Darcy unconsciously and unstoppably brushed his fingers over where the remaining hint of damaged skin had been disguised by an excellent application of some cream by Becky. The covering made the tone of the skin on her bruised forehead nearly match the rest of her skin.

Darcy blushed and drew away his hand. He looked at Becky again, who studiously studied her knitting. The needles clicked against each other.

It appeared he *did* need a chaperone, and not only to maintain a thin pretense of Elizabeth's respectability.

"That's where that big bruise came from," Elizabeth agreed cheerfully. "Cracked him hard, though that was not enough to put him down."

"Every sensible girl should use her head? I do not think *that* is what was meant." Darcy looked admiringly at her smiling face.

"I have been so afeard of hanging. I dreamed about it," Elizabeth said, "but now—"

"Do not say anything on that matter."

"I am so glad he is alive."

Darcy lowered his voice, so that he was almost sure Becky could not hear him, and leaned close to Elizabeth and said in a soft whisper, "You did nothing wrong. Even if you had killed him, you would have done nothing wrong."

"I do not know what to feel. I nearly died. He did not hurt me more than the bruise from a slap. The damage to my forehead I do not place at *his* account, for when I chose to crush his nose with my head I can hardly object to receiving a far milder injury. I did nearly die, and the experience of walking across the cold of London in a pair of house slippers on a sleety day, twice, is not one I shall forget soon. Nor that I would care to repeat. But..."

Elizabeth trailed off. Her mouth was screwed into a small frown.

Darcy worried what she may be thinking. Richard once told him that after the sack of a town, women who were raped often felt deeply stained and shamed by what had happened to them, and that even women who had been simply handled roughly by men, but who escaped worse fate, felt likewise.

And then Elizabeth smiled, brilliantly. "I am exceeding proud. Proud of myself in a way I cannot recall ever being before. Exceeding proud. And I would be prouder yet if I'd killed him, though the consequence of *that* must make me grateful that I did not. To make an allusion to the ancients, I feel as an Amazon must have upon capturing a shepherd to serve as her supposedly unwilling mate. I have beaten the unfair sex at their own game, and though it may be unfeminine of me to exult in having achieved some success at brute violence, I exult in it. This awareness that I can triumph, and that I can use my body to make a gentleman, a peer of the realm, to *hurt* is part of me now, and I am happy it is."

"My sweet warrior woman friend. I salute you then," Darcy grinned, "and *I* am happy for your Amazonian traits."

"Yes, well, I shall endeavor next time I am in a ballroom to hide those Amazonian traits. I *hope* I still can fill a dress with my female traits," Elizabeth spoke in a sly voice that made Darcy both laugh and flush, "And in truth, I would much prefer to be *underestimated* than overestimated. If he'd known that I had some reckoning how to fight, I doubt I could have mauled Lechery so easily or efficiently. And certainly not Mr. Blight as well."

Darcy was quite sure, as he was unable to keep from glancing down to admire her female features, well displayed by the light day dress of Georgiana's Becky had somehow fitted her in, that no one would mistake Elizabeth Bennet for a burly Amazon warrior.

"I shall never underestimate you," Darcy spoke low, looking into her eyes, "Not again, for you once have given me a drubbing."

33

Now was Elizabeth's turn to turn away and flush, hiding her red cheek against a plump pillow. "Have I really? I *hope* you did not hurt so much as I *hope* Lord Lechery hurts from his smashed nose."

"I confess, your words stung, and stung deep. But they stung because they had truth behind them."

"I hope, you know," Elizabeth replied, "that I have long since ceased to give much credence to any objection I held against you at the time."

Darcy smiled wryly. "I hope you have not *entirely*, for that would waste the effort I have put forward upon how to amend myself in accord with your reproofs. You said, *had you behaved in a more gentlemanlike manner.* I confess that notion, that I had not behaved in a gentlemanlike manner, has stuck in my head all these years."

"Dear me!" Elizabeth exclaimed. "I certainly had no notion of affecting you so deeply."

"I should imagine not, you thought me lacking in every proper consideration then, and—"

"I certainly did not. And now I *know* what a man lacking in every proper consideration is like."

They smiled at each other.

Darcy felt in his heart that it would be entirely impossible, and deeply disreputable for him, to push any attention Elizabeth did not explicitly, and unprompted ask for upon her at this time. She was a refugee under his roof. However, he yet loved her, and the passage of four years had done nothing to the love he held for her, and further he thought, that beyond the gratefulness she had for his rescue of her, there was something in her that was awakening to him, and that she responded to his unchanged — no his *grown* — affection for her, with an affection of her own.

"I do not," Darcy added reflectively, "consider it a bad matter that those words were nailed into my mind. Rather the opposite. *You* gave me the impetus to become a better man, a man who might become worthy of the affections of a woman who is worthy of admiration — I do not say I have succeeded entirely, for I do yet have great pride, but I always seek to be honestly concerned in the wellbeing of those around me, I always seek to treat those beneath me in a courteous manner, and I ask myself how I would wish to be treated if I was in such a condition and state as they, and I make that a guide to my actions. Further, I have made an effort to not stick my nose in business where it does not belong, though *that* I confess has in some ways been harder and less rewarding than my attempt to be more courteous."

"You mean to avoid such behavior as what you showed towards Bingley?"

"Aye. I talked with him about the matter, a year or two ago, and he confessed it had been a full year before he ceased to compare every woman to Miss Bennet. I parted a couple with a full potential for happiness. I hope Miss Bennet has not suffered greatly — has she married?"

"She has, to a poor vicar, but she is very happy with him." Elizabeth smiled softly, her eyes dreamy. "I do like him very much. I confess he *looks* a little like Bingley, and has similar manners. And he is loved greatly by everyone in the parish. They have no great store of money, and should the marriage be particularly fruitful it will be a struggle to see the children all settled respectably, but there is a deep contentment in both of them. And I should not overstate their difficulties in matters of money; they have a maid of all work, and a comfortable parsonage. They do rather better than most persons."

"And your other sisters?"

"Ah, Lydia — for a kindness her fate turned out not so bad as we feared. Did you ever hear that she ran off, believing she would marry *another* gentleman lacking in every respectable feeling of our acquaintance?"

"Good God. Mr. Wickham — you do refer to Mr. Wickham?"

"I do."

"I have some guilt in that, for not having denounced him for what he was."

"Nonsense, the blame rests entirely with two people, and you are neither of them."

"What happened — I cannot believe he married her. How was it not so bad?"

"She married in the end, someone else." Elizabeth frowned at the coverlet covering her lap and paused with a sad look in her eyes. Carriage wheels passed along the square outside. "I remember how Papa looked when he came back from searching for her. I miss him very much, you know."

"I still miss my papa as well."

Elizabeth stretched forward her hand and gripped Darcy's. Her fingers were strong despite her illness, and he thought she wished to comfort them both for the loss of a good parent.

"Lydia's elopement seemed at the time the worst fate we could imagine. The trip that year I took with my uncle to the Lakes was interrupted just as we reached so far north by the news of it. Jane at first believed they *would* marry. But with the name of the man she had run off, supposedly towards Scotland with in the letter… I knew in an instant the disaster was certain."

"Mr. Wickham," Darcy stated flatly.

"A single name, all therein described."

"I would I allowed my cousin to run him through after he—"

Darcy glanced at Becky, who stood up as the sun was setting and quickly bustled around lighting a half dozen candles before returning to her knitting.

"Colonel Fitzwilliam?" Elizabeth asked.

"General Fitzwilliam now, but yes. He wanted to."

Elizabeth laughed, her dark eyes dancing in the light from the candles that had been set out as the sunset progressed. "I remember his manner, a charming and personable gentleman. I liked him very much, but he had that manner about him, the sort of man who you would not be surprised in the slightest to hear that he shot a man's brains through in a duel where the right was entirely on his side."

"Mr. Wickham was far too frightened of General Fitzwilliam to face him in a fair duel on any account. And rightly too. My cousin is a capable man."

"And a general now. Employed, I must imagine."

"He leads one of the divisions of the occupying army in France near Cambrai. Though he is in London at present as they are gathering the second battalion of his regiment."

"I would wish to hello him, but I fear that in all cases a secret kept to as few hands as possible is always superior."

"Yes." Darcy frowned. "Though if matters become dangerous, he is a capable man who may help us. I would have already spoken to him, if Lachglass was not his cousin on his mother's side."

Elizabeth stared down at her hands. Her hands clenched and gripped the soft red duvet and then she forced herself to relax the fist. "Things will not turn dangerous. He lives yet, and all other matters will clear up in a decent frame of time."

"Lydia, she was abandoned by Wickham?"

"Yes, or at least that is what I assume. When she did send letters to us again, following her marriage, she did not give any detailed account of that period of time."

"But you say she married?"

"Yes, to a young lieutenant, of no connections, but who had some bravery or talent, as he was raised to captain later following deaths on the battlefield. I do not know the details of the matter, and while Mama travelled to visit her, and see Lydia's child, this was after Papa died, and we did not have the resources to easily allow all of us to travel so far as to Newcastle, where they were at the time, even if just by stage."

"Not a good marriage, but respectable enough."

Darcy was decidedly happy to hear this. Not that he would have hesitated to marry Elizabeth if Lydia was the infamous mistress of an earl. But it was much preferable in his mind for her to be married, and to have the only difficulty associated with her to be that he would likely be someday asked to do something to help establish one of her children.

Elizabeth was silent. "Better, I think, than she deserved."

"Do you believe her to be happy?"

"She claims so. Mama was decidedly unhappy with how low she married, instead of being grateful simply that she *did* marry. That visit was before Waterloo, when he was yet a lieutenant, and an income much less than a hundred a year for a couple with a child."

"And a captain's salary is not so much that one can maintain a proper standard of life upon," Darcy agreed. "But perhaps the man is such that he will succeed over time in his profession."

"I am certain he has no connection to help him in his way, or money to purchase a higher commission."

Darcy hummed and shrugged. "Nothing particularly scandalous in that situation, much better than if her fate was entirely unknown, except that she likely lived as the mistress of some man of barely enough consequence to keep a mistress."

Elizabeth laughed. "I thought that to be her fate after it became clear to us that Mr. Wickham had abandoned her. Or worse. But yet… I do not think I can ever think highly of her."

Darcy could not disagree. "Yes, and I still ought to kill Wickham."

Elizabeth laughed. "Nay, nay. And Wickham, ill as I always have thought of him, late events make me think more kindly of him. I do not believe he had the character to be a rapist."

"To ruin and destroy the life of a silly young girl, solely to satisfy his own lusts and desire for pleasure. I do not know that there is a great deal of distance in wrongness."

"That," Elizabeth replied, "is because you are not a woman. A woman knows that a seductive rake may be a danger, and the objective damage he does may even be greater, but no matter how silly and uninformed she is, the woman has some scope of choice. But when choice is taken away. When violence is used…"

Elizabeth's voice trailed away, but she then smiled that brilliant, proud smile she had used earlier, when she talked about how she felt about successfully fighting off Lord Lechery. He thought she imagined again crushing his nose.

"Both men may be freely despised," Darcy insisted.

Elizabeth patted Darcy on the hand with her thin, still slightly fever-warm fingers. It sent shivers up his arm. "True." She yawned and blinked her eyes several times. "Absurd, but I am tired again, after just an hour awake."

"You were very ill. The physician, Mr. Goldman, was deeply worried, and he bled you several times."

Elizabeth yawned again. "I have never had so much sickness before. 'Twas not a pleasant experience."

"For me neither." Darcy stood up, and he hesitated for a moment, and then he briefly kissed Elizabeth upon her soft and warm forehead before he left her to her sleep.

When he glanced back at her before he closed the door to the room, her sweet eyes were closed and she had a large happy smile.

Chapter Five

The following morning General Richard Fitzwilliam stomped into Darcy's breakfast parlor.

Darcy had been busily engaged in conversation with Elizabeth, rather than breakfasting downstairs when his guest arrived, so he hurried down to meet his cousin as soon as the servants informed him that he'd arrived.

"Where've you disappeared to for the last week?" General Fitzwilliam grunted as soon as Darcy entered the room. The officer was already seated at Darcy's table, slicing a long sausage apart, while sipping a mug of coffee. "Haven't seen your clothes nor your face for a week. And you haven't been to the clubs either. If you were a different gentleman, I'd assume you'd fallen in with a lushly proportioned opera singer, and be happy for you, but with *you* I became profoundly, and, ah, deeply concerned when you ignored your usual haunts."

"Really?" Darcy raised his eyes sardonically.

"Not *so* very worried. But your servants are all buttoned mouthed about something."

Darcy had not been to speak with his cousin in the past days, and not just because he had been absorbed by Elizabeth. Perhaps irrationally, Darcy had avoided General Fitzwilliam because he associated the officer a little with his cousin, Lord Lechery. The two even looked similar, though Lachglass was taller and had a handsomer face, while General Fitzwilliam was his superior in every single other respect.

Should he tell Richard about Elizabeth's presence and ask him to help with keeping her safe and hidden from Lachglass?

"Even if you haven't missed me," Darcy said after he decided that there was no call yet to ask for additional help, and a secret was best kept amongst as few as possible, "I am glad to see you here."

"Haven't missed you? Darcy, course I missed you. Any case, had to come. Had to come. I am damned done listening to my deuced damned mother sympathize with that bleeding, blistered, biting ass of a cousin her father saddled us with. Would have been better if she'd killed him, I think. He deserved it."

"Oh," Darcy said, in as offhanded of a manner as he could manage. "Who would it have been preferable for your mother to kill?"

"Jove!" General Fitzwilliam barked out a laugh. "You have been out of news. Lord Lechery, my cousin Lachglass. An old friend of ours, Miss Elizabeth Bennet, beat him over the head with a vase. A very expensive decorative piece. Lachglass complains to everyone that it was an authentic Ming." General Fitzwilliam laughed. "You *must* remember Miss Bennet, she was a fine fiery specimen of womanhood. She was at Rosings, the Easter a year after Georgie had a kerfuffle with your Mr. Wickham. We all talked a great deal, *you* walked round the park with her a half dozen times. Half expected wedding bells from that. Not your normal habit."

Darcy blushed at that and General Fitzwilliam laughed again. "I see you recall her. Pretty thing, she was. Doesn't surprise me at all she'd beat him over the head like that."

"I do," Darcy replied quietly, "dimly recall Miss Bennet."

"Damned bad luck for her. Damned bad luck all around. I sent my man around to nose out the whole story when I first heard of it from Mother — cannot conceive of why Mama yet likes Lord Lechery, though he is her nephew. Miss Bennet, her father died three year back. I understand her uncle sustained business reverses in the late banking crisis, and then she had the misfortune after all that to be hired by Lechery. Damned bad luck for her."

"What happened?"

"What a girl." General Fitzwilliam laughed again. "Rather wish we'd had her with us in Spain and at Waterloo — I thought from the first evening we spoke that Miss Bennet would have made a fine soldier, if she'd been a man. I respect that in a woman, none of that fuzzy fainting that so many of the female sex respond to danger with. No, she banged him over the head with a vase, straightaway — you should see Lechery, it warms the cockles of my soul, it truly does, to see him with the bandages wrapped around his head like a turban. She broke his skull a little, the doctors say."

Darcy nodded. "Does he have any notion where she disappeared off to?"

"A fine woman. Fine woman, I would have, I think looking back, made a play for her hand, if she'd had any dowry worth the word. What a fine, pretty, clever woman. Very easy to talk to. Smarter than most I've seen, and—"

"The story, Richard. The story."

"Testy are you? I take it you have not been simply relaxing these last days. You *should* find a lushly proportioned opera singer." General Fitzwilliam raised his hands in apology at Darcy's glare. "I will tell you what I know, which is not much. Lachglass claims she beat him over the head for the purposes of robbing twenty pounds from his wallet which he claims is missing. And she also broke the vase, whose value far is above the hanging value. All lies — we both know the stories about him. He finally chose a woman who was beyond his abilities."

"Yes," Darcy said quietly. "But will the courts see it in that manner?"

"Cases like this. Damned cases like this. I've been talking to some Frenchmen a great deal, since we've been occupying their north frontier. And I learned... something else about my damned father a few years ago. Just an example. This is just an example, but the damned rights of the aristocracy need to be stripped down — when I heard the story about Lachglass, and when the name connected to it came out, Miss Elizabeth Bennet. That name, I tell you, it sent a chill shivering down my spine. It feels different. I'd known Lachglass bothers his servants — *bothers* servants. What a disgusting circumlocution. Let's say it straight: He rapes them. He is a rapist. Perhaps some are happy enough to give up their favors and get some compensation for it, but he does not care greatly whether they are or not. My cousin is a rapist; it makes me disgusted to have the same blood flow in both our veins. And my mother defends him, and still swoons over her sweet nephew Arthur."

"Any man of honor would do differently than he does."

"When a man acts in such a way, it becomes the duty of someone to stop him. It makes me feel different about that sort of violence. This should not feel different, but it does. To know that my cousin tried to rape a woman of my acquaintance, a woman who I admire, both as a woman and as a human. A woman who is a gentlewoman, whatever may have happened to her family's money, she is as much a gentlewoman as my mother or sister, or Georgiana. And he tried to rape her."

"It makes me think as well," Darcy replied.

"I'd challenge him to a duel if I had the slightest excuse. I will yet, and do more thoroughly for his skull than Miss Bennet did, much as my mother would hate me for her nephew's death. But otherwise by the law we can't do anything about him."

Darcy grimaced, and he sat down next to General Fitzwilliam. Was there a way to punish Lord Lechery? Perhaps Darcy should challenge him. Once he married Elizabeth... if she would have him. He did not consider it presumptuous to believe that her opinion against him of four years prior was malleable, and likely already changed.

He hoped to marry her, and when — if — no, *when* he married her, he'd have the right to challenge Lord Lechery to a duel over her honor.

Right now, challenging Lachglass would simply point the constables towards where Elizabeth was. Her safety saved Lachglass for the moment from his deserved punishment.

"He is family still," General Fitzwilliam added contemplatively, crossing his ankles in front of him under the table. "I've lately been thinking about blood, its importance, the duty a man has to those of his blood. If I could... if I gain the chance... I will kill him. It is the job of a family to deal with their own. Lachglass is a rabid dog. If your dog starts to go mad, you don't have a furrier shoot the poor puppy. Not if you are a man. If you are a man you shoot your poor animal yourself."

Bang. Bang. Bang.

The sound echoed to the breakfast room from Darcy's front door. The sound of the door opening, and then, without waiting to be escorted, the subject of their conversation, Lord Lechery, the Earl of Lachglass, snarled into the immediately tainted room.

He wore a purple turban wrapped around his head, but the fringe of the bandage was rakishly visible. His nose was a giant twisted purple bruise that looked unlikely to ever recover its proper shape. Lachglass was a handsome man, usually brimming with good health and vibrancy, but at present he looked happily beaten in.

The earl waved a piece of paper in front of Darcy. His voice came out distorted by the completely blocked up nose. "Where is she! Is she here! Did she come to you!"

Darcy's stomach spasmed with terror, while his chest roared with anger.

Lachglass suspected. Somehow he suspected Elizabeth was here. He must protect Elizabeth.

"The deuce?" Darcy replied calmly, sipping his coffee. "Old boy, no idea who you are speaking of. Rather impolite to hound a man at breakfast with such questions. Bad form, Lachglass. Bad form."

General Fitzwilliam glared angrily at his vile relation, but when Darcy started speaking he twisted his face fractionally in confusion as he glanced at Darcy.

"The woman who beat my head in! That damned whore. I can't believe," Lachglass sneered viciously, "cannot believe you offered marriage to such a pathetic creature. Though she is skilled at refusing her betters what they deserve from her—" Lachglass erupted in laughter. He grinned at General Fitzwilliam. "Nice to see you here too, Soldier Dickie, such a lark — and Wickham. Old dear, George Wickham. Letting him run off with that sweet little skirt Georgiana. Both of you." He made a series of kissing noises. "Little Georgie has turned out pretty, pretty. A pretty pity that she has such a fondness for men like *that*."

Darcy went pale and cold.

He now recognized the paper Lachglass waved in his hands. The letter he'd written to Elizabeth after she refused his offer of marriage.

"Lech," General Fitzwilliam drawled. "I am quite put out with you at present. If you say anything, of any sort, about Georgiana, I will challenge you."

"Nonsense. You wouldn't dare."

"Try me."

Lachglass blinked at the officer staring at him with his calm eyes, but General Fitzwilliam sat in a coiled manner that hinted at violence at Darcy's breakfast table. The officer's hand still gripped his sharp breakfast knife.

Lachglass pointed at Darcy again. "Our idiot here — he offered marriage to a governess, and she turned him down! Down straight." Lachglass laughed again. He paced from side to side in the dining room, rather like an angry tiger in a menagerie going from one side of its cage to the other, the tail wrapped around the haunches. "Did she come to you? Did she!"

"I certainly have never," Darcy replied severely, "offered marriage to a governess."

"Ha! You have! To *my* governess. Mine. I'm going to have her hung for stealing from me. Hung you hear? *Hung*." He stuffed the pages in Darcy's face. "Remember this? Remember asking Swinging Lizzy to marry you?"

"Perhaps if you let me examine those papers," Darcy replied as he reached his hand out to grab the letter.

"Nope, nope, nope. Upon my honor, I'll never give them back to you. Mine now. Jove! What a fool you were in love."

"I do recognize my handwriting on the page," Darcy said. "It is quite possible I did write whatever you think I wrote. But I am quite certain this was not a letter addressed to *you*. So you have added the theft of correspondence to your other sins."

"Damn you, Darcy. We are almost related. You ought to help me find her and punish her, for family sake—"

"I am tempted to shoot you, straight through the head, for family sake." General Fitzwilliam calmly poured himself another cup of coffee as he spoke, making that statement as decidedly and casually as he might state a plan to go for a ride in Hyde Park.

Lachglass sidled away from General Fitzwilliam. "What has gotten into you, coz, of late? You weren't always such a mud stick."

General Fitzwilliam made not reply.

"So! Elizabeth Bennet. Darcy, you are damned going to tell me if the woman who tried to *murder* me sought refuge here. Swinging Lizzy hasn't visited her relations, nor any friend I can track, but her aunt and uncle did receive a letter written on fine, expensive stationery, and delivered through a poor beggar boy who disappeared before he could be questioned by the constables. *Someone* with resources is hiding her and protecting her."

"Ah, Elizabeth Bennet. *Now* I remember who you are talking about." Darcy quirked his head. "*She* did that to you? A woman." And Darcy laughed with a pretense of good humor. "What a silly sight you make. If *I'd* been banged over the head by a slight short girl stealing twenty pounds from me, I'd just salute her for her success and never tell anyone that I let a *woman* get the drop on me. What say you, Fitzwilliam?"

The officer grunted and sipped his coffee. His cold blue eyes never left his cousin's face, and his right hand loosely lay over the handle of his knife, in such a way that it was clear he could grab the weapon and stab Lachglass in a single fast motion.

Lachglass looked carefully at General Fitzwilliam and paced to the opposite side of the room from his cousin. It was only when the table was between them that he began to shout again. "Over the head! She beat me over the head. She tried to kill me, just so she could steal a purse full of coin from me. She stole twenty pounds off my body. So did this murdering thief come to you and sell you some story about being raped, needing refuge, and a lie about how she now wanted you—" Suddenly Lachglass broke into high-pitched giggles. "I laughed out loud for twenty minutes when I found this letter. Marriage! To a governess. You offered her *marriage.*"

"If I ever did, it is certain that I would trust her story above yours, had she come here to ask for my aid, which Miss Bennet did *not.*"

"I'll need to inspect your rooms. Let me wander round them. Let me wander round."

"I shall not. And I would kindly ask you to return that letter. It was ill conceived for me to have written it in the first place, and Miss Bennet ought to have taken closer care of it to prevent it from falling into the hands of those who had no business being privy to my affairs. In the unlikely case that I ever meet Miss Elizabeth again, I will reprimand her for doing so."

"Haha! You'll meet her again! You'll meet her when you watch Swinging Lizzy walk the gallows walk. I'm going to have that slut hung."

"Cousin. I think you've stepped past the boundary with that last insult against Miss Bennet." General Fitzwilliam had silently stood, and then he quickly moved so that it seemed it had taken but an instant for him to step inches away from Lachglass, who awkwardly shuffled backwards from General Fitzwilliam. "I too have met Miss Bennet. It is my duty as an officer of the crown to defend all British womanhood. I am challenging you to a duel. Apologize publicly to Miss Bennet, or we will face one another across the field of honor, and I will blow your brains apart."

Lachglass paled further.

And then his face became red. "You are just, just…" Lachglass sneered and turned up his nose. "Soldier Dickie, I have never heard such a ridiculous excuse for duel. I am fully in my rights to not accept such a challenge."

"No? You admit then to being an honorless coward who hides his rapes behind accusations of theft. I shall tell everyone of our acquaintance that you refused to meet me if I do not hear either an apology to Miss Bennet's character, or if I do not see you tomorrow morning on the field of honor."

"Ha! Were you in love with her *too*? You should be fighting Darcy in that case. You'll get to watch her hang as well."

"Lachglass, let me be clear." Colonel Fitzwilliam's voice was quiet and far more menacing for not being raised. "If you are too much of a spineless coward to meet me, I will not be able to fight you in a duel, but I will tell every man in London about your worthless cowardice. If you pursue this deceitful and ridiculous charge against the lady, I shall also testify as to every evil fact and story I have ever heard regarding your character in the court. And I shall testify to Miss Bennet's good character, and your vile and evil one. When I am done, everyone will know to despise your name, and she will be free."

"Your old man would cut off your allowance if you defamed the family name in court. Besides, you'll be back in France and unable to testify."

"*Cousin.*" As General Fitzwilliam spoke, he stepped again and again into Lachglass's physical space, pushing him until he was pressed into the wall, cowering away from his shorter relation. "I despise myself for not acting to curb your propensities before. I was stopped because you are family, and your actions were, by the standards of most in Britain none of my business, and your rank is superior to mine. I despise myself for knowing of the crime, and doing nothing, but let me say this clearly: If I *ever* hear about you abusing one of your servants again, or any other woman, I will splatter your brains apart. You can refuse to fight me, but I will find an opportunity someday when you are by yourself to splatter your brains with a pistol anyways. Do you understand my words?"

He sneered back, but he was clearly rattled by the calm and composed voice of General Fitzwilliam. "You would not dare."

"I pity the girl who will be the reason that you discover I *will* dare. But you, I pity you not at all. Now fucking leave. I never want to see your disgusting face again. And if you say anything against Georgiana, if any information about what occurred between Wickham and her finds light and air after all of these years, I will assume you released the information and I will shoot you dead for it whether you show up for the duel or not. Get out, and damn yourself to hell."

With a pale parting sneer, Lord Lechery retreated from Darcy's house.

Jove, he'd been tense.

Darcy let out a long shuddering sigh. Everything in his room looked nicer, sharper, cleaner now that Lachglass was no longer in the same room.

General Fitzwilliam paced vibratingly from one side of the breakfast room.

"Good show," Darcy said admiringly to his cousin. "That was a deuced good threat. It chilled me. I'll also tell everyone the coward refused to face you."

"Eh, that's not the important issue right now." General Fitzwilliam smirked at Darcy. "Apologies for rather impolitely sending a guest away from *your* house."

"He was not precisely an invited guest."

"Lech never is. Never is." General Fitzwilliam pierced Darcy with a hard, questioning look. "Is *she*?"

Darcy paused. "What do you mean?"

"Don't pretend to be dense. We both know you aren't."

Darcy sat down at the table and frowned at the geometrical pattern inlaid underneath the glass surface. Should he trust his cousin with the information?

He glanced up and sighed. General Fitzwilliam was grinning lopsidedly.

"I would have," Darcy said in a disgusted voice, "immediately denied the question if she were not here."

"I'm only impressed by how quickly you lied to our Lord Lechery. Not much more than a second of hesitation. I *had* thought you abhorred all deception."

"One can only be dishonest when deceiving a fellow human. Lachglass does not deserve such an appellation."

"When? When did you make an offer to Miss Bennet?"

"At Rosings. When we all three were there."

"At Rosings!" General Fitzwilliam chuckled. "I am not surprised by the outcome."

"For myself," Darcy replied with a wry smile, "I have never been so shocked — no, I have now received an equal shock. The evening I found her in my drawing room with the story that she believed she had killed your cousin."

"But why on earth did you tell her about Wickham and Georgiana, and in details?"

"It seemed like the proper idea at the time."

"Oh?" Fitzwilliam tilted his head to the side, and then, consciously untensing his body, he sat back down to the table, and began to eat Darcy's fine sausage again.

A soldier's stomach, able to eat anything, anywhere, no matter what had just happened, because you never knew when the rations might run out. That was what Richard told Darcy about his appetite. For his part, Darcy could not eat more.

46

"She had thrown at me a variety of accusations," Darcy replied a little defensively. "One of which was the story Wickham had given her. I... well I was heartbroken at the time. And I now have come to see my manner, and the rudeness with which I treated her, and her family, and all of her friends gave her little reason to trust in my words."

"At least it has been four more years. And Georgiana is married," Colonel Fitzwilliam grunted. He stood and rubbed the small, growing bald patch on the back of his skull. "It would in truth be more Mr. Tillman's place to defend her honor than ours now. Was he ever told?"

"Georgiana said she spoke to him about it, when he made his proposal."

"Good, good. Despite my threats Lachglass may release this information. Though I will kill him for that if he does, and you may testify that I said I would at the trial, if it should come to such."

Darcy rolled his eyes. "You know I would not do that."

"Eh, I hope my neck doesn't ever depend on *you* deceiving a jury."

Darcy wrinkled his nose. "I should have asked Elizabeth to burn the letter, but I did not think that..."

"That my cousin would steal the correspondence of a girl who you had reason to trust and who had no connection to him at that time. It is only a little your fault. Staring backwards does not help anything. You acted reasonably at the time."

Darcy frowned at his coffee. It was almost empty, and the hazelnut liquid mixed with cream around the bottom of the mug. The friendly, familiar aroma of coffee wafted to his nose.

"Miss Bennet, how does she get on at present? Is she in the house? Was that why you were delayed in joining me, you were busy making love to your guest? Tut, tut. Quite improper."

Darcy flushed, since in rough details General Fitzwilliam's supposition was correct. "She was very ill at first. She walked through London from Hyde Park to her uncle's house at Gracechurch Street, and then finding that the authorities were already present there, she walked back again to my house, all the way," Darcy spoke proudly, filled with admiration of Elizabeth, "on a swollen foot, in slippers and a thin cotton dress on a half frozen day."

"Deuced impressive woman. Is she recovered?"

"Partly, she still is weak, but the fever has completely left her the past two days. I was terrified at first."

"She turned to you," General Fitzwilliam said firmly. "And I can tell by your manner you are once more infatuated with her — these particulars promise well for your possibility of happiness."

Darcy was unable to stop himself from flushing again. "I have spoken nothing to her on the matter yet, but I hope her opinion of me is changed. It would be impossible for me to speak to her while she is lost in the world, and entirely dependent upon my support for her safety, succor, and very survival."

"Good man. Deuced good man. So we must get her out of any chance of the hangman's noose. For your sake too."

General Fitzwilliam walked to the window that looked out from the breakfast room. "Damn. Forgot this window looks over the inner courtyard — does Miss Bennet's room face the street?"

Darcy blinked and shrugged at the quick question. "It does."

"Might I call upon your visitor with you?"

Chapter Six

When Becky told Elizabeth that Mr. Darcy's cousin, General Fitzwilliam, wished to pay his respects to her with the master of the house, and that both gentlemen desired to know if she would be amenable to such callers in her present state, Elizabeth smiled and happily struggled to stand up. She stretched out her arms, though she wavered a bit dizzily.

"Even if I am quite the invalid yet, I will be dressed properly to greet such an august creature — *a general.* I confess, I made acquaintance with him when he was a mere *colonel.*"

Elizabeth's body felt considerably improved from the previous day, and when she restlessly sat on her bed, desperately tired of inactivity, she could imagine that she was almost healthy. In fact Elizabeth barely stood long enough for Becky to throw the beautiful but girlish and conservatively cut dress that Becky had modified for her from one of Miss Darcy's "old" castoffs that had not yet been handed to the servants to make with as they would.

Elizabeth half collapsed into the bed, while she let the maid button up the back of the dress, and her corset was tied in very loosely. She'd look quite frumpy, but she suspected Mr. Darcy rather liked it when she looked that way. And she was becoming quite certain that she liked it when Mr. Darcy liked the way that she looked.

She closed her eyes while sitting on the bed, feeling Becky's hands quickly and nimbly work on her buttons.

Despite having felt full of energy and desperate to stand when she had been in bed a few minutes before, she found herself almost drifting off. She had never been so sick as she had been the past week. Hopefully she would soon be much better.

"There, ma'am," Becky said patting Elizabeth's hair fully into place. "In the chair I imagine?"

Elizabeth shook herself into wakefulness. "You do understand me." She grinned. "No reason to play the invalid more than I must."

The maid moved the armchair that Darcy liked to sit in next to the fire and helped Elizabeth to stand. Then Elizabeth shook away her supporting arm and walked the rest of the way. She felt less dizzy than she had when she stood to be dressed, but she still collapsed gratefully into the warm chair, enjoying the fire that made her skin almost glow with heat.

She would *never* cease to love fires and warmth, and never forget how grateful she was to not be freezing. It had become dangerously cold for her that night after the sun had fully set.

"All right, Becky, you may tell the gentleman that her sickliness is presentable, and ready to receive gentleman callers."

Becky smiled back. "Are you certain, ma'am, that you do not wish to require them to wait yet a little longer — always does a gentleman good to wait a while for a woman. Reminds him of his proper place in the world."

Elizabeth laughed. "Ah, but I think Mr. Darcy can never forget his proper place in the world."

The maid snorted, and then resettled her face in an expression of servantly decorum. She curtsied with her intelligent eyes sparkling with humor and opened the door. As chance occurred, Mr. Darcy and the General Fitzwilliam both stood there already.

Darcy had been pacing back and forth, while General Fitzwilliam, who Elizabeth noted did look a little similar to his *other* cousin, lounged against the wall with a look of amused relaxation as he watched Darcy.

The two gentlemen snapped to attention as soon as the door was open. Becky curtsied to them and announced, "Mrs. Benoit is ready to receive visitors."

The two filed into the room, and bowed to her.

Elizabeth with her dimples said, "I apologize for not rising to curtsey, but I yet am rather weak from my recent illness."

General Fitzwilliam chuckled as he pulled forward one of the other seats in the room and sat. "Mrs. Benoit, eh? I must congratulate you on your recent marriage."

"Yes," Elizabeth laughed. "The suddenness with which I found myself named a married woman surprised *me* as well. Would it shock you terribly if I confess I cannot recall the ceremony?"

"My cousin Lord Lachglass. Damned man — I apologize for my language, but I despise him to the bottom of my heart. He is like a wild dog — I confess we have a slight similarity in appearance, I know that such can often trigger unpleasant memories in one who has been attacked."

"I do not mind seeing you in the slightest," Elizabeth replied with a friendly smile, "but I suspect that our mutual friend would not enjoy seeing my sister Kitty's face, for she is the most similar in appearance to me."

"Is she similar to you also in character? Since your recent marriage removes my chance to pursue *you*, I must settle elsewhere."

"Alas," Elizabeth grinned back, remembering how easily Colonel Fitzwilliam, when he *was* Colonel instead of General Fitzwilliam, could banter and set her at her at ease, "I am given to understand that Mr. Benoit is deceased. So while I am yet, I *think*, in mourning, your pursuit has *some* hope of success."

"Jove, Richard," Darcy exclaimed, "wait till she has fully recovered to flirt."

Elizabeth laughed merrily, and winked at Darcy, who flushed a little.

The dear man was jealous.

General Fitzwilliam laughed. "I think I may have a competitor for your affections who is a little taller, in person and rents, than me."

"Not his *only* virtues," Elizabeth exclaimed, smiling warmly at Darcy.

Darcy noticeably brightened at her saying that.

Without having consciously decided to, she was definitely encouraging him.

"Did you know we had a visitor this morning?" General Fitzwilliam said with a frown.

Elizabeth blanched. "That was the noise beneath? I heard something, but could not make out any of it and fell back asleep."

"My cousin happened upon a letter which our somewhat incautious Mr. Darcy once wrote to you."

"Lord! I had forgotten." Elizabeth closed her eyes. "I always buried the letter in the bottom of my trunk. I — my apologies. Mr. Darcy, I know there is information in those pages you do not want in general circulation. I ought have burned the letter soon as I'd digested the words, but… I liked having the pages as an object of some sentiment."

"In honest truth? You liked keeping it near you?" Darcy replied with a deeply interested smile. "In truth?"

"In honest truth."

"I would not then, no matter the consequence, have wished you to remove such a token from your possession."

Elizabeth smiled back into his beautiful, deep eyes.

"I see that I am outmatched," General Fitzwilliam drawled. "But this means we need you out of England, and quickly. That at least is my view."

"You think he shall be back?" Darcy said to his cousin in an anxious voice. "But—"

"Back, with a warrant signed by a backpocket judge, and with constables to search the premises." General Fitzwilliam stood and walked to the window, pushing aside the wispy drapes. He studied the bare winter road and the square dusted with snow.

He nodded with a frowning visage. "As I thought."

Sweat suddenly stood on Elizabeth's forehead. The room that seemed so warm and cheery was now becoming oppressive and cloying from the too warm fire.

The officer sat back in his chair. "Two men watch the house. One is Mr. Blight, with his delightful new scar. Lord Lechery would have done better to find a different spy; he is obvious at present."

"What can he do to me?" Elizabeth asked, worriedly. She pulled in a deep breath. She would not fear that man, she had prevented him from hurting her once when she was alone, and now she was cared for by Darcy and his cousin, she would not feel frightened of him again. "He is alive, and he hardly would bring a case against me for assault."

"Claims you stole twenty pounds off his person after knocking him out. He is determined to see you hang in vengeance." General Fitzwilliam leaned forward and spat into the fire.

The fire hissed and sizzled.

"I hate him," General Fitzwilliam added. "I'll testify against my cousin's character in trial. But juries. Juries can be strange animals; any true man of action will avoid having excess of todo with them. No, until we have settled matters in some permanent fashion with my cousin, you ought to be out of the country. And without delay. Today I think. My regiment's training cadre and their new recruits are back to France to join the occupation army two days from now, but the ship is ready, and a goodly part of the regiment's complement aboard it. We'll sail off today, and find other means to get my men to Paris. You ought to be on that ship with me, protected by three hundred good British muskets."

Elizabeth's heart beat heavy.

She felt faint, and not from the aftereffects of the illness.

The vivid intense fever dreams she had of the noose came back to her, though she insisted to herself that she would not let herself be affeared to an excess before any such matter was necessary.

She would have accepted the noose, and bravely walked to it, had she killed the earl. It was a righteous act of self-defense, yet he who took up the sword, might perish by the sword, and have no cause for complaint in that.

But to be hung while he yet lived.

That she protested against in her soul.

"We must hide Elizabeth elsewhere in London," Darcy exclaimed. "She is yet too ill to travel."

"Mr. Darcy, my dear, my dearest friend. I thank you," Elizabeth smiled at him warmly. "I thank you greatly for your consideration for my wellbeing, but I am well enough for a carriage to the docks. I *must* be well enough."

Elizabeth stood, and she found her claim was almost true. Perhaps some part of the weakness her body had felt was because she *believed* she had ample opportunity of recovery. But now that drive in her spirit returned which had let her walk six miles through London streets in the freezing cold upon a swollen foot.

Darcy rushed to her side with a supporting arm, and she took it, but she smiled at him, with what she hoped was reassurance.

General Fitzwilliam walked back to the window and stared out, clearly studying the men across the road again.

"We have a little time, but not much. He'll not easily convince a judge to put a warrant against the house of a man such as Mr. Darcy. Not with only correspondence stolen from four years ago."

"Three years and only nine months. Not yet four," Elizabeth replied without thought.

"You remember the date quite precisely, madam," General Fitzwilliam quipped in reply.

Both Elizabeth and Darcy blushed.

"Naturally," General Fitzwilliam added, "naturally you remember that date so clearly as it was the time most recent that you saw *me*."

"You may freely *believe* that," Elizabeth replied with a smirk that showed humor she did not feel.

"The servants. He may need to bribe the servants for evidence that you are staying here before they give him the warrant. But he'll get it sooner or later. Always someone cracks, sooner or later. Even if he needs to hand a judge a bribe of a hundred guineas. He wants his revenge. Miss Bennet, is any stationery in this desk?"

"I have no idea, as my bedridden state has not yet given me liberty to write." Elizabeth shrugged, looking at the dainty desk that General Fitzwilliam had sat down in front of, as he rifled through it, clacking the drawers open and closed. "Mrs. Benoit, please — it shocks me how quickly my husband is forgotten after his decease."

General Fitzwilliam rang for Becky once he gave up finding papers in the desk. She brought the officer a stack of sheets and ink and a sharpened quill. He said as he began writing, "We'll have a group of my picked men, Peninsular veterans, and men who were at Mont St Jean with me when Ney's cavalry tried to run us over at Waterloo."

"How terrible! You were at the very center then of the fighting at Waterloo?"

"Not at very center, madam. At Hougoumont and La Haye Sainte the fighting was much warmer. But warm enough where we were. Warm enough. Three men were killed who stood directly next to me during the fight. I received only a sharp cut across my neck that was not deep enough to even leave a scar — so you need not worry, we are a group who'll get you out of England safely, even if I need shoot a dozen Bow Street Runners to get you free of my cousin's evil."

The quickly written letter was then handed, closed over, sealed with wax and an official seal that General Fitzwilliam produced from his coat.

After he called to Becky, and handed the paper to her, General Fitzwilliam sat back in the thin chair that creaked under him with a moderately worried air.

"Ought I…" Elizabeth paused, and then she spoke quickly, in a single breath, to get the idea out. "Ought I perhaps stand trial for what he accuses me of? There was no money, and I can charge him with his attempt to violate me, and surely a jury would listen to me, and then that would be the end of the matter."

"No. Too unsafe," Darcy said sharply. "If you are captured by the law, we will pursue every avenue of that sort, and we shall destroy Lord Lechery's name, and bring all his enemies out to court to testify as to his character, but a jury is a chancy thing. We are going to do this carefully and systematically. Your safety and your life matter more than any other consideration in this matter."

"Too many blasted privileges for the titled," General Fitzwilliam growled at them both. "Jury of his peers. We ought to be accusing *him*. If England was as well governed as we pretend it is, my dear cousin would be hung by his neck till dead, but that is impossible. Even if a good accusation and case was made against him, he would be tried by the House of Lords, and I greatly doubt that my father and his ilk would be so hypocritical as to condemn him for what the rest of them do."

Lachglass had been here below, in this house. He wanted to hang her. She needed to call on that strength in her again, to remain calm. Elizabeth made herself smile thinly at General Fitzwilliam. "A rather radical opinion you express now. I had not detected such attitudes in you when we conversed at Rosings those pretty years before."

"Hmmph. Hadn't had them, not yet. But even if I had… you've pounded the head of a peer in. Don't pretend innocence, Miss Bennet. I salute you for it. But it gives me a courage to freely speak to you, as freely as I think — Darcy, could you give orders to have your carriage prepared? We'll ride out to the docks soon as my men join us."

Chapter Seven

Darcy paced back and forth and back again on the ground floor room of the house they had gathered in to wait for General Fitzwilliam's soldiers. Anxiety ate at the back of his throat. He'd brought Elizabeth down, supporting her with his arm as she needed help still to get down the stairs. Now she sat pale faced but composed in a winged armchair that she made to look like a throne.

Elizabeth was astonishing, the way she could keep some sort of calmness at such a moment.

He could not.

It was three quarters of an hour after Richard sent his message out when ten soldiers on horseback clattered up to the entrance of Darcy's house. They dismounted as a body. All of them wore the splendid red-coated uniforms of the British army, and they carried the long muskets of the infantry with them, in addition to pistols and cavalry sabers. A splendidly armed and well equipped group.

They entered the house, General Fitzwilliam embraced the young officer who led them, a lean young major with fine sideburns. "Excellent. Are you ready to defy law and order if you must?"

The officer smirked, "If I *must*."

"I'll do my part to keep from getting the whole gang of us hung, but I make no promise."

"Of course not, sir." He grinned back and raised his eyebrows.

Darcy studied the officer, who had the uniform of a major. While Lord Lechery and General Fitzwilliam looked a little similar, looking at this man was like looking at one of Richard's brothers.

"My aide de camp," General Fitzwilliam introduced the officer to Darcy and Elizabeth, "Major Williams."

Darcy shook the officer's hand, while Elizabeth smiled and inclined her head. "A pleasure to meet you, Major Williams," she said in her clear, pleasant voice.

"And likewise, madam." He bowed smiling at the pretty woman, and Darcy had to suppress a jealous instinct.

General Fitzwilliam studied the group of his men with satisfaction. He then said to Darcy's butler, "Around, around now. The carriage." He stepped to the window and peered out again with a frown. "Our friend Mr. Blight is gone. I suspect he is reporting the arrival of the men to his slaver." He clapped his hands. "Let's move. Quick now. Battle waits for no man."

Elizabeth had a decidedly amused smile.

"What entertains you?" Darcy quietly said to her.

"Just that I once considered you to be the one with the demanding, and commanding manner, and him to be the one who served at your leisure." She smirked, mischievously so both dimples showed. "I clearly recall Colonel Fitzwilliam's complaints upon how you put off the date of departure, which was a problem as you both travelled in *your* carriage."

"I had a particular reason to desire to stay in the neighborhood, as you may recall." Darcy smiled back, unable to resist her amusement.

"Now he is commanding *your* carriage. Such is the difference the rank of *General* makes."

"I hope, by Jove, I hope the General knows what he is about."

"I as well," Elizabeth replied.

"Rise, rise!" Colonel Fitzwilliam waved at them both. "Your conveyance awaits, Mrs. Benoit."

Elizabeth took Darcy's offered arm, and she tottered forward. Every moment Darcy watched her, worried that she would become sick again, or faint, or something else horrible.

A freezing wind whipped them, lashing through their heavy coats and scarves as they crossed the dozen feet from the entry steps, over the hard city cobblestones, to the waiting carriage. Elizabeth shivered, and she looked around, as if she was more frightened by the cold than the prospect of being hung.

And then rushing towards them was Mr. Blight, shouting with hints of a Cockney accent, "Halt, stop. Belay that damned whore!" He leapt past General Fitzwilliam's soldiers and hissed as he grabbed for Elizabeth.

She shuddered back into Darcy's arms as Darcy prepared to knock the man off his feet.

A soldier grabbed Mr. Blight by the back of his coat and hurled him around onto the ground.

Behind Mr. Blight two men in the uniforms of the Bow Street Runners, one of them pulling at the pistol in his belt, which he pointed at the man who'd manhandled Mr. Blight. "Stop, halt! As you serve King George, halt!"

Elizabeth's hand gripped Darcy's arm like a claw. The two of them stepped forward quickly towards the carriage. Darcy dragged her forward.

The carriage door was pulled open by the footman as soon as they reached it, and rather than letting Elizabeth try to find the steps and lift herself into the carriage, Darcy picked her up by the waist, and lowered her into the waiting conveyance. He ignored the Bow Street Runner shouting behind him, knowing that Richard's troops all had pointed their muskets towards the officer of the law.

Elizabeth's waist was slender and firm underneath his hands.

He immediately climbed into the warm interior of the carriage after Elizabeth, while General Fitzwilliam jumped in the other side.

A Bow Street Runner pointed his pistol at the carriage, but the soldier who'd tossed Mr. Blight to the ground pointed his musket at the man and said in a thick Scot's accent, "If ye point not tha' dam'd toy elsewhere than at my general's carriage, blow ye to hell, I will. By Jesu, I will blow ye to hell."

The Darcys' driver, an old family retainer who was completely unflappable, shook the reins out, and clicked for the horses to move. The carriage rolled away as the confrontation continued. Half the soldiers continued to point their weapons at the Bow Street Runners and Mr. Blight, while the rest led by Major Williams mounted and formed up around the carriage to provide an escort through the city.

One of the other Bow Street Runners ran in front of the carriage, and pulled his pistol out to aim at one of the horses, but before he could shoot, a soldier batted him calmly in the head with the stock of his musket, as if the presence of the pistol was not of the slightest moment, and the man went down easily. The carriage driver carefully and slowly directed his horses around the downed man, as he started to come to his fours, so that he wasn't trampled under.

The Bow Street Runner who had first shouted put his pistol away, but he yelled pointing at the carriage, "That woman is under arrest for theft and assault upon a peer of the realm. If you do not wish to be charged with a crime as an accomplice, you will stop and let me take her into custody! As you love the king!"

The Scottish soldier spat. "I love me the king. But ye, I believe ye not. Ye are just a common highwayman wearin' some fancy get up, I 'spect."

The Bow Street Runner pulled out a piece of paper to wave at the soldier as the carriage turned around the corner. The last look Darcy had of the two was the soldier spitting on the warrant paper and shouting, "I cannae read ye fuul, but I be sure ye wish to put some forgery on me."

And after just another two minutes they were out into the big avenue of Piccadilly Street.

The interior of his carriage was almost stuffy and over warm from the profusion of wrapped heating bricks and hot water bottles that had been prepared to ensure Elizabeth would stay comfortable. Darcy closed his eyes and breathed in. He could smell Elizabeth's scent, and that comforted him.

General Fitzwilliam laughed. "Did you hear that? Ferguson can read better than any of us, except you, I dare say, Mrs. Benoit. They take their grammar seriously in Scotland, being Presbyterians — but that fool man'll never know. Hopefully we'll be on ship, and floating down the Thames by the time the runners can catch up to us again — by the way, Darcy, I will need a fair amount of money from *you*. I gave orders to the ship to take its departure the instant we all get up on her, but there'll not be time to gather all the men aboard before time, so I've given orders to Major Williams to lay out the regiment's money and credit for the rest of the soldiers to get private transport to Calais, and to meet the rest of the regiment there before we march to Cambrai. *You* are going to reimburse the regiment for *that* expense."

Darcy laughed. "My money will at last be good for something. How much are we talking?"

"Private transit across the channel for at least a hundred fifty, more like two hundred men? That will run you between three and six hundred guineas I suspect."

"Just have the bill sent over. Just have it sent over. Or, soon as we have a stable writing surface, I'll write you a check against my Childe's Bank account for six hundred, and trust your honor to return me any change."

"I swoon at the trust you give me."

"So much!" Elizabeth screeched. "You surely cannot spend so much upon me."

"Shhh." Darcy smiled at her. "Relax. It is nothing to me."

"It is something to *me*."

"You both are only humoring me," General Fitzwilliam said, "by providing an opportunity to laugh at Lord Lechery, and spoil the cream in one of his schemes."

"I am happy to nearly beat a peer of the realm to death, anytime you wish," Elizabeth replied aseptically. "But six hundred pounds is still six hundred pounds."

"A fine tautology."

Darcy placed his hand on Elizabeth's arm. If his cousin wasn't here he would have placed his arm around Elizabeth's shoulder and pulled her closer against him.

"I swear, Elizabeth, I swear by all the trees and sheep in Derbyshire, that you are worth anything to me, to rescue and protect. The money I spend to protect your life shall be the finest money I have ever spent."

"Well, if it is an oath upon sheep and trees, then it appears I have no choice but to accept your aid."

"Not only any sheep and trees," Darcy replied dryly. "The sheep and trees of my home county, the finest in all England, Derbyshire. And a goodly proportion of those sheep and trees belong to me, and it is from that income that I am paying the ferry's bill. So you certainly have no choice but to accept my oath."

She sighed.

Elizabeth leaned back and her head comfortably rested on Darcy's shoulder. She closed her eyes as the carriage rocked them all back and forward. "I do not fear our Lord of Lechery, but I think my six hours in the London cold in naught but a day dress have left me with such a terror of cold weather that it will take more than one long winter walk to cure me."

"Soon it will be spring," Darcy replied.

General Fitzwilliam constantly glanced at the windows, and then every minute or so, he looked backwards through the window in the back of the carriage.

After they had been upon the road for about twenty minutes, he swore. "We are being followed once more."

He knocked on the back of the driver's box, and shouted through it, "Faster, man, don't stop, though they throw all the law at you."

The thin voice echoed back, "Don't teach your old grandpa to suck eggs, General."

General Fitzwilliam laughed, and nodded at the other two inhabitants of the carriage. "Good man, your driver. Deuced good man. We'll make it through to the docks safe and right."

But belying his stated confidence, General Fitzwilliam patted all three pistols in his jacket several times, but he stilled himself, took a deep breath. He glanced back the road and smiled.

Darcy looked back at those following them. "Three Bow Street Runners. I recognize the uniform and Mr. Blight."

"We'll ignore the warrant again. They don't have the force to threaten us, and then on the ship, and out of London. Jove, I hope Mr. Blight tries something that will let me shoot him."

Elizabeth shuddered. "I do not."

"There is a story; he once killed a milkmaid who was sounding out that the earl had raped her. The girl was found, throat slit, with signs of having been despoiled. She had simply been tossed, blood soaking through the straw, onto a haystack in the barn of the big tenant farmer who employed her. The story said that he killed her, as he was seen in the village earlier that day, and then again afterwards. But the thing that chilled me, the physician who examined the corpse. He thought the pretty girl had not been forced before she had died, but after he'd already slit her throat."

Elizabeth shivered at the story.

"Jove!" Darcy exclaimed, pale faced. "Jove, why did you share *that* tale with Elizabeth?"

"Is it her who is too scared to hear the tale, or you?"

"Nobody needs to hear such stories."

"Someone needs to act on such stories. *Great* nobles accumulate violent and vicious hangers on. The sort who hear, 'who will rid me of this chattering milk maid,' and who then go on to do *that*."

"The murderers of Thomas à Becket were not a fraction so monstrous as you imply Mr. Blight to be."

"That places a low value upon the sanctity of church and clergy," General Fitzwilliam replied sardonically.

The carriage continued to bounce along rattling them up and down, despite the fine springs.

Elizabeth asked, "Where are we? Stuffed between you two like meat between bread, I can barely see the windows. Are we close to the Thames yet?"

"Close, yes, another mile to reach our docks at Wapping."

The other soldiers had joined up around the carriage, but they did nothing to threaten the Bow Street Runners again, at least not yet.

The white knuckled carriage ride shook through the endless cobblestoned streets of the great city of London. Workmen dodged out of their way as they did not slow at the intersections, instead having two of the soldiers ride ahead to stop the traffic at each intersection so they could pass by freely.

Darcy could barely breathe. His own safety was nothing. Elizabeth's was everything.

They burst into an open area along the Thames, with vast docks finished only ten years ago. Ships almost two hundred feet long, with towering furled masts stood in lines within the vast wet dock.

The carriage followed Major Williams who pointed the way to go. They were stopped at the gate to the dock complex by several guards in the red and white uniform with a six-inch brimmed hat of royal naval marines.

General Fitzwilliam leaped from the rolling carriage as it came to a stop. He looked deeply commanding in his general's uniform with gleaming gold buttons and long epaulettes. "Open the damned gate. Quick!"

"I must see your authorization."

General Fitzwilliam annoyedly stuffed a sheaf of papers in the guard's face. "My regiment is on the *Orion* waiting to take sail the instant I arrive."

Behind them clattered up the Bow Street Runners and Mr. Blight. Darcy had at some time, without quite realizing it, put his arms around Elizabeth, and he held her tightly against himself.

He thought it was more to comfort himself than her. He had a pistol as well hidden in a compartment of his carriage, but he knew that would be no use against the entirety of England. He could shoot as many Bow Street Runners as he wished, and the only end it would bring was to have him hung whether they kept Lizzy from the noose or not.

His nerves seized up as he gripped Elizabeth's slim form in his arms. She, though, straightened up, carefully watching the action.

"Halt these men!" the Bow Street Runner shouted at the marines, hoping they had at last found someone who would listen to the voice of authority. "By the authority of King George they are all under arrest."

The marine examining General Fitzwilliam's papers looked up from them, glanced at the Bow Street Runners, glanced at General Fitzwilliam, and then looked at the carriage with Darcy and Elizabeth staring palely out at him through the windows.

He shrugged. "Papers in order, General. Papers in order. Open the gate!" he shouted to the other soldiers. He stabbed his thumb dismissively at the Bow Street Runners. "Thems with you?"

"No, not at all. I'd not admit them if they don't have proper authorization. I suspect," General Fitzwilliam lowered his voice, "I suspect they may be infiltrators trying to destroy our ships and are part of one of those groups of agitators, like the Hampstead clubs, or those people who want Napoleon to rule Britain. Best give them a run around before you send for the Captain on duty to look at their papers."

General Fitzwilliam handed the man a coin. The marine nodded, bit the coin, and waved General Fitzwilliam's soldiers and the Darcy carriage through.

"Stop, in the name of the king, stop them! For fuck's sake." The leader of the runners threw his short top hat to the ground in anger. "Are all you all here criminals? These men are disobeying the law and must be arrested."

"He is definitely," said the royal marine, enunciating every syllable, to the Bow Street Runner, "a proper and auth-en-tic general. Now are you calling a general of his majesty's army a criminal?"

"That woman tried to murder a peer of the realm!"

And their carriage rolled them away, towards where a giant ship that had been designed along the same lines as the most modern East Indiamen, with long trees trunks making up the sweeping line of the deck, a smattering of canons stuck in a single line along the gun deck, and beautiful black paint on gold making up the coloration. The sterncastle was painted blue, and the flag of the united Great Britain flapped in the wind.

A wide gangplank made of hewn yellow planks led up to the ship. The railings were lined by red-coated soldiers with their muskets out and settled calmly on the wooden planking of the deck. The cold wind blew stray hair about, but the soldiers kept a firm formation on the mostly stable platform of the ship.

The soldiers who had escorted them dismounted and formed up an honor guard. General Fitzwilliam stepped out into the cold wind; the temperature of the day was cold enough that their breath formed clouds. The slightly rotted, even in winter, smell of the Thames greeted them. Darcy took Elizabeth's arm to help her out of the carriage. To his surprise, and pride, she smiled at him, and she was completely steady.

"A fine adventure, Mr. Darcy," she said, "but one I hope is over, and that we shall not repeat."

"I was never so terrified in my life as when the marine would not open the gate."

Elizabeth smiled softly at him as she let him lift her to the ground from the carriage. "You took our escape with rather less composure than me."

"You merely hazarded your own life, I hazarded *yours.*" His voice was low.

The drummer on the ship took up a rolling military beat to greet the return of the general. The three of them walked up the gangplank together. Elizabeth was now steady and firm in her steps, as though the fear of the last hour had scared away, at least for the moment, any lingering aches and weakness from her illness.

They reached the deck of the ship, and the gangway was pulled in.

The captain of the ship was a bald man with a grey fringe of hair and a vicious scar an inch wide going up his forehead and disappearing under his slightly askew bicorn hat. He wore a coat of a blue wool that was at least half an inch thick. And he was angry.

"What the damned tarnation is the matter with you, Fitzwilliam," he ranted at Darcy's cousin. "Thought you were a reasonable man when we settled matters. In all tarnations! Ordering us off onto sea on an instant. You can't prepare a ship like this to sail without some warning. It just isn't done."

"Do you have the pilot, and all preparations under way? Can we cast off?"

"Damnations, man. Yes I have the pilot. Had to promise him a bottle of my best whiskey and an extra six guineas to show up on such notice. A different ship is being held an extra hour so that we can be guided out, and the stores are not prepared. Damnations and tarnations, man."

"I would ask," Darcy said coldly to the naval officer, "that you might keep your language under some regulation whilst there is a lady present."

The seaman looked Darcy up and down. Darcy smiled pleasantly back at him, standing tall and firm, and unwilling to be challenged on this matter.

"Damnations, man, I *am* watching my language for her sake. Damnations isn't a curse. It's nothing like…" He blushed, which rather surprised Darcy. "None of that nonsense in a lady's presence. Quite outside of what should be said to her."

Elizabeth's merry laugh rang out. "Captain, I am pleased to make your acquaintance. I have a quite particular and personal desire to be out of England soon as might be possible. Are we able to leave?"

"Set sail, set sail." The captain busied himself for half a minute giving orders that Darcy was not quite convinced were in English, but the crew of the ship moved with alacrity, and the sails were unfurled, and movement of the ship started. A prim man of about thirty and five with overly greased blond hair and what seemed like a perpetual sneer stood at the rudder, occasionally calling out his own instructions to the crew. Darcy presumed him to be the harbor pilot.

"Damn — dash it, man." The ship's captain turned back to General Fitzwilliam, since he would have no further business managing the ship till they were out of the shifting and low waters of the Thames. "Ordering a ship hired for a regiment of the king to depart before time to help a tart leave England with her lover?"

"Sir, I will not hear Miss Bennet insulted," Darcy said in a quiet voice.

"I did not insult her. What are you talking 'bout? Besides, why else would a tart and a gent like you flee so quickly?"

"Elizabeth is not a—"

"Cousin," General Fitzwilliam placed his hand on Darcy's shoulder, "I dare say that our friend here thinks that tart is the name you give the most respectable sort of woman."

"Well… not the *most* respectable sort." The sea captain winked broadly and in what seemed like a grotesque attempt at salted charm at Elizabeth, who blushed and winked back at him.

General Fitzwilliam pointed at Elizabeth and then said in a mighty whisper, "She bashed the head of a different cousin of mine in, and beat him near to death. This cousin is an earl, who wants to bring the law against her."

"Oh!" The captain brightened at this. He now smiled at Elizabeth broadly, showing that two of his teeth were gold, and the rest tobacco stained. "You bashed in a true milord? What was he doing? A little handsy?"

"More than a little. I also broke his nose with my forehead." Elizabeth tapped the fading bruise on her forehead. "A real milord too."

The captain peered at Elizabeth's forehead, and then he laughed gaily. "Damnations. Damnations and tarnations. Suppose that really be reason to get out of England fast and quickly. You hit him hard?"

"Hard as I could. I did break his nose."

"I've seen him," General Fitzwilliam confirmed. "Warms the cockles of my soul, it does."

"Damnations and tarnations. Well, well, well. Was the stupid of a milord that gave me this scar." He took off his hat to show them the thick line of the scar that went all the way back to the surviving fringe of hair in the back of his head. "By the sea, worthy reason. But still." He turned to General Fitzwilliam. "Cost me a good deal to get the pilot here. Cost me a good deal."

General Fitzwilliam had a blazing smile. He poked his finger towards Darcy. "Our good fortune is to have a patron present. He has been quite willing to tell me to hand him bills, and he'll pay without asking. So he'll give you a much better bottle of whiskey, and that bottle will have a dozen fine partners to keep it from being lonely, than what you gave to the pilot, and whatever else you need. Mr. Darcy here is your friend in that respect…"

Darcy rolled his eyes and sighed. He owed Richard a great deal, and in a way he owed this sea captain as well. "Yes, whichever Epicurean pleasures a *reasonable* sum of money can provide are yours for the picking."

"Don't be put off by that caveat!" General Fitzwilliam cried out. "He'll consider in gratitude a quite unreasonable sum reasonable for at least a fortnight more."

"Tarnations." The sea captain bowed his head. "At your service, Mr. Darcy. At your service."

By now they were exiting the controlled water of the dredged dock for the main line of the Thames River.

The Bow Street Runners in their caped coats and red uniforms at last ran up to the dock where the ship had been and they incoherently yelled for them to stop. Of course the ship did not, and they knew themselves the entire matter was much too late.

Mr. Blight joined them, and he looked straight at Elizabeth with a vicious snarl that made Darcy protectively put his arms around Elizabeth. There was something of a brutish borderer's violence in the man's face.

"I am quite all right," Elizabeth said, unperturbed. "I have already downed him once. And he is *there*, not here."

Mr. Blight glared across the water at them. He raised his fingers in an obscene gesture and spit into the rushing water of the Thames. He shouted something across, but it was too faint to be heard across the distance.

Elizabeth turned to Darcy, and she laughed exultantly. "Zounds, I hate that man!"

Chapter Eight

The February sun had already half set as the ship floated down the continuously widening Thames towards the sea. The buildings of London were left behind, and on either side was countryside, and eventually fens and marshes.

Elizabeth remained outside the afternoon entire upon the ship deck, with Mr. Darcy stood by her side watching her anxiously for any sign of a relapse, or faintness. Elizabeth feared greatly this would be her final sight of emerald England. And she knew not what next would follow.

If she dared not face the charge against her levied by Lord Lachglass at this time, when would be a proper time to face the claim of such a crime?

At least, Elizabeth smiled to herself, she spoke some French.

The wide river with Thames estuary opened up on either side. The bramble and trees lined the banks, mostly dense brown sticks grown high at this time of year. Elizabeth had read in journals that her father had subscribed to about the peculiarities of this large area where different fish than those in either the rivers or the seas lived, fish that could survive in both the salt water of the ocean when the tides came in, or the fresh (except for the sewage tossed into the river in London) water that poured out from the Thames.

The large cargo ship passed many fishing boats, whose busily working occupants ignored them. Other freighters worked their way up the river towards the greatest city in the world, and occasionally a faster ship, built for speed rather than efficiency, passed them on its way down to the ocean.

Elizabeth's face was cold and chapped from the wind, but Darcy had found a thick blanket to wrap around her shoulders.

He kept her warm.

The reddish sun setting was a beautiful sight, the light gleaming almost painfully off the waves created by their wake in the river.

She had not been scared the entirety of the passage through London. It was strange. But now she felt like shaking and crying, and becoming entirely maudlin. She had not even killed a man, and she was safe, and she trusted Darcy to see she was cared for.

Elizabeth glanced from the corner of her eyes at him.

Darcy stood a few feet away, his powerful forearms propping up his chin on the rail of the ship. A slight manly shadow had appeared on his face. He had a thick head of rich dark hair, and a muscular neck. His face was carven finely, with noble and aristocratic features. He looked less proud when he smiled at her, but she liked the look of him now, as he stared out towards the seashore, thinking thoughts Elizabeth could not guess.

She remembered the smooth feel of his hands gripping her as she thrashed from side to side in her fevered delirium.

She had called his name in that fever. She remembered calling his name.

He turned to her, perhaps realizing that her idle eyes had turned to stare at his glorious features, thus missing the glorious setting of her last *British* sun for an unknown time.

And he smiled at her, that grin making him even younger than he had appeared when she had first known him as a Miss Bennet of Longbourn. It transformed his face, and made her breath catch. There was something in his eyes that made her heart race, and yet at the same time made Elizabeth to feel entirely relaxed, happy and calm.

"Miss Bennet—"

"Elizabeth," she interrupted, shuffling consciously so that she stood just a fraction closer to Mr. Darcy. "You prefer to call me Elizabeth, and you have saved me so many times now."

"Today was the product of General Fitzwilliam's intrepid quickness." Darcy looked back out at the passing riverbank sliding relentlessly away. "I ought to have brought him into the matter immediately. It was his relation to Lord Lachglass that made me hesitate, but…"

Elizabeth softly smiled at him. "You are far more my hero than he is."

Darcy swallowed.

"You do not mind that I title you my hero? My champion. I expect you to slay any dragons I may face. General Fitzwilliam of course may be your second, and he can bring up a cannon from his regiment, but you will need to be the one who puts the final stab to the creature."

"I would happily kill any dragon that might torment you. If only…" His voice faded away.

"Yes?"

"You are very much under my protection at this time. It is not… I cannot speak on certain matters while you are under my protection. But I will, again, and, and… I will then want you to know that gratitude has no place in such a matter. I have done nothing for sake of *gratitude* or because…"

"Fitzwilliam."

He looked her deep into the eyes. They stood so close, and in the cold winter's evening, she could feel the warmth of his breath brushing against her cheeks. An albatross leapt over them from its perch on a railing, cawing and flapping its wide wings.

Elizabeth smiled at Darcy. "I will say yes, and not for gratitude's sake."

"I ask you, say nothing, make no promises *now*. Once you are safe, and once you have some hope of making your way without a dependence on me, and—"

Elizabeth laughed. "You are such a dear man. But as you insist, we shall do such as you wish for the moment."

They stood silent together, so close that their elbows and wrists brushed against each other. The night became dark and darker, and as they left the relatively tame waters of the Thames estuary for the open sea in the channel, the light faded completely, and no more was there sight of England.

All they could see was lit by the swinging brass lanterns of the ship that waved side to side with the rocking motion of the ship, and the brilliant spangled stars high above, as clear as on one perfect night in Longbourn, when she and Papa had taken the carriage late at night to Oakham Mount to test out a telescope he had purchased, and they were able to see the moons around Jupiter, and the rings around Saturn.

That night they had lied there together, with a picnic packed by cook for this expedition, on a warm summer evening, looking up into the sky as Papa told her stories about the constellations, and their meanings, and about the history of astronomical discoveries, from Copernicus, to Galileo, to Kepler, to Newton, to the more recent greats such as Herschel, Laplace, and Lagrange.

Tonight was freezing cold, the constant sea breeze bit through her, and though Elizabeth did not want to leave the deck, she shivered despite the heavy blanket Mr. Darcy had given her.

Fleeing England. Her home. Her life had been overturned and near destroyed. A peer of the land wanted her judicial murder. There was so much wrong.

Yet with the man standing next to her sharing this beautiful clear night, Elizabeth felt as happy as she had that night with her father.

*****

As it happened Elizabeth did not *stay* so happy the entire night.

Not long after they hit the open sea, the far worse rocking of the boat proved to Elizabeth that she did not at present have her sea *stomach*.

She'd been persuaded by Darcy to go into the galley where it was far warmer from those clever stoves that allowed sailors to heat the inner space and cook their food in the shaking seas without more than the slightest chance of lighting the tarred and oiled wooden decks aflame.

Within moments of entering the warm (comparatively) room in the back part of the ship — the stern, as the almost offended sailor firmly explained when she *called* it the back part — Elizabeth was offered a cup of hot grog as a proper welcome to a real ship.

The story had gone round the ranks of what she had done to the earl, and her use of violence both reduced the usual distance and deference men, especially men of a lower class, treated a lady with, and at the same time meant they thought of her with deeper real respect.

Elizabeth sat on her rolling seat next to Darcy and she half closed her eyes. She calmly sipped the grog and listened. She was terribly tired and cold from the day, and happily relaxed in a warm room with Mr. Darcy seated next to her.

Unfortunately when three minutes had passed from when the rocking of the ship increased enormously, she began to feel quite uneasy, and her skin became clammy and she felt dizzy.

Elizabeth shut her eyes, and wished the sensation away with all her power.

Something spun about her. She did not feel right. She pressed her hand against her sweat beaded forehead.

"Lizzy, Lizzy. Are you well? Jove, I should not have let you stand out so long. Not after your illness. You are so pale."

Elizabeth clenched her hand to her stomach and stood. "I think I may be relapsing. I feel terrible. Though not like a fever."

Darcy pressed her forehead. "No fever," he said in a relieved voice.

The sailor who had given Elizabeth the grog cackled. "Ain't nothing but a landsman's stomach. You can beat up a gentleman, but can't handle our lady the sea. But ain't nothing to worry about. You'll be sick today, but well tomorrow."

Elizabeth nodded. She pressed her hand to her mouth, and her stomach churned inside.

"Outside, lady. Best off the *stern* side of the ship. Don't want to hurl out when the wind is blowin' in your face. That be right unpleasant. You believe me."

Elizabeth believed him.

She hurried out back onto the cold deck, with Darcy holding her hand and helping to guide her. She saw the side of the deck and ran, noting from the corners of her eyes at least two dozen sickly pale men from General Fitzwilliam's regiment leaning over the railings and staring sickly out at the sea as if life had betrayed them unexpectedly.

She barely reached the edge when the vomit hurled out. And then the acid came up again, and out.

Her throat burned from the pain of that. She stared out at the sea behind them, the sliver of the moon high in the air. The deck lanterns of another ship swung perhaps half a mile away. Her forehead was so cold and sweaty but she did feel much better with all of that out of her stomach.

Why did anyone ever voluntarily go sailing if *this* was considered a natural and normal part of the process?

A thick horse-hair blanket was wrapped around her shoulders, and then, after a moment of hesitation, Darcy put an arm around her, holding her against his side. "Elizabeth, do you feel better?"

She took in deep shuddering breaths, and then turned to smile at Darcy. "A little."

He handed her his handkerchief, and she gratefully wiped around the edges of her lips, getting rid of any remains. She could not see his eyes and could barely see his face in the flickering light of the lantern. But his arm was strong and warm, and she was very glad he was here with her. She snuggled closer to his body and closed her eyes.

"Can't go back inside yet," she said. "Need the cold breeze, better than the sick stomach feeling."

Darcy murmured something soft and comforting, and held her close.

Elizabeth closed her eyes, and she concentrated with each breath on Darcy's strong manly scent as it mingled with the salty wind.

Darcy kissed the top of her head, and he whispered something to himself that Elizabeth could not hear. But the sound of his voice made her, as he always made her, happy.

They both knew the love which bound them together. They both knew that their future would be the two of them together. It was an unspoken thing; it waited for the right moment, a moment when Darcy felt his duty of honor to protect her had been fulfilled. But if he waited too long for such a moment, Elizabeth thought to herself saucily, she would just use her arts and allurements to convince him that it was time.

Chapter Nine

Lord Lachglass stood in the alcove of a mullioned window in his large townhouse. The light from the afternoon sun fell on his back, keeping his face and his broken nose in shadow. Lachglass kept his face impassive as Mr. Blight snivelingly sniveled out his report.

He always kept his ruined face still and impassive now, because it hurt less. And Lord Lachglass tired of the taste of his own blood occasionally dribbling out the back of his nostrils and down his throat.

Why did he keep a man like Blight as his man of business if Blight couldn't *do what was demanded?* Spitey Blighty had uselessly trailed the carriage, and waved Miss Bennet a fare-thee-well, as she and Mr. Darcy sailed away. With his cousin Soldier Dickie— Lachglass's mind, like an ostrich hiding its head in the sand, pushed all thought of General Fitzwilliam away. *Don't remember how he looked. Soldier Dickie wouldn't ever really kill you, Aunt Fitzwilly loves me too much to let her son do that.*

Mr. Blight finished. Spitey Blighty.

The man of business observed his still master, who carefully breathed through his mouth. Blight's beady eyes looked vaguely worried. He was clearly angry himself at his sniveling failing. Blighty's cheekbone had not broken, but there was still a giant swollen blue bruise, which made the scar swell up grotesquely. Blight had told Lachglass his father had cut that scar in his face before he killed the man. Lachglass did not believe that story though.

Spitey Blighty sometimes lied, even to him.

Lachglass said nothing.

"Well." Blight rubbed his hands together, like Pilate after condemning Christ. "There is the end of it. She's gone; out of the country. Don't speak the French myself, but could try and follow them, and—"

"To France. To France. To France!" A sharp pain cracked in Lachglass's nose at his scream as the rage took him, but he barely felt it, even though blood dripped out his nostrils again. "You let the *slut whore* escape to France."

Lachglass delicately pressed a fresh silk handkerchief to his bleeding nose.

Blight held up his hands defensively. "Ten soldiers. Ten of em, didn't respect the law none at all, they didn't. They rode right over the Bow Street Runner and—"

"She got away! You fucking let her get away!"

Mr. Blight submissively chose to make no further defense of himself, yet there was that in his manner which suggested to his master that

Blighty considered the blame placed principally upon him entirely unreasonable.

Lachglass forced himself to calm.

Spitey Blighty had told him he ought to get the warrant first, and *then* bother Darcy. But he'd been too full of laughter and hope at the prospect of seizing Swinging Lizzy to listen.

He regretted it now, but he still loved the look on Darcy's face as he sneered at the man for getting refused by a *governess* — a governess who was, in Lachglass's disinterested opinion, a whore.

Lachglass would confess that in honesty, he considered *all* women whores, at least till they were so old that no one discriminating would want to rut with them.

He let out a breath and painted again in his mind the comforting thought: Marching that pretty governess out to the scaffold. Watching the hangman put the noose round her neck, as she whimpered and begged for mercy.

He could hear her whimpers: *I don't want to die. I don't want to die. Please, just let me live one more day.*

With a thin smile Lachglass removed his handkerchief from his nose and looked at his red blood. It felt like the nose had stopped bleeding again. That was the best part of the fantasy: The whimpers of *I don't want to die. Pleases don't make me die.* But he then followed it with his mind the rest of the way through.

The lever pulled. The sharp crack of a neck breaking. The cheering of the crowd, as he stood on the platform and promised the rabble who'd gathered to see Miss Elizabeth Bennet off that he'd tap a barrel of wine for them to toast her death.

Lachglass let out a deep breath. His useless anger was gone.

But he hated that this vision in his mind might never come to pass. He *needed* to see her dead. Needed it more than he needed another woman.

It was the way he'd fought off the doctor's demands that he take laudanum, by imagining her hanging again and again. He didn't like laudanum. His father had been addicted to the poppy juice, and he did not want to follow down that dark path.

But it seemed to him that there was nothing he could do.

The French, tyrants they were, had treaties with most of their neighbors, and with the rebellious colonies in America where each side would hand over common criminals in their territory to the other if they were asked. But Britain, free independent Britain, glorious Britain had signed no such treaties. Which meant Elizabeth was gone, gone beyond his hope of revenge, unless he did hire a killer to stab her in the back.

But that was by no means certain… and Lord Lachglass flinched from that course. It would not satisfy him.

He wanted to watch her swing. He wanted to hear her whimpering for mercy that the hard court, that the hanging judge he would find to try her, would never give. Above all he wanted to see the despair in her eyes before she died; he wanted to watch those pretty sparkling eyes, so alive, go dark and glassy.

And he wanted to hear the wails and laments of those who loved that refusing whore.

"All right," he said at last to Mr. Blight. "Have all her family watched — spend whatever is necessary. Know if they receive a letter from her, know if they behave different from their normal, know if they have a strange visitor. She will eventually long for England, and when the time happens, we *will* seize her and remand her to the crown."

"Yes, milord." Blight bowed, his Adam's apple bouncing against his greasy cravat.

"Dismissed."

Blight went to the heavy oak door with a fine nude with exceptional breasts painted onto it. Some classical allusion that Lachglass had long since forgotten was the excuse for the painting. Mythology, in Lachglass's view, was of value solely because it let everyone stick statues and paintings bare as Eve's arse in public areas.

"And Spitey Blighty?" Lachglass added, as the man opened the door, his hand hovering next to the egg white breasts of the nymph on the door.

Blight looked back at Lachglass, hopefully a little wary, though Lachglass didn't think he was.

"Fail me again, and I'll fucking bury you alive."

Blight inclined his head in his own impassive manner, and there was something in the curl of the man's lip that suggested the threat amused him rather than frightened.

Chapter Ten

Fitzwilliam Darcy did not, in the general course of experience, get sick on the sea. He watched Elizabeth vomit with first concern, and then with a fond affection for her when he realized that she was not relapsing, or in any particular danger, but simply sick in the very unpleasant way many, many people had been.

Elizabeth lay on the deck, looking up at the stars, with Darcy next to her, for a half hour. They did not talk, both lost in their thoughts.

But he found himself, almost as though by accident holding her hand.

She gripped his back tightly.

He wanted to marry her. He always did, but now more than ever.

After some time of commune with the cold salty stars, Elizabeth began to drift off to sleep, and Darcy roused her. She looked at him with a smile, such a smile. Her smile was felt more than seen in the dim starlight.

She trusted him to care for her.

He took her arm to help her up. They came to their feet, and he helped her to the cabin that had been set aside for General Fitzwilliam, but which the officer gallantly gave up for the sake of the lady. They didn't have any servants with them, so Darcy looked at Elizabeth in confusion, not sure if he should leave her in the bed to... undress herself... or if he should help her in some way.

Elizabeth seemed to see his confusion and she said with a sweet voice, steadying herself on his shoulder against a sudden rocking of the ship, "I will be quite at my leisure here."

"Are you certain you need no help?"

Elizabeth laughed. "Quite, quite certain."

Darcy looked at her with a smile as in the flickering light of a sea lamp she used her hand to steady her way through the narrow room, and then she sat on the thin bed. He closed the door behind Elizabeth, the tin knob cold on his hand, and went back up to the deck.

General Fitzwilliam joined him, with a freshly lit cigar in his hand, the glowing ember of the end bright against the velvety field of stars high above, and the single sliver of moon.

"Thank you, thank you, and thank you again," Darcy said to his cousin.

General Fitzwilliam grunted and smiled, leaning much of his weight on the smoothed railing of the ship. "My pleasure. Just invite me early to any future like occasions. I like to be involved." He took a deep pull from his cigar, and then blew out the smoke which pleasantly curled with the astringent and almost sweet smell of Carolina tobacco around Darcy before the salty sea breeze took it away. "When shall you two marry?"

Darcy coughed.

"Don't be daft, she adores you. You adore her. What is there to wait for?"

"I can't."

"What do you mean you can't?" General Fitzwilliam ground his cigar out on the railing and peered closely at Darcy. "You don't mean to say you've got a secret wife somewhere?"

"Of course not!"

"Huh. Well after today, nothing from you will surprise me anymore. Hiding women in your townhouse… *and* telling me nothing about the matter. I'd tell you if *I* hid a woman in a townhouse."

Darcy rolled his eyes. But his cousin had earned the opportunity to needle him. "You are the one who always goes on about the importance of family, didn't think you'd like being put in opposition to Lechery."

General Fitzwilliam snorted. "Of course I would, and you ought have known I would — is she secretly your father's bastard?"

"*What?*" Darcy's voice came out at a slightly high-pitched screech. "Who? No! Good god, *no*. No, no, no. What dark crevice of your mind spews forth such ideas?"

"Well then why aren't you marrying her immediately? — does *she* have a secret husband?"

"No!" Then Darcy paused for a moment with a ridiculous and silly feeling of anxiety. *Did* Elizabeth have a secret husband somewhere?

And then Darcy laughed at the absurdity of the idea. "Stop with this — it should be clear to you. It is a matter of honor, she is dependent on me. She came to me for safety, and for protection, and she is now banished from England and her family, perhaps forever. I can't… she refused me once, I can't use her desperate situation, what gratitude she feels for me now to manipulate her into accepting me. I honor Elizabeth too much for that."

General Fitzwilliam did not reply, but from the manner with which he pulled a match out, struck it on the railing, and relit his cigar, Darcy perceived his cousin rather thought he was an idiot for these compunctions.

But he was who he was, and Darcy would never seek to take advantage of the situation that had placed Elizabeth under his protection. That was what being a gentleman worthy of her *meant*. Besides… "I don't want her gratitude, I want her love."

General Fitzwilliam complacently puffed on his cigar, blowing out bursts of smoke that were blown away immediately. "Don't drag things out so long that you annoy her, *she* deserves better than that."

The two continued there, on the deck of the softly rocking ship, accompanied by the slapping of the waves against the ship's sides, and the endless creaking of the wooden beams. The starry infinite sky high above them.

And they talked of other things, as old friends will.

Early the next morning their ship floated into the modest — by comparison with London, or Liverpool — but busy harbor of Calais. An ancient city, with long connection to England. Calais had been an important possession of the crown for centuries, and it remained in good English hands long after everything else that had been united to the crown of England in France had been lost during the Hundred Years War.

And then Queen Mary lost the city. Or King Philip II of Spain, if one was more accurate, and not intent upon being a wag about the deficiencies of female rulers.

A city of famed business importance, and the closest on the Continent to the island of Britannia.

Calais also was a city Darcy had never visited. When he was a young man inclined to travel, England had already entered its two decades of war — hopefully at a permanent *finis* — with France. Instead he visited the capitals of German speaking principalities during his Grand Tour, Berlin, Potsdam, Hamburg, and of course the King's possession of Hannover. And then Vienna, hearing Herr Beethoven perform upon the piano, before the next day watching a performance of Mozart's *Don Juan* and later that day hearing one of Handel's fine symphonies — though Handel could be heard easily enough still in London.

He'd gone to the supposed wilds of the Habsburg crown's Magyar holdings, which despite the prevalence of impressively large mustaches and the paranoia of the Turk to the south were mostly civilized.

Darcy travelled even further to the east, and he visited in winter the Russian capital of Moscow. *That* had been a foolish idea of his. Darcy thought he could stand any cold comfortably, coming from the cold hills of Derbyshire. After those two lovely, if almost frostbitten months, he was not in the *slightest* surprised when Napoleon's army froze to death after capturing the city several years later. The company and conversation had been excellent, though the Russian mind tended towards the dourness demanded by the weather.

Darcy had only been called back to England by the letter which reached him, too late, with news of his father's illness.

He had not had opportunity, or more accurately, inclination, to travel from England since gaining the estate. As he walked down the rough gangplank with Elizabeth's arm nestled in his, he smiled to see her delightedly glance around and around at every sight in the harbor.

Elizabeth grinned with every fragment of conversation in French that came to them.

He would have the opportunity to explore a new, and greatly famed, country with Elizabeth at his side.

When they left the ship, they first went to the customs house, which was thick with the scent of a poorly ventilated fire and musty books. There was a difficulty there. The French clerk who managed the office was not impressed with the old passport of Darcy's issued by the Foreign Office a decade ago. Darcy considered that rather ironic, as the British passport was written in French, and thus perfectly legible to the man.

"No description of the bearer, no information about your conditions or employment — no reference to the lady. No, no, no. This will not do."

"I assure you, we are respectable British travelers," Darcy replied rather annoyed with the man. Elizabeth frowned worriedly.

On the other hand Major Williams, who General Fitzwilliam had sent with them to ensure any problems were smoothed over, grinned.

"You ought to have applied for a proper passport from our embassy in London," the Frenchman said with moderate outrage. He was a small bald man, with a wispy fringe of hair and dried out skin. "How can I know from *this* that you are not subversives, revolutionaries, *symathetiques* of the *empereur*! No, no, no! A proper passport. Why did you not go to the embassy in London and get a proper passport? Go back and get one! — Where are your servants? All most irregular."

Major Williams patted the clerk on his shoulder, the man rather stiffly and prissily drew back from him. The officer said in French that was considerably worse accented than Darcy's own. "Friend, friend. I vouch for them, as an officer of His Majesty. We aren't bringing over sympathetics... uh... what is the word I want... uh..."

"Subversives? Revolutionaries? Radicals? Jacobins?" Darcy offered in French to General Fitzwilliam's aide.

The young man snapped his fingers. "Exactly."

He flashed a brilliant smile at Darcy, which again struck Darcy as a close imitation of General Fitzwilliam's own smile, perhaps... but while he was a young man, Major Williams was much too old for there to be any chance that he was a by-blow of his cousin.

"We dislike Napoleon quite more than you do I would imagine." Major Williams grinned widely. And as he spoke he pulled from somewhere a large yellow coin that Darcy believed was worth ten francs, which he rolled around his fingers with impressive dexterity.

The clerk watched the coin quite closely. He then said, "Well, Monsieur Darcy and you are of undoubted respectability... we can have a passport made here for Mrs. Benoit... you really ought to have followed procedure. That is the procedure for a good reason."

"I know. I know." Major Williams placed the coin on the desk and said again, "I am quite disapproving of Mrs. Benoit."

He winked at Elizabeth.

"We have further servants who will come this afternoon on the Dover packet," Darcy added, "but I have good hopes they will have acquired passports of their own."

"Just send them here, if they do not." He sighed. "You British, how did you ever win the war when you are so disorderly. By regulation, everything should be done by regulation."

Major Williams laughed. "We won with money, we have a great big lot of the yellow stuff — Monsieur Darcy here more than most."

The clerk disappeared the coin Major Williams had put onto the desk into his pocket and he spoke to Darcy, "A two franc fee if you wish me to write up a passport valid for internal travel, and ten francs if you wish one that shall allow passage past borders."

They paid, and then the man, carefully writing Elizabeth's description into the passport, under the name of Mrs. Benoit, filled out the document, and then signed the bottom of it, and he had the chief of the office enter and give a final undersigning of the passport.

Now free of customs. Though when all of their trunks and carriage arrived they would be held here and Darcy would need to return to the office to pay the import fees on the carriage and allow the inspectors to look over his clothes and other belongings to ensure he was not a smuggler.

Based on the timetables for the regular packets to Dover, he'd asked the harbor master about the packets from Dover, Darcy expected to have his servants and carriages to arrive late in the afternoon.

They planned to stay in Calais at least until General Fitzwilliam gathered all his troops and set them off on a march towards Cambrai.

They picked their way along the streets lined with tall buildings painted in oranges and blues. Major Williams led them quite confidently. "First time in Calais, Mr. Darcy? Lovely city. Lovely people — too deuced talented with the use of cannons. Never liked *that* about them."

"First time in France," Darcy agreed.

"Here we are," Major Williams said when they reached a fine park, with an excellent building taking up a large frontage of the street. Several carriages were parked out front, one of them being loaded as they watched. "Dessein's. Best hotel in this city. Or so they say — the rooms being a little above my purse. They have the finest breakfast in town, and excellent wines. The General always dines here when he is in Calais."

Though everyone referred to the hotel as Dessein's the sign in large letters above the entrance to the building proclaimed it to be the *Hôtel d'Angleterre.* When they reached the coach yard, they found a fashionably dressed English gentleman with a face ruddy from too much drink and beer, waving a gold tipped cane as he oversaw the loading of his carriage.

Darcy almost winced as the gentleman leapt eagerly towards him, not liking him in the slightest, even though they both attended White's in London, and both had accounts at Childe's Bank. However, always polite, any such sentiments were kept from Darcy's face.

"Allo, Darcy, damned fancy, pardon miss" — said aside to Elizabeth — "seeing you here. Thought you were stuck on our side of the little river that kept the little ogre away. France." He took a deep breath. "Stinks to the soggy heavens, of course, but they have the best clothes here, whatever Beau says. What's your business, old chap?"

Darcy shrugged.

"Just to look-look the sites, eh? Maybe *voir-voir* their women in Parii?" He chuckled good naturedly and almost good naturedly elbowed Darcy. However something about Darcy's foreboding expression stopped him. "Most beautiful, neatest dressed women in the world. With their curves… even if they all are radicals, even those of fashion."

"That is not my purpose in visiting," Darcy replied stiffly.

The gentleman laughed. "Second time here since the peace. Off to Paris. Nothing in the world like the *Palais Royal* — covered like a market hall, but bigger than any, with a half mile walk and fine shops on either side, and the gambling upstairs." The gentleman sighed happily. "Best gambling in the world. And the girls they have there…" And then he coughed embarrassedly and looked at Elizabeth. "Who is the lady? And your fine martial companion?" he added inclining his head to Major Williams.

"Major Williams, at your service." Major Williams bowed to him.

"Lord Wakefield at yours."

"I'm afraid I have no time for chatter — the General has need of me. Till we meet again, Mr. Darcy. Dessein will set you up nicely in the hotel, and tell you what room your cousin breakfasts in — my apologies," he added with another bow to the gentleman. "But military matters demand urgency."

"Of course, of course."

And with a satisfied air Major Williams went off leaving Darcy and Elizabeth alone with Darcy's acquaintance.

Feeling a little odd with the lie, which he was not at all sure was still necessary here in France, but General Fitzwilliam had thought would be best to continue as they had begun, Darcy replied, "Mrs. Benoit, the widow of a relation of mine. Mrs. Benoit, Lord Wakefield."

"Benoit. That's a French name — didn't know you had any French relations, Darcy. Hahaha. Well met, Mrs. Ben-waa," he said ridiculously overexaggerating the pronunciation of the French 'oi'. "When'd you pick up French relations, Darcy?"

"Ah..."

"My husband's family were Huguenots," Elizabeth replied smoothly, from her voice she found it a much easier task to pretend than Darcy did. "They have been on our island for a hundred fifty years and almost entirely forgotten anything about France."

"Ah, no Papist tendencies then. Good. Not that the French are very Papist anymore. Hahahaha."

Elizabeth politely laughed with him.

Then Lord Wakefield shouted in English at the man loading his carriage, "Not that way! That trunk is worth more than your head, you fool! More than your head!"

The hotel's servant replied in French that he had no idea what he was being asked, but that he was offended by the foolish Englishman's tone. Or at least that is roughly what he said.

"Eh, ah, *mais qu'avez-vous dit?*" Wakefield replied first and then he angrily strode over to the servant, smacked him on the back of the head, and demonstrated with big gestures and slow half shouting in English the way that he wanted it to be done.

Darcy caught Elizabeth's eye, and she laughed. "In truth, it seems I do not speak so good French as I thought I could... I can read easily, but..."

"It takes a bit to get the knack to hear them speaking, but don't worry, you'll manage sooner or later."

"I hope." Elizabeth looked at the ground and frowned.

Darcy extended his arm to her, "Shall we?"

He gestured his head to the hotel where they were to breakfast with General Fitzwilliam and decide just what their next plan was.

As they started towards the ornate doors of the fine large building, Wakefield jogged back up to them. "Charmed, Mrs. Benoit. Charmed. Busy now, so apologies, Darcy — you are coming to Paris, right?"

Darcy again opened his mouth, not sure what to say. It would sound deuced strange to admit he had come across the channel with no plans about what he was to do after he'd crossed. That sort of answer was acceptable for a youth of nineteen or twenty on his Grand Tour who was quite ready to just fall in with whichever friends fate presented to him, so that he might let chance show him the adventure and culture he longed for.

A man past thirty was expected to be somewhat more deliberate though.

"We are," Elizabeth's clear voice said from beside him. "I am eager to see the *Notre Dame* and walk along the Seine. See where those famed events took place."

"Of course you are — best city in the world, better even than London, because the cits in Paris aren't trying to pretend to be one of *us*. Call on," Wakefield pulled out his card, and scribbled on the back of it with a nub of pencil he pulled from a little book that he apparently kept for the purposes of tracking odds during games of chance, "I'll be settled on the *Rue de St Denis,* quite near the Isle. We servants of King George must hang together eh? Charmed, Mrs. Benoit. Charmed."

Wakefield took her hand and kissed before he returned to shouting at the servants.

Elizabeth smiled, a little melancholically, "If I am to be exiled from the Albion, at least I need not miss for *John Bull.*"

Darcy laughed, and walked her into the hotel.

The decor was elaborate, pretty, and very ornamented. Endless detailed patterns, all done in gold and blue, with chairs that looked too thin to support the weight of a man of Darcy's size. It was like the hotel had been decorated by a Lady who'd become obsessed with French fashions and threw into some rubbish heap all the good solid furniture made of English oak.

Which was fair, since this was *France.*

Likely anyone who bought sensible furniture here was laughed at by his companions for adopting the English style — *à la mode Anglais.*

There were large mirrors built into the walls, from ceilings to ground, like he'd been told were in the old palace of the king at Versailles. And there was no carpet, but instead a hard brick floor, which must save on the expense of cleaning the carpet, at the cost of being quite uncozy when the weather was cold.

Monsieur Dessein himself was at the desk, and something about Darcy's manner led him to brush aside his servant to serve Darcy himself.

Their host's English was completely clear with an almost affected French accent. "The rooms General Fitzwilliam asked for you are prepared. We have a good collection of bathing rooms here, large and commodious, and there is a passage to the theatre. If you have any needs at all, simply ask me, and I shall provide — do not worry about gaining French money, it is simple. I shall give you Napoleons for your guineas, and then when you return, when your sojourn in our fair land is complete, I shall give you guineas for any Napoleons that remain to you."

Elizabeth looked down with a slight frown and a little turning away from him.

She was thinking again of the money he'd promised to pay to transport the rest of Colonel Fitzwilliam's troops to the continent, and what they paid now for this fine hotel. Each time he gave her anything it put Elizabeth deeper in his debt, and he did not want that. He wanted them to be one, so that there was no talk of debt or obligation.

Darcy frowned as he ran over what Dessein had said. What were the values he usually received in his business dealings? "Is not a Napoleon twenty francs?"

"It is, Monsieur Darcy."

"I shall refrain from having any money changed for the moment."

Monsieur Dessein laughed. "You'll not find a more convenient way to change your money, but I confess, as I can see you have already established in your mind, you may find a *cheaper* way to do so. Sign the register, and I will have you shown to your rooms, and then shown to the breakfast parlor where General Fitzwilliam and his aide are at present — both of you, please."

Elizabeth frowned. "Is it necessary to sign?"

"Quite, I am afraid." M. Dessein replied. "One of our local peculiarities."

"*Que faisiez-vous avec eux?*" Elizabeth asked stiffly as she signed her false name of Mrs. Benoit. Elizabeth had apparently decided now was the time to practice her French, with a Frenchman.

M. Dessein tilted his head in confusion.

Elizabeth repeated her question, with an air of frustration.

"Ah," M. Dessein replied in English, "Dear Madame, whilst your accent is perfect, I fear my hearing is poor. Perhaps you might repeat your question in your own noble language."

Elizabeth laughed, and it made Darcy glad to hear that she could be distracted from her worries easily. "My accent is not perfect, while your hearing is, I suspect."

"Were it so, I would not confess it," M. Dessein replied with a smiling bow of his head.

"What is done with the register, why is it necessary to sign?"

"Ah the police require it of me, that I inscribe every stranger staying with me. My boy runs the pages down to the *gendarmerie* each morning, so they can know who stayed the previous night, and then they copy out the names, and return the register. It simply means that if you *did* commit a crime, they would be able to find you. But, mademoiselle, the only crime a woman such as you could ever commit is the theft of a heart."

Elizabeth laughed nervously, and made a pretense of blushing at the compliment.

They then went to the breakfast room, where General Fitzwilliam and Major Williams already sat over their coffee.

Chapter Eleven

Elizabeth looked around impressed by the breakfast and the room.

They'd dined in a private first floor room, overlooking the garden ten feet below. The garden must be splendid in spring, a proper English style courtyard garden, with lawns, ample beds of flowers and several varieties of trees. There was a fine fountain of a nymph ready to spit water to the skies.

The sky was grey, and so were the plants. All grey sticks with their leaves fallen off.

Inspired by the scene, Elizabeth intoned, "Upon those boughs which shake against the cold, Bare ruin'd choirs, where late the sweet birds sang." Darcy frowned at her worriedly, and she laughed. "There is hint of at least one early bloom in that garden, near the wall there, so not quite the proper poem."

"Not proper at all. No dourness," General Fitzwilliam said. He and Major Williams had risen at her entrance. "You are alive, and safe."

"Safe enough." Elizabeth nodded and she eagerly sat down to breakfast, finding herself drained by the meandering from the bay and down the crowded avenue that led to the hotel.

The table was piled high with food and drink. There were decorated carafes of coffee and small jugs of milk to pour into the coffee. There were brie cheeses, squares of mouth-watering butter sitting on small china plates, an ornamented jug of honey with a little bee on the outside, and piles of freshly baked bread, still warm from the oven. A few hothouse fruits were also available. There were French style tarts and a pile of croquants with almonds in them.

The smell of rich bread was divine, and Elizabeth had by now completely recovered from the nausea of her boat ride, and she was ravenously hungry.

Darcy busied himself filling a plate for Elizabeth. He delighted in asking her which of the breads looked the most appealing, and in quickly and expertly piling them with more melted butter and honey than she would have dared to give herself.

The coffee tasted fresh, and was mostly clear of grounds. Elizabeth wondered how Dessein managed to make such smooth coffee for all his guests, their cook when she had lived at Longbourn never had the patience to pour the cups back and forth, or use isinglass to clarify the grounds out of the coffee.

"Add more milk, Miss Bennet, more milk," General Fitzwilliam demanded of Elizabeth after she took her first sip. "The French always take their coffee with an almost disgusting amount of milk — *cafe au lait*. You shall commit a crime against this fine country if you do not add more cream."

Elizabeth laughed. "If it is a requirement of politeness."

"Just ask in any *cafe* for *cafe au lait*. They also serve chocolate, tea — anything. It is quite the proper thing for women to frequent the French cafes, though I hear that was not so before the revolution."

"I shall *certainly* in that case frequent one myself."

Elizabeth did not want to think of money being spent for her entertainment by Darcy — since she assumed his cousin would leave him with the entirety of the bill at the hotel.

"Is there…" Elizabeth bit her lip, and then shrugged. "You shall need to go to Cambrai immediately, I believe, General Fitzwilliam."

Major Williams answered for his commander, "Not so quickly, we'll wait till all the regiment, the men left in England, come by ferry from Dover. Best to all march out in a body. That will take a deuced long time — you have no notion how *slowly* a large body of men can move."

"Do you think… shall it be a great problem for me that my French is… ah less than perfectly polished? I swear, I can *read* anything in the language, but while I made an attempt to teach it to my pupil, it seems I needed a teacher myself. I have not had much occasion to speak to authentic Frenchmen — this establishment is well equipped for English travelers, but—"

"Not a problem at all," Darcy replied. "My French and German are excellent but on my Grand Tour I travelled to Russia and Poland and through Bohemia and Hungary. You can manage well enough *anywhere* with shopkeepers by pointing and showing a few coins. You must also angrily shout and wave your arms about if you think they wish to cheat you."

"Here in France many speak decent English, the better to take advantage of our leisured classes." General Fitzwilliam laughed and patted his Major Williams on the shoulder. "Fitz told me that you encountered your old school chum, Lord Wakefield."

Darcy's sour face made Elizabeth laugh.

"He is," she said, "the sort of man who appears to have walked off a satirical drawing — it is easy for you to say I need not worry about speaking French, but I am trapped here. How is *your* French, General?"

"I get along well enough. Always have," General Fitzwilliam looked at Major Williams with a smile, "My governess ensured I had it pounded into my head."

"You know," Major Williams said, "I asked *her* if you were such a diligent student as you pretend you were, and while she confesses to believing you were already as charming as at present — not that *I* believe that you are charming in the slightest—"

"I do," Elizabeth laughed. "But how are you both acquainted with General Fitzwilliam's governess?"

"She is my fine and fantastical mother," Major Williams replied with a smile.

Elizabeth's attention was drawn to Darcy drawing his breath sharply in and looking with a close frown at Major Williams.

"Yes," General Fitzwilliam said grandly to Darcy. "My father's bastardy. Also why she was dismissed. He's my half-brother."

Darcy blinked. And then he extended his hand to Major Williams. "That makes us cousins as well. As close related as I am to Richard."

The young officer laughed. "I'll accept *that* connection a little more nicely than most — I'm not terribly enthused by a great many of my noble *connections*."

"Ha," General Fitzwilliam said, "but you are still a Fitz William."

"Wait," Elizabeth said with some surprise. "Your father acknowledged him?"

"No." Both Major Williams and General Fitzwilliam laughed.

Major Williams lounged back in his seat. "My Christian name is Fitz. That makes me Fitz Williams — my mother wished to claim the old earl as my father when she Christened me, but he had threatened to remove the little support he offered her — the bare least that he *could* do. She was not such as to stand upon noble but unadvantageous principles when the happiness of her child was at stake, and I am glad for this, for my life could have been significantly worse had she fought for the principle in the matter — what education I did receive, and my commission as an ensign and then a lieutenant and captain were purchased through that means."

"Perhaps, as he did support you, you ought not be so angry him, as I perceive you and General Fitzwilliam to be."

"*I* am angry at *dear* Papa," General Fitzwilliam said, "for certainty."

"'Twas the normal story, as I understand it." Major Williams said, "I asked my mother what occurred once, when we'd returned from Spain, before Waterloo. She was not raped, for she did not scream or fight as you did. But she was neither willing. Such is my belief. Perhaps I am wrong. You cannot speak with a parent in any detail about such events, but... I have never once met my father. He did not wish his wife to know of his indiscretions, and the reason why the governess was dismissed without her say so."

"And she then named you Fitz Williams. To spite your father?"

"A joke, a two-fold joke — my mother has a fine education, her father was a poorer vicar. It has always been a common thing to name bastards by appending Fitz to the family name. My father's line starts with a favored mistress of a king — but to name me *Fitz-Fitzwilliam* would have been more ridiculous than even Fitzwilliam. Fitzwilliam," Major Williams poked General Fitzwilliam as he said this, "is sufficiently pretentious and nonsensical."

"I would not say that," Elizabeth replied, herself nudging Darcy. "In my ear there is a sweet sound to it."

Darcy smiled widely at her saying that. He was her savior, so of course his Christian name had a sweet sound to her ears.

"I've been thinking," General Fitzwilliam said, leaning forward, and rather viciously sawing his meat with a knife. "How to convince my loose, leaky, lecherous cousin to forget charges against you? Public pressure is the thing: The people love stories of aristocrats proving their rights should be taken away. Let's have the story told clear and simple so everyone in London hears it and knows what sort of creature Lord Lechery is."

Elizabeth sat straighter, her hand holding her cup of coffee. It tasted nice, but very milky with this much cream in. "I would like his reputation to be generally known, so he cannot simply hire another woman who will enter such a place unknowing of the risk."

"Ha," General Fitzwilliam said. "You have that fire in you, to want some revenge against him."

"No, no." Darcy placed his hand on Elizabeth's elbow briefly, and she smiled at him, enjoying the comfort of his incidental touch. "Let's not wish to splash a bad reputation for you about town. Lechery will not drop his plans that way; he will pursue them assiduously, because he *must* prove that he was right."

"He'd be a laughing stock. A nitwitted object of scorn — think, Darcy, think." General Fitzwilliam growled, "How will they speak of him in White's? Already laughed at — already despised. Simply the whispers about the story. Everyone will make him an object of fun, for having been beaten to a pulp by a woman who he tried to force, and then they will sneer at him for trying to use the courts to rectify a private loss — nay, I tell you, it will hurt him."

"That isn't the point. I don't give a damn about Lechery. I'll challenge him one day, and then—"

"No!" Elizabeth felt a stab of anxiety, and a flash of seeing the two of them, with smoking pistols staring at each other across a green field on a foggy morning. "I do not want *you* to be injured, or to face the hangman like me."

Darcy dismissively made a cutting gesture with his hand. "Juries never hang duelists. Much as the judges would wish them to, never happens. I voted to acquit once myself, at the Derbyshire assizes. None of us assembled for that trial demurred."

Elizabeth took in a shallow breath. "I do not want to see anyone dueling. He would have a gun too, and… no, no, no. I could never bear it if you were shot. And he is a vicious man. He would try to kill you."

Darcy had a mulish expression and that frightened Elizabeth. She knew that she could not keep him from making the attempt. Darcy said, "I would have made a challenge to him the instant I learned he still lived, if it would not have informed him of where you were hidden. But now—"

"Now I am lost, unable to return to our Green England, and I need you to protect me." Elizabeth did not *like* being dependent, but she was enough of a woman to use her weak position to her advantage. "You cannot return to England and leave me alone here and friendless."

General Fitzwilliam said calmly, "In any case, Darcy, you forget that I have priority, he is my cousin, and I already challenged him to defend Miss Bennet's honor. He did refuse to face me, like a coward — he might refuse you as well. Not a man who wants to fight with one of equal strength is my cousin. He prefers to fight women, and given the end of his most recent attempt along those lines, I suspect the coward may become too cautious to even do that."

"Oh, you challenged him?" Elizabeth grinned at General Fitzwilliam, for some reason having vastly less anxiety for *him* dying in her defense than Mr. Darcy. Probably because she loved Mr. Darcy, while she did not love General Fitzwilliam. And General Fitzwilliam had an air of being well capable of killing a man without feeling much remorse or hesitation. "What a hero."

Confirming *that* sentiment, General Fitzwilliam replied, as he filled his coffee again, "My pleasure entirely. I must confess that I was more motivated by the hope to give my cousin a wound that would spout crimson than to make defense of your honor. Cousin Lechery annoys me. Always has. He'd intentionally wing birds when we went hunting as lads, just so they'd flitter to the ground in pain. He is family, and family ought take care of its own — both in good and in ill."

"Hear, hear." Major Williams raised his coffee mug, as though he were toasting with a glass of wine. "And Lachglass is no relation of *mine*."

"It would do no good for Elizabeth — Miss Bennet — to sound the story about," Darcy said. "What we must do is…" He frowned and trailed off.

"Darcy." Elizabeth put her hand briefly on his arm, so that he looked at her with his beautiful and startlingly deep eyes. It was rather hard to think about anything with the way her stomach twisted and jumped in delight with his eyes upon her.

"I just want," he said, "I just want you to be safe and happy, and able to return to your family in England, and be in such a position that you need not depend on me, and then…"

Elizabeth nodded. He felt as if his honor would not let him ask her again to marry him while she had such reasons as gratitude and necessity to suggest she must say yes.

Silly man — didn't he know by now that she was quite talented at refusing men in cases where her interest suggested she must accept them?

"Well," General Fitzwilliam said. "There would be value in making a scandal of Lachglass — he is one of the junior ministers in the government. A reward for bringing his rotten boroughs with him — a damned disgusting thing how our parliament works. That *one* man controls more of the government of our country through those MPs than all the people of Manchester."

"I," Darcy said, "would not be terribly enthused with giving the radicals amongst the workers in that city *any* say within the governance of our realm. *You* fought the French. You saw the sequel."

Elizabeth smiled. "May I suspect this is a matter of regular contention betwixt you, since you have determined to become a radical, General Fitzwilliam?"

"You have ample proof yourself, from your own life, for why the privileges of the aristocracy should be trimmed back," General Fitzwilliam replied.

"The system of pocket borough's appears quite reprehensible, but in truth it is simply another manner of ensuring the greatest landowners in the country — those who have the deepest interest in its long term wellbeing — have a proper say in her governance." Darcy replied seriously, "Such is the way that our constitution has settled for us to be ruled, and so it has been for many centuries now. We have prospered under this way of law, and we have defeated France many times despite its greater size. The landed interest must not be able to ignore the mercantile interest of the city, but the power of the land should always be predominant."

General Fitzwilliam laughed. "Spoken exactly as one would expect a man who himself controls a rotten borough to speak."

Darcy rolled his eyes. "You now have the nonsense idea that *everyone*, man of consequence or wandering vagabond, ought equally to have say in who is their MP. I would rather keep my head, and avoid the inevitable sequel of a tyrannical British ogre rising from the masses."

"Nothing of that sort happened in our colonies — I insist, every man is a soul equal before God, and I think there is no necessity to believe the negative consequences you believe would follow from an extended franchise are necessary."

"Wide suffrage has *already* been put to the test. And then the French chopped the heads off all their betters—"

"Men such as Lord Lechery."

"A few were such, but many were the most glittering flowers of civilization." Darcy shook his head annoyedly. "In her bed, they grabbed Marie Antoinette from her bed, whilst in her bed clothes. A queen. And then they murdered her, in cold blood, whilst making the pretense it was justice."

"Men such as you — and in general such as I — tend to have a rather narrow application of that sympathy Adam Smith argued was so vital. You have sympathy for the queen who is pulled from her bed. You can imagine those women who you love in such a case. But you have little sympathy for the vagabond who has no bed—"

"I do have sympathy for the poor, at least those willing to work; you know how willingly I pay my poor rates, and how I offer charity above that when needed for those round about Pemberley."

"In any case," General Fitzwilliam said, "I know what I'd be expected to do if there was revolution in England. Any attempt at that sort, and I'd be expected to murder every gathered weaver in Manchester, every 'prentice boy in London, every washer woman who tried to shout for her rights. There was some justice in the fear Robespierre had of reaction."

"Nonsense. In the end the French king proved that Robespierre's fear of mass murder following the victory of the better sort was insane, since when *we* placed him back upon his throne once more—"

"Not 'we', Darcy. It was me. It was Major Fitzwilliam. It was brave lads recruited from your farms, and from amongst the workmen of Manchester and London. Your only part in placing a king once more on the French throne was to pay your taxes."

"And now you wish we had not done so."

"I did my duty. I always do my duty. Do not think I will not do my duty — my duty as I see it before the Lord — I take no joy in this anymore. And Napoleon was a tyrant, and Napoleon needed to be removed."

"And when he was removed there was no reaction such as you fear. There were not thousands of French peasants murdered. The women of Paris were not brutally shot by the new King."

"Of course not, because he was scared they would rebel again, and remove him. Which they did the instant Napoleon bared his breast and dared the soldiers to shoot their emperor. Why do you think the French are willing to pay for our army to sit in Cambrai? It is because the king and his ministers fear their own people, drained as they already are by the wars. But mark my words — if Louis's government outlasts twenty years, and I live to see it, I'll eat my own hat."

Darcy sighed and sat back. Elizabeth's eyes were dancing. *She* had enjoyed being an observer of this argument a great deal.

"So then," she said with a delighted smile. "Not to interfere with your chance to bare swords of words against one another, but Mr. Darcy's question should be replied to: What is your purpose in spreading the story about Lord Lachglass about, beyond protecting other innocent women from ignorantly entering his clutches?"

General Fitzwilliam blinked and shook his head. "Ah that. The government is worried — you should hear my father rant upon the matter — the government worries about an uprising. There were few hints of any such chance whilst we maintained the war, but during the war, though prices were high, wages were high also."

"It was those such as my mother who were hurt by those high prices," Major Williams said. "Those who had all their income from the consols or a pension — Matlock gave her some eighty pounds a year to maintain herself and me after my birth, and he would not raise that just because the necessities rose in price."

"Yes," General Fitzwilliam nodded. "There are always those harmed by every change, but then at least everyone who could work had a full belly and full purse. Now employment is scarce, and a hundred thousand discharged soldiers wander the cities and countryside with no honorable place. A story like yours, Elizabeth, of an earl who is a minister in the government who first tried to rape a woman, and then attempted to use the court of law to murder her because she fought back. This sort of story might light a spark to the dry tinder of the already riled masses. The prime minister will push Lachglass to make terms with you, so that the story will go away."

Darcy sighed. "This is hardly a certain route to protect Elizabeth, to enable her to return to England."

"Have you a better notion?"

Darcy sighed. "I'd rather not see her name bandied about by the lower orders."

"'Tis my choice." Elizabeth said, "And I am not so delicate — I have worked for my supper, myself."

"It is entirely different to be a governess. That is still a respectable position, living in close terms with a proper family, rather than hiring yourself out by the day."

Elizabeth patted his arm. "I thank you for your concern, but I truly have no worry on that account — But how would such a story be passed around? No newspaper would print such a scandalous story about a peer of the realm."

"Well, well." General Fitzwilliam scratched at his sideburns. "I know a few men who are well… ah, they have access to a printing press. Or *they* do not. But they know people who do. You know…"

"Good God!" Darcy exclaimed. "You have friends amongst the suppressed scurrilous press."

General Fitzwilliam shrugged. "Not friends… friends of friends. Tell the story of what happened, and I'll see it printed and distributed widely in London, and elsewhere in the country. Miss Bennet, *you* want that to happen, so Lord Lechery's next governess will know what to expect."

"I do." Elizabeth tapped her foot on the brick tile floor a few times and looked out at the empty winter garden. "For my part, whether it helps me return to England or not, I like your plan."

Chapter Twelve

Elizabeth's first order of business during her stay in Calais was to pen an essay for pamphlets, or newspapers, and any other libelous and rebellious press that might print it. She was rather proud about her treatment of: *The Tale of an Evil and Rakish Noble who wanted to Violate and Murder an Innocent Governess.*

Her story, with rhetorical flourishes, was readied and sent out the afternoon of her second day in Calais. It had been written with the reluctant help of Darcy (who had a fine turn for the invective), and the eager help of General Fitzwilliam (who was a surprisingly *poor* writer given his ample other talents), and Major Fitz Williams who suggested many puns that were hilarious, but would not contribute to the desired effect if entered into the text.

The essay packaged and sent to General Fitzwilliam's friends amongst some subversive organization of The Young and Privileged Against Tyrannical Excesses — Elizabeth had begun to think satirically in Capital letters about everything after penning her account of her experience.

She found this laughter cathartic, and it helped to banish any demons which may have lurked in her soul after such an unpleasant experience.

Though she liked to think any would-be demons had in the main been banished by the simple fact that she *won.*

Elizabeth also spent an hour each morning in attempted conversation in French with a servant M. Dessein provided who *almost* spoke English, and who was willing to correct Elizabeth each time she made a mistake. She made mistakes of grammar almost never, and mistakes of pronunciation almost always. The servant also repeated everything she said in French *veeeery* sloooowly until Elizabeth understood the sentence.

Becky came over with the Dover packet, along with Darcy's valet, Joseph, the Darcy carriage with its driver and footmen, General Fitzwilliam's soldiers, Darcy's man of business, a pile of correspondence from Darcy's lawyer about what he was doing to stymie and annoy Lord Lachglass, a supply of Georgiana's modified clothes for Elizabeth, Darcy's own clothing, ample odds and ends, and most remarkably to Elizabeth, a stack of large denomination bills in the French currency that was six inches high.

The man of business explained to Darcy, when he arrived, that they had been all changed by Childe's as a courtesy at the rate which prevailed on the market.

Darcy nodded, idly rifling through the stack of bills that Elizabeth watched with wide eyes.

More than a thousand pounds were sitting on the table, except in French, that is in franc. "How badly would I have had my ears trimmed back if I let Monsieur Dessein give me Napoleons for guineas?"

"Is that his offer?" The man of business chuckled. "Quite badly, a matter of more than a tenth of the value, sir."

"Still, a fine establishment."

"Yes, sir," the man of business, whose name Elizabeth had already forgotten but who was a far, far more friendly and honorable looking man than Lachglass's Mr. Blight, replied. "A fine establishment. Mentioned by Sterne, you know. In his *Sentimental Travels*. Though I believe the building that the family occupied then may have been different."

"Oh, really!" Elizabeth exclaimed with a small clap. "I adore Sterne. I must find a copy of that to read."

The man of business bowed with a friendly air to her. "I shall send for my own copy, madam, if you wish."

After penning her story, Elizabeth was at liberty to enjoy the touring delights of Calais. She walked along the shore a great deal with Darcy. She looked at every part of the harbor. She was properly repulsed by the smell of the fish market late in the afternoon after all the catch worth selling had been sold. She admired the half medieval, half modern town hall. She listened to the church bells from the cathedral chime every quarter hour. The church had, she was told, been built during the English rule, three or four centuries before. And Elizabeth visited the neighboring town of Bourgoine, which had seemed to be half English in its population.

On the fourth day of their stay in Calais, which they planned to be the last, as General Fitzwilliam's regiment was to leave the next morning, an event of some importance occurred.

Darcy had taken her arm in arm for a walk out along the long wooden pier that extended far out into the sea from the land. General Fitzwilliam was this day occupied arranging matters before his men marched off to join the division he commanded in Cambrai.

However Darcy and his cousin planned to meet for fencing at a salle patronized by many English gentlemen of fashion and leisure, and that General Fitzwilliam promised was exceedingly well equipped, at around four o'clock.

The pier delighted Elizabeth like a ball of yarn delighted a kitten.

She had never had the opportunity to properly enjoy a beach resort town, as Papa had a general disinclination to travelling, even so far as London, and he kept the family mostly fixed during the summers (and winters) in Longbourn when she was a girl.

The salty sea wind flapped loose strands of hair against her face, and the waves propelled by the wind splashed against the big round tree trunks that made the frame of the pier. Seagulls and albatrosses placidly sat on the roughhewn wooden railing of the pier. Despite the cold weather and winter season, every few yards some man with a bucket of stinky bait fished from off the pier. The hooks hung down off long twine strings, and the already caught fish swam helplessly in tubs, awaiting their final doom.

Quite sad for the poor fish.

Many ships were moored along the line of wood, floating slightly up and down with every wave. There was also that peculiar slightly pleasant and slightly rotted smell of decaying sea life everywhere.

The waves made the pier moan and sway which gave Elizabeth the delightful sensation that the entire structure was about to collapse under her and toss her and Mr. Darcy into the sea. It gave her an excuse to cling close to his arm (her other hand needed to cling closely to her hat, lest it *actually* be tossed into the sea by the blowsy billowing wind).

At the very end of the pier there was a small wooden bench that they could sit on. They contemplatively looked out at the endless sea — not actually endless. The white cliffs of Dover, with the afternoon sun gleaming off them, were easily visible in the distance on this clear day.

Elizabeth sighed. "Just a few hours' carriage ride away."

Darcy took her hand and comfortingly squeezed it. "A little over twenty-seven miles. Or perhaps a little under, given the length of the pier, we are some appreciable fraction of a mile out into the sea."

"Twenty-seven miles." The white cliffs of Albion were beautiful. They were as beautiful as every patriotic poet or writer describing this scene, of looking upon his home from a foreign land had ever claimed. Something caught in Elizabeth's heart, and she wanted to cry. She squeezed her lips tightly together.

Darcy was a calm presence, confident and caring. He sat with her quietly.

"'Tis strange," she said to her companion. "I had anticipated I would be purely eager and happy to be in a new country, a new land. I thought I would need at *least* a few weeks simply to explore every new sight, sensation and smell before I had the slightest longing for our green home. But…"

"You shall enjoy every sight, despite this longing, and I shall be at your side, to protect and care for you," Darcy said, "I promise you."

Elizabeth nodded, but she also pursed her lips with a little dissatisfaction.

Yes, he promised to be with her so long as she was separate from England. But he did not want to marry her. At least not yet. Thoughts in *that* direction would lead to a sensation of disappointment, and annoyance.

And annoyance at her savior. At a man she owed her very life to, and in no metaphorical sense, for she would be dead of two causes, and likely a third as well without him.

"Well at least you do not guarantee I shall return to England soon as I may wish."

Darcy smiled wryly at her. "I am not in the habit of making promises whose fulfillment I cannot guarantee — however much I may wish to comfort the person I make such promise to. Besides," he grinned at her with a playful light in his eyes, "nothing simpler than to return to England, you can take any packet boat back to Dover."

Elizabeth laughed. "I would very likely not be *pleased* with the reception I gain in England."

"That is entirely possible," Darcy replied smilingly.

"Thank you for making a joke about such a matter — though it is too serious to joke about such things…"

"If a matter is too serious too joke about, perhaps then it also is too serious to take seriously."

"It is very like to what Anne of Boleyn said while she laughed afore she was executed, 'I hear the executioner is very good, and I have a little neck.'"

"They will not execute you."

"Did you know, King Henry had a swordsman who was obtained in France to execute his wife? Perhaps it would have been some sort of *Lese Majeste* if one of his *English* subjects were to do that to his queen."

Darcy squeezed Elizabeth's hand.

Thankfully, he refrained from insisting once more they would not execute her. She *knew* they would not. Elizabeth loved her life too much to return to England whilst that was a hanging chance. She was not one of those sad foolish men, on the run from the law, who returned in disguise just so that they could see their mother one last time before she died, and who were then seized by the law and hung for loving their parent too well. And also, presumably, murder.

No, she was one of those just as sad, and perhaps not wiser, persons who would stay in unhappy foreign climes though her mother begged to see her daughter one last time before she expired.

"I would not be in any particular hurry to return to England, if only I knew that I *could* return. It is the *inability* that makes me long for it."

"That," Darcy said, "is a reaction in no way out of the ordinary."

Elizabeth laughed, deciding once more that she would never permit herself to descend into moroseness. "A perverse reaction, despite its popularity. But I have no taste for *perversion*, though we are now in France, and we all know what they say about France, I shall endeavor to enjoy my time in this country though I know not for what extent the duration of my stay shall be."

"What *do* they say about France?" Darcy asked as he and Elizabeth stood to walk back down the pier.

"*You* know." Elizabeth waved her hand and replied with a smile. She bit her lip and looked up at him from under her eye lashes.

Darcy swallowed.

The wind had kicked up. Clouds rushed towards them worrisomely fast.

Oh! But the view of the city was one of the grandest Elizabeth had ever seen. Lines of tall houses along the pier, and the brown wood of the pier for hundreds of feet, and the tall masts of the ships in the harbor, and birds circled high in the sky, their lonely cawing distantly audible, and the bell tower of the cathedral rang an hour, and the water lapped and slapped the pier.

Oh, so, so lovely.

The walk took the best part of ten minutes from the end of the pier all the way to the safe stone of the city. The clouds, which had not been present at all when they started their walk down the pier, opened up with soft sprinkles and Elizabeth was cold, and also terribly tired from the wandering of the morning.

There was a cafe next to the pier, which looked quite warm — the people, more women than men inside, had mostly put aside their coats as they sat at their coffee.

"Let's go in," Elizabeth said eagerly. "A real one of France's famous cafes!"

Darcy's face screwed up at the suggestion — Elizabeth knew that he did not consider this establishment, with some peeling paint and a sign proclaiming the prices in chalk, as meeting the fine standards to which a member of the Darcy clan, and those under his protection, were entitled to.

"It'll be ever such a lark. Look at how many people are reading — and they are all dressed quite fashionably in the French way." Elizabeth grinned widely at Darcy.

Darcy shrugged, and he then smiled with that brilliant familiar, heart turning smile of his, that he reserved mainly for her. "This location seems very much the sort of venue *you* wish to patronize."

"Exactly." Elizabeth shivered violently as a gust of wind blew. "Oh, I am so cold, and I need to sit down."

"Oh, Elizabeth—" Darcy looked slightly miserable, as though he considered it his chief employment to keep the winds and rains from bothering her — or at least to ensure she stayed safely indoors if there was a chance of such rains coming down to bother her.

He rushed her into the cafe.

The air in the room felt like a blast from an oven upon their entrance, and they quickly closed the door behind them.

"I should have paid better attention," Darcy said frowningly, "and made us to return from the pier faster. Are you tired also? — You need a great deal of rest. Mr. Goldman insisted you must rest for at least two weeks the last time he examined you."

"You care for me excellently — even without Lord Lachglass's interference, there is no chance I would have remained abed for longer than necessary. It is my conviction that the principal cause of ill health is enforced inactivity prescribed by doctors."

Darcy smiled as he helped her to a collection of winged chairs around a low table. "I sound like a worried mother hen. But I do worry — your eyes rolling up when you fainted is an image which shall stick in my brain forever."

Elizabeth gratefully sunk into one of the chairs and closed her eyes for a moment of ecstasy at no longer being on her feet and at the warmth in the cafe. She said, without opening her eyes, "You are right. I overexerted myself today — *don't* make yourself anxious. I shall be entirely well in twenty minutes if I do not *continue* to exert myself so."

"Do you want tea, or should I ask if they have a cold *dejeuner* laid aside?" There was that slightly snobbish frown in Darcy's voice again, as though he was quite skeptical of this perfectly respectable appearing establishment being able to furnish forth meats delicate enough for his lady's palate— anyone in Elizabeth's family would have happily patronized this place when they had money.

She loved Darcy very dearly.

Elizabeth opened her eyes to find Darcy's deep worried eyes on her. Something happy in her chest fluttered. She loved even his snobbery. That snobbery was as deeply bred into him as his honor. "Just *café au lait* and a little *pain avec beurre*."

Elizabeth smiled twistedly to make fun of herself for speaking in English, except for the words for food.

Darcy almost absently replied, "You must roll the Rs — are you sure?"

"Quite. This is a lovely place."

The cafe had a big tiled stove with a pile of firewood next to it in the corner merrily radiating heat into the air. There was a counter like in an English inn, behind which were stored a variety of wine and whiskey glasses, bottles of spirits and wines, and there was a hot pot of water boiling on the stove. Several pairs of well-dressed young women talked eagerly to each other in French, after glancing at the English party that had just entered the premises.

There also was, delighting Elizabeth, a man in one corner with the delicate features and wild hair of an artist, furiously scribbling away with a nub of pencil on a thin stack of papers, pausing every so often to mutter angrily, and take his rubber out to deface the perfectly excellent rhyme Elizabeth was sure he had already created.

She was not used to being weak like this.

Elizabeth sighed and stretched her arms wide, noticing happily how Darcy paid close attention to her as she displayed — unintentionally, she would swear — her body. The waiter came up to them, and Darcy ordered for them the *café au lait* and *pain avec buerre* which Elizabeth had requested.

Outside the cold sea wind flapped the furled masts of the trading vessels and private yachts moored along the pier. The sky was grey and overcast, and quite beautiful in the way Elizabeth always found bad weather beautiful — except when she had to walk through it in her slippers, of course. She admired the waves splashing along the entire length of the pier, whose end almost disappeared in the distance.

Darcy smiled at her, and Elizabeth smiled back at him.

She sunk a little deeper into the comfortable armchair, and the warm air from the hot stove baked her back into comfort.

The waiter presently brought their hot coffee and the bread with butter that had been requested. The cream had been heated and was placed in a delightful little jar with flowers on the side. There were squares of sugar cut off of a sugarloaf and placed in a little pyramid with a pair of silver tongs set next to them.

Elizabeth exerted herself to sit up and take on the hostess's duty, and she mixed Mr. Darcy's coffee as she had noted over the past days he liked it. It was oddly intimate and thrilling to mix his coffee and to know how he liked it without asking, because she now knew him well.

Darcy smiled brilliantly at her when she pushed his cup and saucer towards him, and he lifted up the cup and took a sip of it.

It had always seemed to her a ridiculous little game when scheming mothers contrived to learn by bribing servants how their wealthy quarry liked to take their coffee — and it *was*. But there was a truth underneath the game. There was something special about knowing how a man liked things, and being able to arrange them to his comfort.

Elizabeth had a flash of insight in that moment about how Darcy must feel to be in the position of having been her rescuer. No wonder he seemed so generally cheerful now that he had saved from extreme danger the woman who — she allowed herself to believe — he loved dearly.

"Very fine, better coffee even than what Dessein provides for our breakfast spread." That was Darcy's judgement. "I was being ridiculous, and a useless peacock when I did not wish to enter — you saw my hesitation. No chance to deny it—"

"You may trust me to never hide your flaws from you."

Darcy laughed happily. "Which makes your compliments the more precious by far that I can trust you to abuse me directly to my face any such time that I deserve it."

"I *am* an exemplary woman."

"Yes, yes you are."

Elizabeth flushed with happiness at that simple compliment, delivered smilingly by Darcy.

To hide her blush she buttered her bread — fine butter and fine bread, but in truth no better than what she was used to in England. And perhaps the bread was *slightly* stale. Not that Elizabeth would *ever* let a matter like that damage her enjoyment of this fine moment. Only a fool, in her opinion, would obsess over trifles while she was alive, drinking fine coffee and fine food paid for without the necessity to work for a disreputable earl.

Elizabeth frowned at that thought.

Why couldn't she simply accept the situation and be happy? Why did she need to ruminate over her position of unspecified dependence upon Darcy when her ruminations would do no good?

The coffee was as good as Darcy said it was, clear through, with none of the ground remains left in it.

They chattered over coffee, talking about a play and about the pier, but Elizabeth subsided into silence and yawns as she finished eating her bread and drinking her coffee. A little food and a little fat in her body, and she was already halfway to sleep. Elizabeth leaned against the wing of the chair and closed her eyes, lulled by the rhythmic splashing of the waves.

Darcy briefly took and squeezed her hand before releasing it.

Elizabeth snuggled deeper against the side of the comfortable chair, wishing that Darcy would squeeze her hand again.

She was woken some time later by the ringing of the church bells calling out four o'clock.

Elizabeth stretched her arms out, and rolled her neck side to side to get rid of the slight crick in her neck from the upright posture she'd slept in.

Darcy still sat by her side, though he'd taken out a book, which he now also put to the side. He looked between her and the street running along the harbor. The rain had stopped and the late afternoon sun shone across the waves. "I meant to meet General Fitzwilliam, but I could not bear to wake you. Now it is too late to escort you back to the hotel and still meet him according to our arrangement."

"Just go off, go off," Elizabeth laughingly said, rubbing her eyes. "You can meet him there easily in time — leave your book so I have more than the view to entertain myself with."

"I can't leave you alone in a cafe! Unprotected, and unguarded."

Elizabeth laughed. "What do you worry will happen to me?"

The cafe was clearly a respectable place, and at least one other conversation was conducted in English. The waiters looked quite fashionable in their uniforms, and with the prices drawn on the menus there was little chance of a rowdy low clientele visiting themselves upon her.

Which she would *also* survive if they did appear.

Darcy frowned and did not answer her question.

"Are you wracking your brains to think upon every terrible thing that might happen to me if I am left alone for the span of an hour and a quarter in this place, or are you frowning for a different reason?"

"I just… I would never leave my sister without a maid or a footman — or best both — in such a place as this."

Elizabeth laughed. "A caring and careful brother! 'Such a place as this' — I hope neither the waiters nor the regular patrons can understand English, else I *will* be in danger."

"I confess…" Darcy scratched at the back of his head, almost confusedly. "You are alone; a British gentlewoman in a foreign country. Women must be protected… that's the place of gentlemen, our purpose is to care for and ensure the wellbeing of those of the gentler sex around us. Especially when… especially a woman who I…" Darcy hesitated, he clearly wanted to say more, but also could not without directly declaring himself.

Infuriating, sweet man, Elizabeth thought both fondly and annoyedly.

"You saved my life, Mr. Darcy. You saved it at least twice — from the illness, and when you snatched me from under Lord Lachglass's nose."

"That was principally my cousin's doing."

"And you are a man who never wishes to take credit undeserved — which is a stance the easier for you to take since you deserve so very much credit, and you know it. You *hid* me from Lord Lachglass at the least; you called the doctor for me. You allowed me without a question of anything but friendship and concern to occupy one of your bedrooms, and your time and your care. You protect me, and you care for me exceedingly well. I… I depend upon you in this foreign, half familiar, half strange and different country."

"However?" Darcy smiled at her. "I hear a however in your tone."

"However, if someone in this cafe tries to bother me, I will first butt them with my head, and then bash a coffee cup over their head, and you shall need to spirit me to Denmark, and pay the dear owners of this establishment some extra money for damages caused."

Darcy laughed. "I forget in a way… that you are not so defenseless. You *look* fragile and everything that is spirit and beauty. But…"

"I like to think there is animal and flesh and muscle within me as well. I am not just a spiritual being."

"You are not," Darcy replied admiringly.

He looked towards the road again. "Still enough time. If you *insist* I can leave you behind, with just a book for entertainment, I'll do so, but know it makes me feel uncomfortable."

Elizabeth took both his hands in hers and kissed his knuckles. "I thank you very much."

Darcy went to the chief waiter and handed him one of those big French bills that he'd gotten from his man of business while saying a few words to him. No doubt ensuring that this man would keep a very close eye on her.

And then he was off to beat General Fitzwilliam into a friendly pulp.

Or the other way around.

Elizabeth would not care to wager bets on who would win in that conflict, but from the eagerness both of them had evinced when General Fitzwilliam mentioned the possibility of fencing, she was quite assured both would end with bruises.

She tried to read Darcy's novel, and as the sun set the now obsequious waiter immediately set several beeswax candles out for her to read by. But rather perversely she put the book aside shortly after.

The relationship betwixt her and Darcy was filled with such an odd mixture of the awkward and the delightful, and at this moment her annoyance at the awkward was predominate.

How could she endure months at least — perhaps much more — halfway the chosen companion of Darcy's life, and halfway a helpless distressed maiden, a piece of driftwood fate had tossed on his shore?

She *understood* Darcy.

He was honorable. He wanted to do the right thing. He would act to protect his friends when he thought they made the wrong decision. But Lord! This was the same sort of mistake that he had made with Jane and Bingley.

Mr. Darcy thought it was his business to ensure she made no enforced decision. That there was no necessity tying her to accept him, and no excess of gratitude that influence her in his favor when her natural preference would have been in some other direction. It was *ridiculous*.

Was this really where his hesitation to declare himself came from?

Maybe, despite Darcy's evident and clear affection for her, his infatuation towards her, his desire for her, perhaps he did not want to have a wife who would be forever barred from England. Or perhaps he was rethinking the entire matter, and not at all sure if he wanted to marry her with the poverty and the scandals.

His first instinct, she comforted herself in this dour speculation, had of a certainty been to ignore her changed circumstances. But his pride held him back further and further the longer he pondered on the matter.

The brutish fact was that her circumstances were worse by far, and her family would need far more of his support than when he had asked her to marry him the first time.

And Darcy had not come easily to the decision to marry her then.

And thus he had concocted in his mind this notion of it being important for her to not be dependent upon him for her life and safety as an excuse to avoid admitting to himself that he did not *actually* wish to take her on as a wife, with all that would entail.

Elizabeth shook her head annoyedly, and asked for a glass of wine and some of the cheeses and sliced meats that one of the other patrons dined on from the waiter when he ran up to her to beg if he could do anything to be of service to her.

The blue veined cheese with freshly baked bread, made for the evening crowd, tasted exquisite, an explosion of taste in Elizabeth's mouth.

On consideration, it was not in Darcy's character to engage in *that* level of self-deception.

The uncertainty scared her. Until he declared himself, she could not know that he *would* declare himself.

Elizabeth wanted to know. She didn't want her heart to be tortured in this almost engaged state. If he yet loved her, and loved her enough to take her despite all the reasons against such a match, she wanted him to do it now.

But it was impossible for a lady, even one so daring as she, to simply say that brazenly.

There were matters of money, but she could survive without *much* money.

In any case, she was *not* so desperately dependent upon him.

Certainly, her French was not so good that she could easily seek some sort of employment at present in France, but her command of the language also was not so bad that she would require a great length of time before she *could*. She had improved enormously in just the past few days. She could make an effort as a governess again, to some family which never returned to England, or to a French family which wished to ensure their children spoke English perfectly — this time she would find a widow to employ her.

Or she could become the companion to some widowed or unmarried lady.

Darcy had an extensive acquaintance. He could foist her off on some friend of his.

Elizabeth brooded.

Frowned and brooded.

And so she was frowning, and slightly tipsy from the excellent red wine she had drunk a glass of, when after just an hour's absence Darcy returned with General Fitzwilliam in tow.

"See," General Fitzwilliam said loudly, and with a wink at Elizabeth, "Miss Bennet is flowering and in better spirits than she ever has been. You needed not to worry about her."

"We did not stay away too long?" Darcy asked, in a slightly worried tone, as if she would choose to disappear if he did not constantly keep her in sight.

"No." Elizabeth knew her voice was irritable.

Beyond everything else that she had faced in the last weeks, including being assaulted, nearly dying, and becoming an exile from her country of birth, she could feel that she was only a few days from the commencement of her monthly bleeding.

It was all quite enough to make a woman cry.

Darcy flinched slightly at her voice, while General Fitzwilliam phlegmatically raised an eyebrow.

"I am not a child in your care, who depends upon you for everything. I *can* protect myself."

"I know, Elizabeth."

"You do *not*. I can defend my own honor. I can entertain my own self. I can plan my own decisions."

"I know, I know—"

"I don't need you!"

Darcy swallowed and looked hurt.

"Oh," Elizabeth reached her hand out shakingly, "I do not mean to yell — that is not what I meant to say, I… what I meant is that I am sure I could find a position for some employment in France if I needed to. Maybe risk being a governess again, to some sympathetic French widow who wishes her children to speak English particularly well."

"Perhaps…" Darcy swallowed, and his eyes looked suddenly hollow. "Elizabeth… perhaps, even if you do not need me, perhaps I need you. I… I have never been to Paris. Never been to France at all. I… I would wish you to stay with me until we have… have seen the country. I do desperately want to see Paris… you and me. And then if you yet wish to find employment as a governess… afterwards. I shall understand… and I—"

"Oh, you sweet, wonderful, silly, dear man. I… I do not mean I want to become a governess, either. I don't." General Fitzwilliam was grinning widely at her, and his amusement was distracting, and they were surrounded by the crowd of evening guests who had made appearance at the cafe for an evening bite and coffee and wine now that the work day was done, but she had to say now what she desperately wanted to say for Darcy's sake. "What I mean is that…"

Elizabeth swallowed.

She felt a terrible hesitation in her gut — a fear of what his reaction would be. Best to know now. Best now. "What I meant to say… what I really meant is that, I… I want to marry you. Mr. Darcy, you are dear to me… and my opinion of you has changed so completely since that day I mistakenly refused you."

He blinked at her in confusion.

"That's all I meant. That I want to marry you." She swallowed and waited for Darcy to proclaim her fate.

"Oh." And his brilliant, heart stopping smile came out, like a sunbeam through the clouds. "Oh, *that's* what you meant by 'I do not need you.' I apologize for the difficulty I had interpreting your words," Darcy was grinning so widely that he had to pause, "but now that you have explained, the meaning is perfectly clear."

General Fitzwilliam snorted. "Was clear enough to *me* from the start."

Elizabeth glared at him; this was *not* the time for his humor.

"Elizabeth, my dear, darling Elizabeth." Now everything was gone for Elizabeth except Darcy's beautiful sparkling eyes, and his flashing happy grin. "It seems like I have been a fool once more, I shall often depend upon you to tell me when I am behaving as a fool. Can I depend upon you to tell me?"

"You can always depend upon me." Elizabeth's heart stuttered, as though it both wished to race fast and stop in contemplation of Darcy's handsome visage. "You can depend upon me for anything."

Darcy glanced for an instant at his cousin and the other patrons of the cafe. His smiling expression seemed to say, *I had not expected to do this in such company.*

With his color high and a serious voice he said, "Elizabeth Bennet, you do *not* require my help. That is true. You can survive and you can choose for yourself. That is who you are, a woman worthy of being admired. But I desperately want to help you, whenever you can use help. I desperately wish to live with you, during every trial and tribulation of our lives. However since you do not need my money, since you shall find way to survive without my aid, I have only one thing I can offer to induce you to stay close by my side — for I do need you by my side — my heart. Elizabeth Bennet, you have my heart. I beg you not to crush it, for I do ardently admire and love you. I have missed you every day since we parted last, and now that I have seen you again… Elizabeth, perhaps I might survive without you, but I do not wish to. I ask you to make me the happiest of men, and accept my hand, my heart, and my soul. Please be the companion of my life. I beg you, tell me that I have your heart and then I shall be — and this is no poetic exaggeration — the happiest of men."

"Oh, oh, oh! Of course I will. Of course you do. My heart is yours."

Darcy stood to his feet and pulled Elizabeth to hers and then he kissed her solidly on the lips, in front of everyone, and then he lifted her in his arms and swung her round three times, laughing with happiness.

There was a mixture of laughter and cheers from the French cafe goers at this behavior from the English gentleman and his lady in their midst, and in his happiness Darcy promptly paid for dinner and champagne for everyone in the cafe.

Chapter Thirteen

Darcy was deliriously happy two days later when he married Elizabeth.

There was an Anglican chaplain in the city. According to this chaplain, as they were not in England they did not need to have the banns sounded, or gain a license from a bishop, if they married in a French civil ceremony first.

To be married by French law Darcy and Elizabeth needed to swear before a notary as to their family circumstances, the location of their births, and their names. And most specifically they were required to swear that there were no barriers to the performance of a marriage between them under the laws of France.

Both Darcy and Elizabeth were aware of none under the laws of *England*, and so Darcy hoped very much that French laws were not so different they perjured themselves when they made that oath. The notary assured them that there was nothing strange, and that the French laws on this matter were in general more liberal than those of the United Kingdom, or at least he thought they were.

In the morning after they acquired the documents from the notary, they went to the town hall with General Fitzwilliam and Major Williams.

It was strange to Darcy to find he suddenly had a new and previously unknown cousin, though he liked Major Williams a great deal. General Fitzwilliam and Major Williams were to witness their marriage, and then immediately ride off to the southeast to catch up to their regiment which had started the previous day its slow march to join the rest of the occupying army.

The happy couple duly presented at the town hall their documents from the notary. They had cost Darcy two hundred francs to be written up and prepared on such short notice. The mayor himself came out to administer the oaths — this apparently was unusual, and only occurred because Darcy was a great gentleman, and the mayor was an acquaintance of General Fitzwilliam.

The usual course was for a couple to have the oaths administered by a minor city clerk. They were made to swear their wedding oaths in French, and after Elizabeth and Darcy had replied *oui* to each question, the mayor popped open a bottle of effervescent *vin de Champagne* that actually had been grown, aged, and bottled in Champagne.

They toasted their marriage, and happily smiling to each other they walked arm in arm out into the mostly cold February sun. The couple then needed to walk several blocks, holding a paper certifying their marriage, to the rooms the Anglican chaplain had rented to serve as a church.

The chaplain then properly married them before God, and the Church of England — which in Darcy's view was a matter of somewhat more importance than being married before the laws and King of France.

They signed the register, which was just a single sheet instead of a whole book.

The chaplain had explained the previous day that their marriage would be properly registered in England under Hardwicke's Marriage Act of 1753 — the law which made Gretna Greene the most popular destination for wedded bliss in all the land. The Bishop of London kept a book in London to which the chaplain sent the register of each marriage he performed to be recorded there officially and properly in England herself.

After the chaplain married them, and they'd said their proper English "I do's" in accordance with the well-known words of the book of common prayer, the chaplain also popped open a bottle of champagne. This bottle was furnished by the cellars of a decidedly lesser gentleman, and was not *quite* so fine as the one the mayor of Calais offered them.

Darcy and Elizabeth still happily toasted themselves and their happy future once more with General Fitzwilliam and Major Williams.

On the street their carriage awaited them, with Becky and Joseph waiting to travel south with them. Also Darcy's coachman, grooms, and his footmen all were gathered round to travel with them as well. Being rather tipsy, Darcy shook hands once more with his cousins, profusely thanked General Fitzwilliam for his help, kissed Elizabeth on the open street in full sight of everyone, and handed her into the carriage.

And so they set off into a happy future.

Darcy's man of business had ridden ahead on horse the day before to rent a house in the city for them. He would prepare everything for them to stay at least a month's time in Paris. As they travelled south, at each postal station the couple needed to show their passports to be allowed to rent the horses, and every single time Elizabeth smilingly took a walk about the French town. She made an effort also each time she stopped to talk to someone in French.

She had improved enormously, having already a solid grounding in the language and reading a great deal in French, but she had just lacked the knack for the proper, and frankly strange to an English ear, pronunciation the language required.

Darcy loved each single minute of their travel south. He and Elizabeth were constantly affectionate with each other, as they sat together in the carriage, his happy arm around her happy shoulder. Elizabeth often rested her head on his chest. She usually smiled, and her smile was his favorite thing in the world.

Her body nestled soft against his, and he was filled with an infinite sense of protectiveness and affection, and he was very, very satisfied that she had — wise woman that she was — convinced him that it was better to be her husband than simply her guardian.

Elizabeth laughingly complained that the scenery did not look *nearly* different enough from England to be worth the price of the trip. All hedges with leaves lost for the winter, and she could see *those* in England any day of the year.

"That would only be true," Darcy replied dryly, his hand upon Elizabeth's — his wife's! — leg, "were it a day in winter."

Elizabeth laughingly kissed him. "Pedantic man — you have no love for the poetic."

In actual fact, the landscape of France was *not* remarkably dissimilar to that of England.

There were of course differences, mostly in terms of the color of the paint preferred and the style of building, but it would take an architect to be able to really explain how French village construction differed from the British style.

There was a great similarity Darcy thought between all Christian cultures, even the Catholic ones. The style of building and life was similar also in the Germanies — the same types and cuts of clothes worn by the fashionable, the same Beethoven and Mozart were beloved everywhere, the plays of Shakespeare and Goethe also. No matter where you went in Europe, cultured men spoke French with some facility.

Only when one reached as far east as Russia did the appearance of the people and of the churches became really distinct. And if one entered the lands of serfdom, the peasantry was entirely distinct from good English cottagers.

Even in Russia the cities seemed to Darcy a little like the rest of Europe, likely because the cities were filled with merchants and aristocrats who travelled and imitated what they saw in foreign lands, whether for good or for ill.

In Russia Darcy had heard repeated twice the story of how Peter the Great had early in his reign gone to visit the more Occidental nations, so that he might learn the secrets of their wealth. And then upon his return, he promptly banned the wearing of beards, because the Dutch went clean shaven.

Spending every night in the same bed as Elizabeth was magical, everything he had imagined, and yet somehow more tender, and more dear and more special than he could have imagined.

He had had some worry that she would be shy or frightened of him because of natural maidenly delicacy, and because of fear occasioned by Lord Lachglass's attempt to attack her. Yet she was quite the opposite, warm and eager to explore and passionate with him. However when Darcy had suggested such an idea to Elizabeth, she laughed and said that being with him was entirely different, and there was no reason she could see to be anxious with *him* when an entirely different man had attempted to attack her.

"Is it the normal and expected thing for a woman to be frightened of congress with a good man if once an evil man tried to force it upon her?" Elizabeth laughed. She then frowned and rested her head on Darcy's chest. "I can see in truth very easily see how such a fear *could* arise, were my nature different, but I am who I am and it has not."

The weather had been unseasonably warm for February since the day Darcy asked Elizabeth to marry him (or had she asked him to marry *her?* — it was quite like Elizabeth to jump over such proper forms, and he loved her for it). The winter fields were yet empty and grey, but there were hints of blooms and early green buds if one looked, which they did, as they took regular walks round the countryside.

The couple travelled slowly and took the road by easy stages, often just going twenty or thirty miles in a day and spending hours in each city or town of any interest. They arrived in Amiens before noon, and stayed there the rest of the day, as Elizabeth was charmed by the large gothic cathedral. Another time they simply stayed in a village where they were changing the horses because the station master mentioned that the sunset was beautiful from a hill a mile from the town.

It was.

They came into Paris early in the evening, a little before sunset.

Darcy's man of business met them at the postal station at St. Denis. He had made arrangements for the rental of a fine set of apartments occupying two floors of a building on the *Rue de Richelieu*, with just a few minutes' walk to the Palais Royal, and from there a few more minutes' walk to the Palace of the Tuileries and the Seine.

Elizabeth and Darcy explored the town of St. Denis for an hour before they took the carriage the rest of the way to Paris. They about the town walked arm in arm, trailed by a guide to the town who attached himself to tourists at the postal station.

Darcy had a smug and self-satisfied smile everywhere he went. He always enjoyed being able to parade Elizabeth around upon his arm, none of the gentlemen he saw had quite so pretty a wife as he.

Elizabeth on the other hand sighed. "How fashionably dressed all the women are."

"Nothing to you, my dearest love."

She laughed. "You need not dissemble upon such a matter — the deficiency is one I shall correct with *your* money over the next weeks. But however good a job Becky has done with it, the dress I am wearing was not designed for me."

"You are beautiful."

Elizabeth kissed his hand in reply. He wished they could kiss freely here on the road. He loved the taste of her mouth. Her taste was soft and fragrant, and he would never, never get tired of it.

"You are perfect, no matter what you wear," he insisted.

"*Precisely* my point," Elizabeth replied, her eyes sparkling. "You can admit the truth about my deficiency in clothing without me taking it as an insult upon myself, as it neither is an objection to my taste — these are not clothes which I chose for myself — nor an insult against my person, for I am, as you solemnly stated," she squeezed and kissed his hand delightedly, "beautiful no matter what I wear."

Darcy had to laugh.

Elizabeth was so clever, and so ready to win any argument. "I confess you have won your *point*, but I do not see how your clothes are in any wit less splendid than those of the others here. Your beauty I believe blinds me to all else — are you certain you *must* spend so much money upon clothes, since you *do* look beautiful, no matter what you wear?"

Darcy winked at her. He'd happily let her spend his entire fortune upon clothes (maybe not *happily*, if that were her *actual* plan), if such would make her happy.

St. Denis was a walled town five miles or so from Paris. It was dominated by a large cathedral with a fine white marble façade and two tall bell towers.

When they went to enter the cathedral, they were informed by the guide that all the kings of France had been buried in this church. And then, in one of the most despicable of their many, many despicable acts the Revolutionaries had desecrated the sacred tombs of those kings and removed them from the church.

There was a certain light in the eyes of this guide, a bald man of middle years now, as he described in language so hyperbolic that it could not be taken seriously the horror of the crimes of the Revolutionaries.

Darcy wondered if he may have been one of those young revolutionaries twenty-five years past.

After describing with this passionate and detailed voice the desecration of the cathedral, the guide sighed. "But alas, happier days have arrived upon us. Our monarch, Louis XVIII, now in the twentieth-third year of his reign" — Darcy and Elizabeth shared a laughing meaningful glance at this description of the length of time for which Louis had ruled France — "He has only this month previous gathered back together all of the bodies of his ancestors and entombed them once more in the church."

They entered the cathedral and took the opportunity to see the line of white sarcophagi, each with the marble effigy lying above the tomb, in which those luminaries were encased. It was a fine church and their guide shared many anecdotes about the kings buried there, with emphasis upon their royal excesses. They returned to their carriage, and Darcy handed their guide a five franc piece as a tip.

Then with fresh horses attached to his well sprung carriage, they went to Paris.

Along the whole distance between St. Denis and the gates to Paris the avenue of the Rue St. Denis was planted with a double row of trees, and you could see straight to the crowded buildings of the outskirts of the great city. There was a great deal of traffic upon the road.

Young farm laborers in simple clothes carrying heavy packs on their backs, either to sell, or which they had bought, going in both directions. A few carriages as fine, and one far finer, than their own. A vast array of carts containing produce, winter grain, tiles, bottles of wine, tools, and everything else which a great city required.

"A similar look to London, I think," Elizabeth said as they went through the outer rings of buildings. "But principally in the city, and not so much the outskirts."

"Perhaps," Darcy said. "Much like the City, but somewhat busier than anywhere else in London, with the buildings somewhat taller on the average."

"What a fine park!" Elizabeth exclaimed as they passed a large wide space, filled with trees.

Darcy from that point entertained himself more with watching the expressions on Elizabeth's face and the delicate color which the reddish fading sun brought to her than with the city itself.

The sun was setting when the man of business indicated to their driver that they had reached the house.

From the outside it looked much the same as every other building around, tall and made of brick.

"Oh, how beautiful! All this for us?" Elizabeth whirled on Darcy and kissed him soundly as soon as they were introduced to the large entry hall, which took up both floors that they had let. The room was palatial and the floors were covered with thick rugs. There was statuary and paintings in every corner, and all of the ceilings fashionably high. Elizabeth wandered around, while Darcy kept her hand in his as she smiled and looked at every corner.

"A *comte* maintained this as his Paris residence prior to the revolution," Darcy's man of business said with pride in his voice at a job done well, "And a Prussian aristocrat of great rank vacated the previous week. We were lucky to find such a place."

"Oh, so delightful!" Elizabeth exclaimed again. "I am almost afraid I shall break something by accident."

"Don't worry about *that*," Darcy said with a laugh, and he took her hand and spun her about like at a peasant dance before he kissed her again.

The cook which had been hired with the house came out to announce in French to Monsieur and Madame that he had prepared a fantastical welcome feast for them, and that they must sit to dine quickly, lest the food become cold, and unworthy of his name as a chef.

Chapter Fourteen

As Elizabeth and Mr. Darcy explored the ancient township of St. Denis, hundreds of miles to the north, in Meryton, Elizabeth's mother received an extraordinary letter with the afternoon post.

She sat in the upstairs sitting room of her younger sister, Mrs. Phillips's, house. Mrs. Bennet still often thought with unhappiness upon how far she had fallen from the days when she was the wife of one of the largest estates in the neighborhood.

If only Mr. Bennet had never become sick. If only, if only, if only...

If only she had borne a son.

A son who would have inherited the estate instead of letting it go to those scheming Lucases.

Despite the occasionally selfish and bitter tenor of Mrs. Bennet's thoughts, she was usually cheerful and happy — she had after all not starved in the hedgerows, and the human mind can adjust to any circumstance and treat the new as normal.

Mrs. Bennet was in fact grateful to Mrs. Phillips and Mr. Phillips for taking her in. She was grateful also to Mr. Gardiner and the help he had provided. And she still enjoyed visits and gossip, as the consolations of a life which had not turned out as it ought have.

Two daughters married, but entirely wrong.

Jane could have done far better than a vicar whose living ran to maybe two hundred in a year, and that only if he aggressively made an effort to collect all the tithes owed him — which Mr. Chawson did *not*.

Jane had nearly married Mr. Bingley and his four thousand a year, in that last year of Mrs. Bennet's happiness with dear sweet Mr. Bennet. Mrs. Bennet would never be able to forget that Jane ought to be married to a man with such an estate.

Mrs. Bennet could never understand how such a promising attachment had fallen apart. At least, Jane was delightedly happy now in her poverty, and she had produced one lovely babe, a son, already.

And Lydia... Mrs. Bennet did not think often of Lydia.

She always blamed Lydia for what occurred to Mr. Bennet. And now that the war was over, and all hope of advancement through the French happily shooting inconvenient superiors was gone for him, she did not expect to see Captain Dilman ever *Major* Dilman.

Any man willing to marry such a girl as Lydia, with such a past, and with such charms as Lydia had, could not be a man focused upon his own advancement.

At least Lydia *had* married. That was better than Mrs. Bennet had ever expected.

Mrs. Bennet at least liked her granddaughter from Lydia, though she had only seen them twice, while Jane and her son were very happily settled within an easy travelling distance of Meryton.

Kitty still lived with Mrs. Bennet. She was the comfort of Mrs. Bennet's desolation, though Mrs. Bennet would of course prefer that Kitty had married as well.

And Elizabeth and Mary… why had they gone off to become governesses?

Both wasted every chance to snag a husband. Mary… Mrs. Bennet accepted Mary's choice. She'd never expected better from *that* daughter, and Mary sounded in her stuffy letters as though she enjoyed her position. Even though her life sounded dreadfully boring.

Elizabeth had always been wild and ungovernable. It was *her* fault the scheming Lucases took Longbourn in the first place.

Mrs. Bennet could hardly comprehend how even Elizabeth had been involved in such a great scandal, and she hardly knew what to believe. There had been *soldiers* and *Bow Street Runners* here to visit. And they accused Elizabeth of stealing from the earl who had employed her. And all she had was a single letter from Elizabeth written in a shaky hand, promising that she was well.

What nonsense.

What had her dear girl gotten herself into?

Mrs. Bennet always expected Elizabeth to get into some sort of problem, but never to be *hung*. It would be such a scandal, and she would cry and weep, and be desolate at the shame of it. And then no one would *ever* marry Kitty or Mary, and Kitty was pretty enough that she might do well for herself if she ever had a proper chance.

Mrs. Gardiner had told Mrs. Bennet that there had been at least two tradesmen with respectable positions who had shown interest in Elizabeth, and that she had discouraged them both. Mrs. Gardiner at the time was rather frustrated with Elizabeth's unwillingness to accept the necessity that she would not find a man who was both a decent match and who looked decently well.

Mrs. Bennet was rather proud of Elizabeth. She had lived in the world long enough to have a decent notion of what happened. Only Elizabeth *could* have defended her virtue from such a man. Mrs. Bennet was very glad after the Gardiners had visited with the entire story that was running wild round London that Mary was employed by a widow with only daughters in the house.

If only Lizzy wasn't going to be hung for it!

Mrs. Bennet was quite pessimistic enough to be sure Lizzy would be hung, just as she had been sure years before that her husband would find Mr. Wickham and duel him and be killed while searching for Lydia.

Mrs. Bennet was quite shocked when Mrs. Phillips ran into the drawing room with Kitty and her husband in tow, "A letter from Lizzy to you! From Lizzy! Posted from *France.*"

Everyone pushed the letter into Mrs. Bennet's face, and they eagerly waited for her to open it, so they could find out what the news was.

Mrs. Bennet looked at the letter, sealed with red wax imprinted with a half familiar symbol. Her daughter's name written on the outside, Pas-de-Calais was marked as the city the letter was sent from.

Something in her heart unclenched, and Mrs. Bennet could not help but smile. Whatever news the letter contained, her daughter was *safe*. She hadn't even realized how deeply anxious she had been for Lizzy's fate until that worry was gone. "In France. She is in France."

Kitty smiled too, and Mrs. Phillips.

"Yes, yes." Mr. Phillips said, "Open up so we can know what her circumstances are — I dare say she has written asking for money to support herself out of the country." The country lawyer was happy enough at seeing that his niece had escaped her enemies that he did not even sound particularly sour at the prospect.

Mrs. Bennet found it difficult to understand what the letter said, for it was too fantastical to be credited.

Dear Mama,

I am sure you have worried very greatly for me these past weeks, but I am now entirely safe and well, though still I cannot return to England. I have some news which shall surprise you greatly.

I am to be married tomorrow morning, and I shall be long since married by the time you receive this letter. Now that I have safely escaped from England, I may tell you that I sought refuge after Lord Lachglass attacked me with an old friend of ours, from many years before, Mr. Fitzwilliam Darcy.

He holds an affection for me that has lasted all the years since we saw each other last, and in the course of the past weeks I have realized I too have a deep and abiding affection for him. I know this shall shock you, as you always believed I disliked him, but I learned many years past that much of the source for my dislike for Mr. Darcy was based upon false pretenses.

He asked me to marry him yesterday, and I accepted gladly, and we are to be married tomorrow morning before we set off to Paris.

I have spoken to Mr. Darcy at length about your situation, and we wish to ensure you, and Kitty and Mary all can live happily and well, and maintain your positions as gentlewomen. Mr. Darcy has a large cottage on his great estate which has traditionally been used by the mother of the master if she outlives her husband. We wish to offer for you to freely live there, and Mr. Darcy will provide a pension to you to pay for your expenses. Attached to this note is a check that can be drawn on Mr. Darcy's bank accounts at Childe's for six hundred pounds to provide the funds necessary to move, and also to purchase some new dresses for yourself and Kitty and Mary.

I am certain that my uncles Mr. Phillips and Mr. Gardiner will help you in making business arrangements, and I have asked Mrs. North, the housekeeper at Darcy's home in London, to call upon you in a few days, to explain the situation of the cottage and further matters.

Mrs. North was exceedingly kind to me during the time I spent ill and quite destitute in Mr. Darcy's home.

Tell Kitty that I miss her very much, and she must come visit us in France in some four or five months if matters have not changed such that I can return to England.

Your loving daughter, signing her name for the last time as,
E Bennet

After she finished reading the letter aloud, Mrs. Bennet stared ahead for a period of several minutes without being able to say a word, such was her shock.

Mr. Phillips recovered first and took from Mrs. Bennet the check that had been packaged in the envelope. "Looks like the real thing. Looks entirely like the real thing. Heh. Did not expect that from Miss Lizzy."

Kitty clapped her hands. "Oh, new dresses! I am so tired of this old material!" She pinched her woolen dress with some annoyance. "But Mr. Darcy? Didn't Lizzy dislike him very much indeed?"

Mrs. Phillips sighed. "'Tis so romantic. He was very tall and handsome, whatever he may have said of our Lizzy. I remember he had said he did not like her appearance, but I fancy men often say that of the women they are the most fascinated by when they wish to hide their sentiments."

Finally Mrs. Bennet comprehended the happy fate that had fallen upon her family, after so many years of ill luck. They finally had such a stroke of good luck so nearly to make up for it all. This marriage did make up for every ill luck, except the death of her husband, for though she had never understood Mr. Bennet, she had loved him.

Mrs. Bennet exclaimed aloud, "Ten thousand pounds a year! As good as a Lord!" And then shortly after she exclaimed again, "Oh, if only Mr. Bennet were alive to see how well our Lizzy has done for herself!"

Chapter Fifteen

The morning after they arrived in Paris, Elizabeth and Darcy set off on foot eager to explore the city.

Elizabeth felt full of energy and enthusiasm that morning. The lascivious nighttime marital activities they now enjoyed, being happily — very happily that is — married got *better* each night as she became more used to Darcy's body, and he to her desires.

This morning was a sunny bright day, though the air still felt thin and cold whenever one stood in the shade. Unfortunately it was still cold enough that Elizabeth needed to wear a heavy coat yet. There had been no rain for the previous several days, so there was little of the horse droppings turned into a particularly grotesque mud by the rain waiting to be thrown up by the passing carriages careening loudly through the city center.

They walked down the *Rue de Richelieu*, until they reached the area around the Palace of the Louvre and the Tuileries. There the couple paused to admire the large and fine triumphal arch Napoleon built there to celebrate his victory at Austerlitz.

They also admired the Palace of the Tuileries where twenty years prior the famous battle between the king's regiment of Swiss guards and the forces of the National Assembly had occurred, and the Swiss guards had been killed almost to a man following their defeat.

"I can imagine those proudly uniformed men standing there, shouting refusal to the offer to surrender." Elizabeth shivered. "I wonder what went through their minds in such an extremity."

"They knew their duty to their king, and they fulfilled it," Darcy replied, admiringly.

The palace was at present the residence of King Louis XVIII. After a moment's discussion, wishing to enjoy the sunny morning, they refrained from inquiring of the staff if they might be given a tour of the public rooms of the palace.

Directly adjacent to the Palace of the Tuileries was the large Palace of the Louvre, and the two palaces together formed a massive C. For Elizabeth the *Museum du Roi* in the Louvre was a far greater draw than seeing that portion of a royal residence which the general public might visit.

They resisted the pull of famed art — though only for the moment, Elizabeth knew she soon would return to admire all the paintings in the great gallery of the Louvre — and instead walked through a passageway built into the Palace of the Louvre, and out to the bank of the Seine.

There was a busy traffic of carriages and street vendors along this area, and the river rushed merrily along lightly murmuring. Many bridges crossed the river, all filled with traffic.

Elizabeth had command of the guidebook, and Darcy had declared that he was in her hands today in determining which way to go. She looked both directions and then studied the map before her. The choice was whether to go east along the riverbank, and reach shortly the Garden of the Tuileries, or to go to the west, and cross to the Île de la Cité, which was, according to the guidebook, the oldest inhabited part of the city.

The island contained a great many churches, most notably the Cathedral of the Notre Dame, which the guidebook insisted was well worth looking upon, and the tourist ought, it said, inquire of the doorman to be admitted in to admire the paintings.

However the promise of a garden which looked upon their map to be similar in size to St. James's Park, though far smaller than Hyde Park, won Elizabeth's preference.

She quickly grew disillusioned though with the garden. The bulk of land was made up of squares of evenly ordered trees trimmed so that the branches and leaves did not grow low enough for even Mr. Darcy to ever need to duck his head, and the tops had been trimmed so that they were all of an even size and did not interfere with each other.

All this order and unnatural attempt at perfection surrounded several giant ponds whose borders were made up of giant circles of concrete, without any irregularity. "This is the French mode of formal design at its very worst!"

Darcy laughingly replied, "We are in a royal garden in the center of France, what else could you expect?"

"I have never seen a place of such an artificial appearance, with such false adornment," Elizabeth replied heatedly. "I have never seen a park where nature has been permitted to do *less* and where natural beauty has been so much counteracted by awkward taste."

Darcy laughed. "I like to see you so passionately determined upon a point — especially when it is not a passionate determination against me."

Elizabeth smiled brilliantly at him, her anger forgotten for a moment. "You really do like to see me in such a mode?"

"Exceedingly well, it brings out the fine color in your eyes, and the sparkles in your cheeks, and makes your dewy skin to glow yet brighter. I do dearly love to see you, in all your modes and expressions."

He took her in his arms and swung her around, giggling.

"Ah, well in that case," Elizabeth said smilingly to Darcy, still leaning against him with her arms around his neck, and feeling her breasts pressed against his muscular chest. "In that case I must rage against many more gardens for your entertainment."

"Not so bad, I think." Darcy replied, "Perhaps if we saw it in summer, or in spring, with all the flowers abloom, and the full growth of leaves on the trees. I believe the smell might be quite delightful."

"It would yet be hideous. Designed by a geometer! Each tree the same distance from every other tree, in a square grid. When I ask you, when, whilst wandering in a forest, have you ever encountered trees which grow in a square grid?"

"You shall like my estate at Pemberley exceedingly well — the philosophy of design there was entirely the opposite of here."

Elizabeth smiled at him. "Do you really think — I do hope one day I can return to our home, and see it with you."

"I as well, but even if that day of safety never arrives, I would far rather live in exile with you than in Pemberley itself without you."

Arm in arm they walked to the end of the park.

The section on the far side from the Tuileries palace, while still not to Elizabeth's taste, permitted more of irregularity. Then they crossed the street, and walked back along the high embankment built up to contain the flow of the Seine towards the bridge at *Pont Neuf* which was the first place they could cross over to the island.

The Île de la Cité was filled with tight packed streets, even tighter than the *Rue de Richelieu*, and the tall buildings occluded the sun, and left Elizabeth and Darcy to shiver at the sudden return of winter, but when they had walked through the whole island, they found on the far side a large square with the large Cathedral on one side of it.

They joined some worshippers, and a fair number of other tourists, some English, but also German and Italian, and possibly French extraction inside. At least Elizabeth believed that several of the people talking too loudly for the interior of a church in French while pointing eagerly at the paintings and the beautiful stained glass ceiling had more interest in the artistry of the place than its value as a location for sanctified Papist worship.

The interior of the great cathedral took Elizabeth's breath away with a sense of the sublime. The late morning sun streamed through the great circular stained glass windows.

There were many statues and tombs with effigies, and there were fine religious paintings with scenes from the life of Christ, and from the lives of the Catholic saints. And Elizabeth loved the fine altarpiece in the center of the building, and the endless wooden lines of pews.

They had the opportunity to climb to the top of the bell tower, and see the entire city from that height, which was quite as impressive of a sight as the view from the dome of St. Paul's or that from the top of the monument to the Great Fire in London.

"An exceptional building," Darcy proclaimed, when they had returned to the ground and left the great cathedral, and turned to looked back at it. "The equal of St. Paul's, in size and beauty, though entirely different in style."

"No, no! Far superior," Elizabeth replied, smiling at her husband. "Sir Christopher Wren's masterpiece has nothing to it."

"*You* would prefer the Gothic style of flying buttresses and tall bell towers to the more prosaic, and I daresay practical, large dome of St. Paul's."

"Can you not see the romance in those bell towers? In every bit of statuary and every *bas-relief* decoration of that building? Can you not see with your mind the endless generations of monks ringing those massive bells — there is some great story about this building, which only awaits the proper poet to tell it."

"It would serve you right if one day someone writes a great novel about the cathedral."

Elizabeth laughed. "The story I imagine would take a poet to write, even if he told the story in prose."

"Does it make up for the ugliness of the park, the beauty of the cathedral?"

"It is more than passing strange to me, how they can build a church, a monument to their saints, which is of such surpassing beauty, and yet make their gardens so ugly."

"They both are evenly structured and balanced in their core, but a well-balanced building is a thing of beauty, while well-balanced nature misses the purpose of nature, with is profusion, and freedom."

"No, no, there is enormous *irregularity* in the cathedral, and that is the source of the beauty. I believe the solution to my mystery is different. This was produced in the so called dark ages, before the rule in France was regular and orderly, under those weak kings that we bashed about at Agincourt, and Crecy and Poitiers. But then came the age of their absolute monarchs and it was *they* who designed the Louvre and the Tuileries, and the ugly regularity and order of the whole. This building reflects a weaker, happier, more human time. And the Tuileries reflects the tyranny — ah but I ought not say that here. It reflects the nature of modern king, and whatever virtues such a king may provide, with it is a loss of real beauty; real and human beauty."

"And *that* is why England shall always be superior to France, in fundamentals," Darcy said laughing.

"That is your interpretation, not mine!"

They were somewhat tired of being continuously on foot by this point, and they had heard many good reports of the *restaurateurs* and the cafes in the Palais Royal, which in any case was close by their apartments.

Darcy hailed a *fiacre* which took them back across the Seine, and then they trundled through the crowded streets of Paris up to the entrance to that remarkable structure.

The one part of the Palais Royal was a colonnaded building surrounding a large garden with fountains and trees arranged again in far too much order for Elizabeth's taste. Along three of the sides there were shops and cafes set along the galleries covered by the colonnades.

The remarkable part of the building was on the fourth side. There was a double line of columns set as far apart as a road of moderate width, with a wood structure covering the whole, and a massive number of shops filled with books, dresses, fine jewelry and all other manner of goods on either side. There were large numbers of restaurants fine enough to even appease Darcy's taste.

Though the wind could blow into the open aired structure it was comparably comfortable inside, much warmer than the air outside, and the entire hall was packed with finely dressed Parisians promenading or shopping.

Elizabeth and Darcy found the fanciest appearing cafe along the first floor and took the private room upstairs in it where they could look down on the crowds pleasantly walking below. They ate an excellent repast, liberally seasoned with the tart and creamy sorrel sauce which the French tended to cook everything with.

Later Elizabeth went into several shops at Darcy's encouragement. She was measured by a dressmaker who had been recommended as being at the height of fashion.

Silk ribbons, swathes of cloth, varieties of patterns, compliments from the madame who managed the shop, gloves and bonnets and hats, and shoes and boots, and clothes for every conceivable occasion, and one or two which Elizabeth was not quite prepared to conceive of.

All a heady, delightful mix.

After a while, Elizabeth began to believe she might be perhaps ordering too many dresses. However, at almost that moment Darcy came to the shop to ask after her, and his encouragement ensured she *did* order too many dresses.

They then found another cafe in the Palais Royal where some very fine chess players had met to compete against each other, and they spent a tense hour watching two extraordinary games play out.

That evening when they returned to their apartments, while they waited for supper, Darcy had his valet retrieve a travelling chess set from his bags for them to make an attempt to replicate the mighty contest they had witnessed in the cafe.

The chess set was made of the finest marble, with exquisitely carved pieces, and as Darcy set out the pieces she admired it.

"Unexpectedly heavy," Elizabeth said smiling as she nearly dropped one of the smooth marble knights. "Such perfect carvings. And those tiny rubies in the eyes." She eagerly turned the knight over and over, admiring the tiny lines, and little details, the way that you could feel the locks of the horse's mane, the way that the grain of the marble was perfectly polished away. She carefully rubbed her finger over the horse's nose before putting the almost ebony black piece back on the board Darcy had neatly arranged. "How many dozens of pounds did *this* set cost?"

"I have no knowledge of that, as this set is… not quite an heirloom, but it was purchased by my father, and—"

"I am very glad then," Elizabeth interrupted with a laugh, "I did not drop the piece."

Darcy laughed in reply, and he tapped a pawn on Elizabeth's side of the table. She liked how his hand waved just a few inches in front of her chest as he did so.

"This one was replaced after Georgiana dropped it a few years ago, you can see how the color is not *quite* the same. And this piece," he tapped another with his fingers brushing her fingers, "this bishop once fell, but only the head came off, and very neatly, so a craftsman glued the pieces together again in a cunning way, but," he picked up the bishop and handed it to Elizabeth, "you can see the line if you hold up the piece right to the light. But he polished away the rough edge so that it is almost impossible to *feel* where the hole came."

She did so, and saw as he said. But what caught her eyes more was the giant bible held by the Bishop, looking as much like some witch's grimoire as a holy book. There was a line of tiny words on the open pages. But the letters were too small for Elizabeth to read.

"It's from the gospel of Matthew. My father's favorite passage. He gave the order to be carved so."

"How did the artist make such tiny scratches, and on a black surface?"

"With difficulty, I would imagine." Darcy shrugged. "I once studied the pieces under the lens of my microscope, and—"

"Under the lens of your microscope, I imagine every boy has one."

"Your father did not? He always struck me as the sort of man who might have scientific interests and leanings. It is not so expensive to get a decent one. Papa believed it was most important I gain a thorough understanding of the modern scientists, and my tutor had written several notable papers and he was a member of the royal society."

"And your tutor was a member of the royal society?" Elizabeth grinned, looking at Darcy. So casually wealthy that like the wealthy always did, he hired the service of the most interesting and best persons. Of course she now was so wealthy herself.

A microscope, Papa certainly could have afforded a microscope if the desire had crossed his mind, but a tutor who was a member of the royal society?

Whatever the cost, such men had the opportunity to find more prominent patrons than Papa. "I think my father had a preference for the less modern. He put his money into antiquarian books in the main — and stars. We had a fine telescope."

"Ah. We also extensively purchased books. In such days as these I cannot countenance the neglect of a family library." Darcy grinned boyishly as he picked up one of the delicately carved white pawns and settled it two blocks forward on the heavy marble board. "I sound quite conceited with that tone."

"Only a *little*," Elizabeth replied. "But an advantage that accrues to the very wealthy is that they can both pursue antiquarian books and microscopes and scientific learning."

Elizabeth moved her own pawn, and Darcy made his move.

"I do not think," he said, "that I am so *very* rich. Do not get the idea that I am one of the greatest fortunes in the land. A great fortune, yes, but there are at least a hundred estates of greater extent than mine. I cannot compare to a duke for example. Or to a Rothchild."

"Merely to an earl?"

"Merely to an earl." Darcy quirked his lips, and his eyes twinkled.

He picked up his bishop to move and then hesitated, frowning. He asked in a half embarrassed voice, "You have not played chess frequently of late, have you?"

"What?" Elizabeth looked down at the board again, and at Darcy's bishop, and at her king, who had already been checkmated through the passage she'd opened up by moving her pawn. She laughed and groaned. "Just like Papa used to do to me. I forgot that trick."

She laughed and pushed Darcy's pawns back into their original spaces, enjoying how now it was *her* turn to brush her fingers against his. "That was merely a, ah—"

"A practice round?"

"Exactly! This was a round to warm the fingers up, so that we could safely move the heavy chess pieces. It does not count."

"Certainly not. Certainly not. One must exert great caution in lifting such heavy objects lest one injure oneself."

Darcy grinned at her and Elizabeth grinned back.

They played several more games, all of which Elizabeth lost, but she got much better over the course of the games. That night, as she lay in bed with Darcy, Elizabeth said to him, "Though it is not England, I think this can be home for us, at least for the time."

"Yes," Darcy whispered back, "I like Paris very much."

"Do you think… we should stay here for now, for a while?"

"Yes," Darcy kissed her and pulled her body against his. "We shall."

Chapter Sixteen

On a fine day late in May, three months following the event which left him with a permanently bent nose, a great official of the government, second to the Earl of Liverpool, came to visit Lord Lachglass in his home in London where he yet remained for the season.

Parliament was still in session, and Lachglass had an important position with the government, but he rarely bothered to do much *work* associated with his position — though he had been able to turn it into thousands of pounds of income through emoluments and the sale of favors to his friends.

These past three months had not been kind to Lord Lechery.

He often had a ringing in his ears, and his memory was not quite right. He sometimes felt as though he lived in a strange fog. The doctors, when he demanded they fix everything, suggested he had acquired a nervous complaint.

A nervous complaint! Like a weak willed woman?

Real men did not have nervous complaints.

The doctors laughed at him once they were away.

He knew they must. They sneered behind their hands, and chuckled when they went home to their stupid ugly wives. "Dearest, I saw the Earl of Lachglass today, quite a womanly man, you could beat him to a pulp like that governess who *fucking married fucking Darcy*."

That *worm infested, slatternly, sluttish, worm infested whore*. He hoped she gave Darcy the French disease.

How *dare* she undo her refusal of that upright, disgusting, tall arse Darcy? That had been the sole beauty of the matter — that the woman who had refused his kindly blandishments had also refused Darcy when he offered marriage to a governess, and Lachglass had giggled to himself every time he thought about it.

Somehow it wasn't funny when he heard that the woman was now married to Darcy.

She was delightfully happy in Paris. His agent sent to the city returned with the full information: She was the darling of the city. She dressed so fashionably. She danced at a ball at the Tuileries.

She was *happy*.

The worm infested whore.

And Lachglass? A laughing stock. And worse, he knew it.

How could a man who allowed a woman to beat him to a pulp be anything *but* a matter of humor at every man's club in London? *Everyone* somehow knew the story. Not only those in the clubs, but his doctors. His footmen. The street urchins who stared at him when he drove his curricle round Hyde Park. They knew too, and they thought as they watched him. They thought: *Even a woman could draw his cork and leave him bleeding.*

Lachglass obsessed over his nose. His ugly, ugly nose. Never straight again.

He had taken to going out rarely, practicing with his boxing master for two hours each day, with a vague sense that he would pummel her into a bleeding, crying, gasping pulp if he ever met Elizabeth Bennet again.

However this day Lachglass was present at home for a different reason, one of Lord Liverpool's chief ministers had demanded the pleasure of an audience with Lord Lachglass.

It was twenty minutes after the specified time for the appointment that the gentleman's carriage rolled to a stop in front of Lachglass's townhouse.

Lachglass this day was particularly irritated, his room was hot, stuffy, and had one of the frequent headaches which tormented him since he'd been attacked by that vicious wormy whore, Elizabeth Bennet.

He wanted to throw the painting that stood over the fireplace through a window.

That would show them.

That would show the hot weather. That would show the disdaining, maddening crowds.

The great politician stepped into Lachglass's drawing room, without having taken off his gloves.

"To what may I attribute the pleasure of your company," Lachglass said, stiffly standing to meet him.

"No pleasure, lad. No pleasure."

"So then what deuced reason do you have to demand my time—" Lachglass took a deep breath. This was an important man who he could not shout at like he could Mr. Blight. This man was senior to him in the government, and he did not wish to lose the extra income he gained from his position. "I mean, sir, I await your pleasure."

"You are done. We have no place for you."

"Whatever do you mean?" Lachglass replied haughtily.

The angry white-haired man stomped back and forth, not caring about the value of Lachglass's carpets. "You are finished. Nothing in our government for you anymore. Your position is to be given to Windham. I will see your resignation tomorrow. Tomorrow. In the hands of Liverpool. We can't have you anymore, not with these stories. And I dare say, for my own part, I don't want you."

"I have provided my support to the government consistently. There is no stauncher defender of our British institutions than I, and—"

"Coddleswop. Think I give a damn? Think I give a *damn!*"

The piercing shout cut through Lachglass's headache, and somehow, against his desire to be angry and defend his own rights, it cowed him into a silence, and he despised himself for that. He despised himself for it even more than he already despised himself.

"Bother the *maids* if you must." The politician's voice fell quiet and conversational. "A gentlewoman in reduced circumstances? An actual lady of breeding — someone a man like *Darcy* would marry? You disgust me. I'd not let my daughter attend a ball you were present at. And then to bring the matter to the courts when you were just a damned fool."

"She robbed me and beat me, and—"

"I don't believe that. You don't believe that. Nobody believes that. It makes you even less of a man if it is true. No jury will believe that — Jove, pathetic. You are pathetic. We have the Hampden clubs organizing against us. The lack of work drives vagabonds to the streets. Secret groups whisper revolution and *you* must prove every false claim about the excesses and wrongs of our aristocracy true? You are the sort of man who led to our French friends meeting Monsieur le Guillotine. *You* are one of the chiefest problems with the state of Britain at this time."

"I will not listen to such insults. I will not listen to such lies about—"

"You were beaten by a woman. And you planned to force her, which you could not even manage. You are done. *Done!*" The old politician's voice snapped again loudly enough that Lachglass vibrated.

The minister added in a disgusted tone, "If you must bother anyone, let me say it again: *bother the damned maids.* They can't write to the papers. They don't have rich friends who are politically useful. Have you any idea how much trouble a man like Darcy could cause for us if he threw his lot in with the Whigs? He has two boroughs in his own pocket and he is exceedingly well respected. Exceedingly. If *he* talks about a need for reforms to curb the excesses of the peers, others amongst the commons will listen, and then where will we be?"

"I don't give a damn. You show yourselves to be low dogs deserving of being shot like low worm infested whores deserve to be shot. You show no loyalty to a man disdained and despised, viciously and violently, by the low seditious scribblers of the press, who deserve to be shot." Lord Lachglass sneered at the powerful government man before him.

The politician sneered back. "For once the scribblers speak sense. I don't want a man who'll let a woman knock him on his ass in my government."

The minister was such a short man. With an ugly folded and wrinkled face, he'd never been handsome. Never been much of a man either.

And now that was how everyone saw Lachglass. Ugly, with his bent nose, and the scar whose fringe was visible on the top of his forehead. No longer handsome.

SHE had thrown him from the position of power and influence he'd cultivated for himself.

They'd tossed him aside. Without so much as a "by your leave". With a simple, "You can take yourself and the votes you provide, and we'll manage nicely without them, because we want to *court* Darcy more. *Darcy* is respected, unlike you."

Darcy, who married a *governess* whore.

Shouldn't *that* make him a laughing stock? Wasn't *Darcy* the one who was less of a man, who would ask the same woman twice to marry him?

Darcy was seen as a romantic hero by the newspaper eating crowds of cits. *Darcy* was seen as a man worth cultivating. Lachglass knew how pathetic Darcy was. He couldn't do a damned thing with a woman without someone literally holding his baby hands to propel him into the room with her. And he'd probably still not manage to stick himself in her.

And now *Darcy* had the upper on him.

Lachglass wanted to murder the politician in front of him. He rather wanted to murder everyone in London.

But instead he did the only thing he could, he sneered. "You have earned my permanent hatred, and one day you'll rue this."

The man laughed. "Going to hurt me like you hurt Mrs. Darcy, eh? Just make sure your resignation letter is handed in by tomorrow midday or we'll have a cabinet vote to throw you out of office."

He left out, chuckling, his grotesquely oversized stomach wiggling side to side with each wormlike laugh. "Scared of your revenge? A man who lets a woman beat him up? What a molly."

Lachglass clenched and unclenched his fists as the sound of the minister's laughing departure faded. And then, without thought, he picked up a vase, almost as expensive as the one Miss Bennet bashed over his head, and he threw it through his gilt mirror. He picked up the fire poker and he bashed out each of his windows, the shards of glass falling onto the scurrying pedestrians on the road below his townhouse.

He kicked five holes in each wall of the drawing room.

A giant globe with a map of the earth painted on it that had cost more than ten pounds was beaten until its remains looked like a giant wooden cracked egg that had been painted blue and brown for Easter.

If one of his servants had entered the room at this moment, Lachglass would have tried to kick them to death.

And then, the cold wind blowing through his ruined windows, Lachglass curled up in a corner of the drawing room and cried.

Naked and exposed.

Everyone could see straight through to him. Humiliated, worthless, he'd shamed the family name. He was known by everyone as the man who was beaten up by a woman, and who then wanted to set the courts on her for his own crime.

He rocked back and forth unable to speak. Everything had fallen completely apart.

Tears flooded his cheeks, dripping in big puddles onto the ground on either side of Lord Lachglass. His legs were too weak for him to stand, and he felt dizzy, as if the whole world spun around him, and he was going to fall off and choke on his own vomit, like a vagrant drunk given a guinea by an impecunious and foolish gentleman.

His ribs squeezed together.

Lachglass tried to vomit, but nothing but acid flooded up into his throat.

The door opened and Lachglass put his hands back on the ground, and like a cat in a corner he hissed at the intruder.

Mr. Blight stood in the door. The tears made it impossible for Lachglass to see clearly, but he thought that the back alley knifer who had become his man of business had a look of contempt upon his face.

He'd show Spitey Blighty. He'd show them all. He'd show every one of them.

He'd make them regret everything.

With a stumble Lachglass rose to his feet and said to Mr. Blight, "Call my boxing master. I need to beat someone."

The attempt to resolve his emotions through fighting did little good for Lachglass. He realized almost instantly he did not want training.

He wanted to use his fists to pummel a man.

The training room had pastel painted walls, and it smelled of sweat. Lachglass held his hands out, and the servant wrapped heavy leather around the fists to protect them.

As soon as he was ready, in a thin linen shirt and flexible pants to fight, he swung an angry wild punch at the heavily muscled professional pugilist who he'd hired to train him. But even though he hadn't waited for the signal to start, the man had simply stepped out of the way of his fist, and with a cluck of his tongue he said, "Bad form, bad form."

Lachglass angrily swung at him. Again and again.

No matter how furiously he punched, the pugilist always kept his hands interposed, or he ducked below the punch. Several times he punched back, though not hard enough to do more than wind Lachglass, but it knocked him back.

Lachglass became more and more frustrated. More and more hateful.

"Damn you, man. You work for me. Let me get a clear blow!"

"You'll not learn anything that way. Aim for the torso, Milord, unsporting to hit a man in the head."

"Damn you, man. I do not want to learn a damn thing."

His face was flushed with raw anger, and his veins throbbed.

"You're in no fit state today." The boxing master stepped back. "In no fit state at all to benefit from a lesson today."

Lachglass snapped five more punches towards the man, all of which were easily blocked, leaving his hand sore and tired despite the heavy gloves wrapped around them.

Lachglass motioned for the servant who watched them to wipe off his sweaty forehead with his fine towel. "My damned man. Let me beat you over the head with my fists, or I will dismiss you and tell everyone of my acquaintance to have nothing to do with your instruction."

"Ha, you think your acquaintance any longer gives a pence for your opinion?" The boxer sneered at him. "Is that what you want? A helpless opponent? That why you like raping little girls? But found one who knew how to fight better than you, and she beat in that misshapen nose of yours. Well I'm no women. But then it seems you can't even beat a woman."

"I'll have you killed for what you say to me. You know who I am! You know what my position is. I can—"

The pugilist screwed up his beefy face and spat on the wooden slats of the training floor. He stripped off his bulging leather gloves with his teeth and threw them to the floor, like a bizarre modern version of an ancient knight tossing his gauntlet to the ground in challenge. "I'll not be insulted by a rapist. I'll not teach a rapist either. Real gentlemen don't use force on women. Real *men* don't need force to get a woman's favors. I'd rather starve than train a helpless, pathetic tyrant who wants to beat a man over the head without earning the skill to do it."

"I'll destroy you! I'll destroy you! You'll never be employed again! Never! You'll starve, and all those muscles will waste away to nothing, and you'll sit on the side of the road, begging, and no one will give you any money or food. And you'll rue the day you disobeyed the Earl of Lachglass!"

Lord Lachglass ranted till he was red in the face.

He ranted until the pugilist was long gone.

And he stood there, abandoned in the training gym, alone except for Spitey Blighty watching him with his blank face and contemptuous eyes.

"Kill him!" Lachglass clenched his teeth so hard that one of them audibly cracked and part of the tooth that had been hurting on and off for a month broke away. "Kill that damned, insulting boxing master. Stab a needle in his back."

There was the sneer again. Like Spitey Blighty was considering refusing the order. But he bowed and left the room.

Lachglass rang for his valet to help him dress and gave orders for the carriage to be prepared. He had no purpose for London.

"Also," he ordered to the servant, "have the windows of the carriage blocked with black drapes, so no one can see within."

Now that he was dressed, Lachglass stepped up to a mirror to properly tie and arrange his cravat. He looked into his own eyes, red from his unmanly tears. His eyes, they glittered, speaking to him.

They demanded revenge. His eyes demanded revenge on *her*.

Lachglass bared his teeth at the mirror, and he growled at his own image.

Chapter Seventeen

Late at night early in June two women prepared to go to sleep in a solidly built house of three stories — the uppermost floor was only used by the staff of domestics. This building was called a "cottage" by the owners of the magnificent estate on which it rested. One of the women was middle aged, and one young.

"Lord! I'm so fagged," Catherine Bennet smilingly said to her mother. Kitty still luxuriated in the feel of cashmere shawls and tightly woven fabrics she now enjoyed because of Elizabeth's excellent marriage, "we were up so late at the assembly last night."

The letters of introduction for his new family that Darcy had sent to all of his acquaintance, and the letters of praise for Elizabeth from Mrs. North and Becky to Mrs. Reynolds, had done a great deal to make the entrance of Kitty and Mrs. Bennet into the society round about Pemberley easy and smooth.

Mrs. Bennet's middle daughter was not present with them, as Mary had taken her share of the money Mr. Darcy and Elizabeth gave them to stay in London with the Gardiners. She attended improving lectures, read the improving books she bought ample amounts of, and improvingly practiced the piano. And she described all this in improving letters to her mother, written in perfectly straight lines.

Mrs. Bennet was generally liked, as she was friendly and talkative, and if she was vulgar, the plain reality is that many of her new neighbors also were.

Kitty was pretty, not so pretty as Elizabeth or Jane, but a fine looking girl, with bold flashing eyes, and an easy confidence about herself that had not been ruined by the years of poverty after her father's death. She liked to be able to dance and wear pretty clothes once again, and to be seen as a Miss of modest consequence.

Mr. Darcy had allowed it to become known through the medium of his lawyer that he intended to do something — though nothing exceptional — for his sister-in-law when she should marry. So Kitty's circumstances were sufficient for those families not on the hunt for a splendid match for their sons, while her beauty and vivaciousness drew the attention of many of those sons.

These were not the dark days of the war, when the absence of gentlemen off serving as officers with Wellington, or upon the wooden walls that barred the English channel from the little ogre meant that even a pretty girl would often sit out half her dances at a ball, or be reduced to making the circuit with one of her sisters or female friends. Kitty could dance often as she wanted at the assemblies, and she had made new eternal boon companions from amongst the other young women of the neighborhood.

Miss Kitty was quite as happy as she could wish to be.

At present she was not eager to *marry*, instead she was eager for a planned visit to Paris with Mama and Mary in the fall, when she would see Elizabeth once more and be able to thank Mr. Darcy for his kindness to them.

However as the great Scots poet of a generation prior said, "The best laid schemes o' mice an' men gang aft a-gley."

A group of six men hunched in the bushes outside of the cottage, waiting for the candles to be extinguished.

Five of these men were ruffians of the worst sort, four of them had worked the noble trade of the highwayman upon the High Toby in the past. Three would in the future, and two would be hung for it. Two more were London back alley knifers, both of whom had killed a man.

The sixth had once nearly been a gentleman, but he had fallen in the world since then.

One of the Londoners had killed more than one man in his time on this earth.

That man was the scarred Mr. Blight. He had never healed quite right from Elizabeth's blow, his jaw ached right in front of the ear, and he fancied that he now bit his tongue far more often than before.

He hated Elizabeth for that, and for that reason, even though Lord Lachglass's plan was ridiculous, and doomed to see him destroyed, likely with Blight himself, Blight was happy to hunch in the shrubbery outside the house where *her* mother and sister lived.

When the lights were extinguished, and the sounds of movement ceased, one of the ruffians worked the locked latch open on the door.

The wooden door popped open fast and easily, just a simple latch, nothing like what a man in London would use to blockade his castle from the evil ones outside.

One man hung back in the darkness of the woods, keeping an eye about for any sign that they'd attracted attention from the big house. This man was the one who had once been a gentleman, and he had no taste for violence.

If he had not considered himself to be in particularly difficult circumstances he would not have agreed to aid the others, and he felt something like pangs of conscience as he watched the line of rough bestial brutes (as he thought of them) file into the breached house.

The others snuck on tip-toeing feet through the house and up the stairs to where the bedrooms of the family would be. The underling who'd killed a man was placed to stand inside the darkened servant's stairway, to stab in the neck without warning any servant who was awakened by the noise and ran down to see what was the matter.

A clumsy country oaf accidentally kicked over an incidental table sitting where no rational table would sit in the middle of the hallway leading to the staircase.

The man on guard against the servants stiffened in the deathly silence that followed that clatter.

But no one wakened.

Led by Blight and carrying thieves' lanterns that only showed their light in one direction, the others went up to the rooms. They softly tested the doors to each bedroom, and none of them were locked.

They easily found the quiet peaceful sleepers.

A quick movement by men used to violence, a knock over the head of each sleeping woman, and then before they could return to themselves, efficient gags were forced over the mouths of both women, making it impossible for them to scream, and difficult for them to breathe.

Hands tied together. Feet tied together.

And then the two burliest of the men in this gang slung one woman each over their back and carted them down the stairs and out into the estate's large park.

This group of men had not been bothered at all while sneaking their way onto Darcy's estate, following the line of ground, and avoiding all of the houses of cottagers, and the occasional roving of the groundskeepers. They had moved so well through the estate that one might wonder if they were guided by a person who had grown up on the estate.

Which they had been.

The man who had led them to dowager cottage was the man who had waited outside. He stood masked to ensure he was not recognized in the dark when the criminals led by Mr. Blight emerged from the now emptier house. This man's eyes flicked over the two captives, blindfolded and gagged, being carried on the back of Mr. Blight's friends, and something like regret for his actions and the past flashed in his eyes.

He led the party quickly over hills and through hedges and out to the blind where highwaymen had hidden in the old days before the Darcy family had suppressed them, and before the king's justice was more than a laughable word.

A carriage awaited them, standing empty with a team of four ugly horses purchased more than twenty miles away. The coat of arms on the carriage had been carefully removed, but the gap in the paint where it had been, and the bolts that it had been attached to, were almost visible in the dark.

Mr. Blight sourly looked at the carriage. Still recognizable.

Would have made a damned sight more sense to rent a separate carriage for the night's work, or better to purchase one, like he had the horses, and then push it off an isolated cliff into the sea in Cornwall when the business was done. But Lachglass had insisted that it be *his* carriage which would carry the captives to his estate, because somehow that would make it more his own revenge.

Blight had prepared a hideaway, where he could flee to after the inevitable end had come, and Lord Lachglass was thrown in prison for a time, and all his associates arrested and hung.

They'd not hang Lachglass of course. Not a peer. Nor chop his head off, not for any crime lower than rebellion against the mad king and his fat son.

Would give the crowd ideas, it would, if aristocrats could go around being hung.

Blight spat on the ground after he saw the two women stuffed into the carriage. The crowd would hang him faster than Lachglass if they knew everything, and he could not blame them. He'd shout for himself to be hung, if he ever was asked.

He turned to the man who had guided them, and who stayed carefully out of the light in the shadows — to avoid being recognized, because even with the large syphilis sore sitting on his forehead, he was yet a handsome man.

Ha.

Blight wondered how long it would take the disease to ravage the man and kill him off. The pox tended to carry off a man slow and painful like. Drove them mad before it killed them too. Would drive them mad like Miss Bennet — she had been a pretty thing — had driven Lord Lachglass's brains out the back of his head.

"Here's the dirty ready." Blight placed into Mr. Wickham's hands the bag of guineas that was the agreed upon fee. Mr. Wickham had bargained hard for his help, but then the poor man was destitute these days, no longer as capable of charming those around him. Anyone who knew the signs would know exactly what was behind the makeup hiding the pox.

Didn't matter none to Blight in any case. Weren't his money, and Lachglass wasn't holding to his money, or his wits too close no more. Not after he'd been hit over the head. Blight was particularly glad Lachglass hadn't asked again after the boxing master he'd been ordered to kill.

Blight made an effort, he did. But the pugilist was constantly with friends or in open daylight for the three days Blight watched him.

Ha! He might like to kill a man twice as much as the next bloke. But Blight wasn't going to get pinched and hung for Lachglass's whim. Not old Blighty. That's what'd happen if he stabbed or shot the boxer in front of witnesses.

So Blight gave up, he had other things to do — the boxer knew Lachglass wanted to have him murdered, and wasn't likely to give him an opportunity for at least a month or two.

And, Lachglass, poor tupper, he'd forgotten plain about the screamed order to murder the man.

Upon receiving the ready, Mr. Wickham bounced the bag of coins up and down in his hand and he then counted them out, one by one.

Worthless half gent tosser.

Blight'd given serious thought to just killing Wickham after they were the done with him. He'd have liked to give him the poke or the blown open head. But the noise of a gun would be too much, and there was something about Wickham that said he knew how to handle a dagger himself. Half likely he had some friend with some letter to send right to the authorities.

That'd upset his Lord of Lachglass's notion of how to manage his revenge. And it'd put neatly paid to any hope Blight had to pretend he was simply a sad fellow being forced to go along with his Lordship. A simple sad fellow who definitely didn't deserve to hang.

Mr. Wickham bounced the clinking purse up and down in his hand one last time, and then put it in his coat. He said in a whisper, and a low gravelly voice that sounded nothing like he normally did, clearly in hopes his voice would not be recognized by their victims, "The amount. Off with you all, off. You don't want to be caught here."

There was something tense in how Mr. Wickham held himself.

"Hahaha, what, worried I'll stab ye in the back?"

Wickham did not reply, and his face could not be seen in the dark.

Blight laughed again, climbed into the carriage, and they set off.

*****

Mr. Wickham was left alone in the little secluded ravine. He laughed and pulled a coin out from the purse and waved it high in the air, smiling at the old friend in crime who he'd hidden in the hills above this blind. An excellent man with a gun that friend.

The friend bounced down from the hillside and, laughing, took off with the guinea that was his fee for the night, and Wickham collected his horse.

Damned business for a night. This was a terrible way for a gentleman to make his way in the world. But such was what Darcy had driven him to. It was all Mr. Darcy's fault, preventing him from gaining the proper position he deserved. Darcy had no one to blame but himself.

No one else.

Like as not Lord Lech was going to shoot the all of them. The entire point was to kill Elizabeth Bennet, he knew. Course, Wickham still liked the girl. She was a woman to be admired, crushing the nose of a gentleman.

Participating in this was a betrayal of himself in a happier, freer time. God, he sometimes hated himself.

Poor Mrs. Bennet — she had always been kind to him — and Miss Kitty.

He'd fucked Lydia Bennet many a time before they parted, and that should mean a *little* to a gent.

Jove, he had not been nice to leave her like that, but he'd been out of money, and the damned woman liked money. It was not his fault her father died, supposedly of a broken heart at the crime of his daughter. Wickham didn't believe that at all — not Mr. Bennet. He was a cold man, who didn't care anything for anyone. Wickham didn't have any guilt for *his* death.

But he did have guilt for tonight's crime.

Wickham patted the purse. He lit a lantern to light his way, and set off down the road towards Derby at a canter. He hadn't been back to Derbyshire for ten years now, and he wondered if Madame Berry's brothel was still there in Derby. Fine establishment.

Such women.

Oh, he had known such women in his life.

Like as not the madam wouldn't let him sleep with any of the girls. Or she'd force him to sleep with one her poxy whores. Some houses did that. He'd not be allowed to touch a clean girl. Not with the sores. Wasn't worth the patronage. He hated women like that. Wasn't his money good as the next gent's? Didn't he deserve a chance to tup a pretty girl, even though he had the pox?

Damned disease, he had only observed the first signs in the past year. His wickedness catching up with him.

But it wouldn't catch him. The mercury treatments helped a great deal, and he could afford more of them now with this bag of the ready he'd picked off Blighty's employer. Just for seeing Mrs. Bennet stuffed blindfolded and gagged into a carriage that was to drive her to a madman.

Wickham felt that chill, and it ached in his stomach, as though he'd made a mistake.

He'd heard what Lachglass had become.

And he had already done wrong to Mrs. Bennet once.

Fortunately for Mr. Wickham, he was not a man to dwell on those wrongs he committed, and he was quite pleased with himself by the time he reached Derby, where he was in fact forced to choose amongst girls the madam knew to already be suffering from the French, or Spanish, or Italian, *or* in some places on the continent, English complaint.

Chapter Eighteen

Three days later in Devon

"Lord! I am so scared. Please, please, please, sir. Just let us go. Let us go. Let us go. My son-in-law, Mr. Darcy — Mr. Darcy loves us dearly. He is rich. Heavens! Very rich. He'll pay any ransom for my daughter… and for me. Just let me and Kitty go."

Mrs. Bennet had not ceased speech from the moment the gag was taken off.

Mr. Blight comfortably ignored her. Perversely he liked the voice, mainly because he hoped that she would continue to chatter in such a way when she met Lord Lachglass.

Her captor was not disappointed by Mrs. Bennet's performance upon meeting her true captor.

When Lord Lachglass arrived to observe "the goods" acquired by his man of business, his headache precluded any possibility of *him* ignoring the chattering of Mrs. Bennet.

"You know my daughter did not mean to hurt you. She is the kindest woman in the world! All a mistake, a misunderstanding. And she married Mr. Darcy. Everyone respects Mr. Darcy — they say at Pemberley there is not a better landlord in the country. And I know that is true, why he's as good as a Lord. Like you… a Lord. Just please… You have scared me so! Lizzy will apologize to you. I'm sure she will… all a confusion. Just a simple confusion."

"By jove! The deuce! No more words!" Lachglass spoke in annoyed tones similar to how Mr. Bennet used to speak to her. Then he slapped the side of Mrs. Bennet's head so hard it jarred her bones.

That was entirely unlike how Mr. Bennet used to treat his wife. "You hear me? Shut your fucking lips, you ugly old hag."

"Please, sir, please. Please. Please. You must realize it is all a misunderstanding. Why are you hurting us? You are a gentleman, an earl, you must surely realize in such a position that…"

"Shut up!" Lachglass screeched.

As Mr. Blight watched grinning inside, Lord Lachglass grabbed the pistol he had on his belt.

"Lord! Lord save us! Not a gun. Not a gun — oh I am so nervous, on normal occasions. So very nervous. I never complain, of course, but I am—"

"Fuck, fuck. Fucking shut your mouth!"

Lachglass clenched his jaws. His face was red, and Mrs. Bennet was quite sure that he was not a healthy man.

She was finally silent.

With sudden jerky movements Lachglass brandished the gun at her angrily. "Told you! Shut your fucking mouth. Told you. But you wouldn't. You wouldn't shut it. Oh, no you wouldn't." He gestured towards Kitty whose hands were tied behind her against a chair. "Only need one of you. Your daughter will care more than enough for *her*, since she is pretty, while you should have been drowned like a cat the day you were no longer worth tupping. You worthless, worthless, useless, useless, fucking woman. And you are full of worms. And this is all *your* fault. Because *she* is your daughter."

The barrel of the gun danced wildly.

Suddenly, pointed right between Mrs. Bennet's eyes from just two feet away. "Only need one of you. Only need one."

Mrs. Bennet stared into her fate with big wide eyes.

He cocked the gun and pulled the trigger in a single fast motion.

Bang.

Frances Bennet honestly for a half dozen seconds believed that she was already dead.

But the screaming was not from her, it was from Lord Lachglass.

The expensive and fancy pistol had misfired and exploded in his hand, and he threw the remains of the piece aside, as he held his scorched hand and howled in pain.

He blubbered as he left the room, leaving Mrs. Bennet to what remained of her life, and he shouted for his servants to call a physician for him immediately, in between the howls of pain.

Mrs. Bennet looked at Kitty, and Kitty looked back at her.

Both of their eyes were very wide, and very scared. They both knew that they were still in grave danger.

Mrs. Bennet shivered violently in the chair, as she whispered praises to God for her, possibly temporary, salvation.

Neither of them knew if the mad earl would return to shoot her through the eyes properly as soon as a physician wrapped up and bandaged his hand.

Chapter Nineteen

It was one of those grey and rainy days in Paris.

Everyone along the crowded *Rue de Richelieu* held huge umbrellas out. Big black umbrellas, red umbrellas, multicolored umbrellas. The people hurried back and forth in front of Elizabeth's happy eyes, as she curled up in her armchair right next to the window. Her mind wandered from the view to her husband.

Her Darcy.

Elizabeth sighed ever so happily.

It looked like there was a little pure river, several inches deep, flooding the road below her. The thick drops lashed her mullioned window panes.

She saw him walk up the road, and glance up at her window from under his umbrella. She waved at him. He reached the door, and there was the click of it opening.

Darcy entered the room slightly damp despite his excellent umbrella from the walk back from the fencing club he had entertained himself at for the past hour. He whistled as he opened his arms for an embrace and a kiss.

Before their reunion — after a whole three hours today — went further than a deep kiss, there was a sharp knock on the front door to their apartments. A few minutes later the housekeeper brought in a wiry young man who wore a riding coat and had the lean appearance of an athlete.

He had a leather pouch and said in a clear English voice, "Express sent from England. From England! Express."

Elizabeth felt an anxiety as she stood next to Darcy. He reached to take the mail pouch from the young man.

"Apologies, sir." The messenger shook his head. "The instructions were quite precise. To only give into the hands of the lady who is the recipient. You—"

"Who sent it!"

"Well, was his lordship, Earl of Lachglass. You be Miss Elizabeth Bennet?"

"I was, I am Mrs. Darcy now." Elizabeth was surprised at how calm and steady her voice was.

Perhaps, some tiny part of her mind thought, he wrote to declare that he had realized the wrongness of his ways, and repentantly wished to assure Elizabeth she could return to England and have no further worry of being bothered by him.

The messenger drew out the still crisp letter from his oiled leather pouch that had protected it from the rain, and any other inclement conditions that may have been encountered on the journey from England. He handed the letter to Elizabeth and then looked between the two of them with a sort of expectant smile.

"Find a different employer than that man if you wish a tip from me," Darcy harshly said.

"Now, my dear, that comes perilously close to punishing the messenger." Elizabeth stared at the letter, and the deeply imprinted wax seal of the earl. She did not yet feel in sufficient command of herself to simply tear open the letter and look at what message was given to her by her enemy. "Give the poor boy what you would have if this letter had been sent by a man we are on some friendly terms with."

Darcy grunted with annoyance and fished a small silver coin from his purse.

He stepped closer to Elizabeth who had made no move to open the letter.

She recognized the stationery. It was the same paper she had used to have his daughter practice her letters with during her brief time in Lord Lachglass's employ.

Fine and thick paper. And really excellent wax that gleamed even in the rainy grey light from the windows. If she were of a different temperament, she might lever off the reddish purple wax, with the seal perfectly pressed into it, and store it in a collection of pieces of sealing wax she had received as one of the best in her collection.

The messenger was gone from the room, along with the housekeeper.

Darcy took the letter from her numb fingers, and he efficiently ripped it open, destroying the red wax and smearing a little bit into his fingernail.

He read the paper with at first a deepening scowl and then a completely blank emotionless face. No sign of what he felt was openly visible.

Elizabeth thought her Darcy might receive the promise of his own death from a physician with a similar expression. A proud and firm expression, but one that could not hide his worry or his feelings from Elizabeth, not from his Elizabeth who knew him so well.

"What news?"

Darcy put the letter down on the table. At first Elizabeth thought he was about to crumple the paper and toss it into the fire, but he thought better of that and instead just pushed the pages away.

"Your sister Kitty, and your mother. He has abducted and imprisoned them," Darcy said at last, after a pause that was dreadful to

Elizabeth's feelings. "He swears that he shall have them killed if you do not come to his estate in England. The letter has some other threats within it, but that is the essence of the matter."

Elizabeth grabbed for the letter.

"You do not wish to read what he wrote. Believe me, you do not." Darcy held the white fluttering pages away from her.

"What can we do? — do you think. Oh, God. What can we do?"

Darcy put the letter away in his waistcoat. He opened his mouth to respond, and for an instant Elizabeth felt a surge of hope that her Darcy would have some notion of what to do that would immediately rescue her mother and sister.

But he then closed his mouth.

Elizabeth shivered, like she had when she sat in his drawing room, awaiting Darcy's return after walking six miles on a swollen foot in a freezing London without a coat or proper shoes.

"At the first we shall contact a judge in his county to send constables to his estate," Darcy said at last, pacing next to the rainy window. "This is not a sort of matter which he can expect to escape punishment from. This letter alone is proof that he is the one to cause the disappearance. He has been deeply incautious. When the magistrates descend on his house—"

"He will simply do what he swears, and kill my sister and my mother."

"Elizabeth…" Darcy walked up to put his arms around her.

His touch was not enough to comfort her. She felt her skin crawling, and part of her wanted to shout at Darcy to leave her be.

Her mother. Her little sister.

Elizabeth panted horribly. She felt like a bare-knuckled punch had been delivered to her sternum, and the air would no longer come in.

"Breathe, Lizzy." Darcy gripped her tightly, holding her body comfortingly against his solid mass. "Deep breaths. One breath in. Breathe out. One breath in. And then breathe out. Breathe, Lizzy."

She followed his orders, and breathed in long shuddering breaths.

He kissed her hair. "We'll rescue them. We'll find a way."

Her mother. Her sister.

Kitty had grown to look very like Elizabeth. Would Lord Lechery slake his lusts on her now that he could not touch Elizabeth? What did he plan to do with Elizabeth when she came to his estate — for she knew she must, even if he killed her.

She was shivering, feeling scared and unsafe, despite Darcy's hold.

She saw her mother, her nervous anxious mother, who despite everything she loved. She imagined her mother caught in this terrifying situation, trying to complain of matters to her captors like she would to all her friends, and them screaming at her to shut up.

"I must go, as he ordered."

"He means to kill you, or worse."

"There is nothing worse than him killing me." Elizabeth pulled out of Darcy's hold and walked to the window. She hunched her shoulders.

The sky was still grey, rainy, and ugly.

Darcy walked up to her, but while he had a firmness in his face, she could tell from his manner that his mind was endlessly spinning, and not coming to any conclusion.

She gulped air repetitively, and she pressed her elbows against her sides, as though that pressure was the only thing which kept her from dissolving into a million pieces.

Then Darcy's distraction faded away. He stood taller, with something that was almost a smile.

Yes, she saw him mouth to himself.

Darcy said, "Do you trust me? You have claimed me as your champion. Your dragon slayer."

"He will kill my family. I must go. I see no other way. I must go."

"Perhaps, we must go." Darcy put his arms around her once more, and he held her tightly against him. "But he shall not be permitted to win. Yes, we must go, and I fear that you will be the bait to draw the vile dragon out of hiding, so that he may be trapped and his hoard seized. But we can slay this dragon."

"Do you mean that?"

"I mean it. I have a scheme in mind. We'll win through this and turn the tables on him."

Chapter Twenty

A week later

"Jove I wish I could go with you," General Fitzwilliam loudly proclaimed, as they all stood in the midst of the town in Cambrai where his regiment was accommodated. "Would be a nice chance to see the old boy again. Have a friendly-like talk with my cousin. Alas, the Duke would not give me leave for such a family manner, not after I only so recently returned."

"I understand," Darcy replied with a quiet voice. "I wish you would be with us as well."

He embraced his cousin, and then he entered his carriage into which he had already handed Elizabeth.

They would immediately travel to Calais, where a boat waited to take them to Brighton. The regiment of a friend of General Fitzwilliam's from the Peninsula was quartered there, and they planned to gather a substantial escort of soldiers which they could take to the Kentish estate of Lord Lachglass.

Lord Lachglass had demanded Elizabeth come to meet him, and meet him she would. But she would not meet him alone.

*****

A week later yawing and creaking their ship sailed into the harbor at Brighton, pulling against the pier on a calm early summer day. "Are you well, my dear?" Darcy whispered to Elizabeth.

She shook her head no. Elizabeth still felt queasy as the gangplank was extended out to the pier.

Her stomach had become no stiffer since the she had left England on General Fitzwilliam's ship to Calais. She had eaten nothing since leaving Calais the previous evening, and the billowing sea breeze felt cold against her sweaty face.

Darcy stood next to Elizabeth with his arms around her as they waited to disembark.

"I shall not make this journey often," she groaned. "Hardly worth the illness to see what is on the other side of the ocean."

He squeezed her closer against his side and kissed the top of her bonnet. Elizabeth sagged against Darcy and closed her eyes until he tugged her to walk towards the gangplank when everything was ready.

When they reached the end of the pier, twelve soldiers waited for them in fine redcoats, with their muskets loaded and pointed upwards.

They had delayed for two days in Calais before sailing to Brighton, so that arrangements for the arrival could be made via letters sent express before they arrived.

The letter General Fitzwilliam had sent to his friend in Brighton had arrived by then, and the soldiers were here to meet them to ensure that no ruffians hired by Lord Lachglass could attack them the instant they stepped onto British soil.

There was still the threat of the Bow Street Runners, but after discussion with a lawyer Darcy had called from London to Calais, they had determined that at this time that while it would be a very frightening event if Elizabeth was put up for trial, there was no longer any practical chance she would be found against.

Elizabeth had nightmares each night since they had received the letter.

Nightmares of Kitty shot, blood gushing from her skull. Of Mama, crying in her natural complaining way, "If only you had been quiet and let him have his way with you, it would have quickly been over, and I would still be alive."

Now Elizabeth felt for the first time something like guilt.

She had been a little annoyed at first with General Fitzwilliam, wanting to blame him for the essay she had written to destroy Lachglass's reputation. The timing of the abduction of her family suggested that his dismissal from the cabinet — Elizabeth and Darcy had cheered and toasted with fizzing champagne when they heard of it — had triggered his choice to seek revenge in this new way by abducting her mother and her sister.

Elizabeth swallowed.

Much as she hoped everything would turn out well, and that Darcy's scheme would succeed perfectly and in the end they would all be alive, she was not in any sense entirely persuaded it would.

An odd beggar in a giant shaggy coat stood near the soldiers who waited for them on the dock. He had a huge bulbous nose, and a giant scar across his neck that he pointed to whenever anyone stepped near. He then extended his hand out pathetically asking for money without being able to speak.

Elizabeth smiled at the beggar.

Another person caught her eye. She stood beside the captain who commanded the platoon of soldiers sent out to meet them. A young woman Elizabeth had not seen for four years.

Her sister Lydia.

Elizabeth tottered down, her stomach forgotten, to stare at Lydia, who in turn stared at her with a half smile, and a half worried expression.

They stood across from each other, and Elizabeth hardly knew what to say. She had been angry at Lydia for long after she had disappeared with Mr. Wickham. Though Elizabeth knew that there was no actual connection in cause, a little part of her had always thought it was somehow Lydia's fault when Papa became sick and died less than a year after she disappeared.

At the same time... at the same time.

Suddenly tears started in Elizabeth's eyes. She and Lydia embraced each other fiercely. "My dear sister," Elizabeth cried.

Lydia at the same moment exclaimed, "Lord! You look quite the same as ever."

Elizabeth could not help but feel happy. Lydia was her sister, and she could see that she was well and happy.

While the soldiers grinned at them, Lydia turned to the officer leading the men. "Lizzy, this is Captain Dilman, my handsome husband."

He bowed to her. "My pleasure to meet you, Mrs. Darcy."

"And you as well." He was a handsome man, but not at all well dressed in the way Mr. Wickham had been.

There were spots of patching on the elbows of his uniform, cleverly sown to be almost invisible, and in spots the fabric was worn rather thin. He also was missing half his ear and had a light scar on the cheek on the same side. When he noticed Elizabeth looking at the injury, he laughed and tugged at the remainder of his ear. "At Waterloo. Wrecked my handsome looks, but at least my Lydia still loves me." He embraced his wife from the side and smiled at her.

Lydia looked at Mr. Darcy and exclaimed with a laugh, "La, what a joke that you two married! I remember how you disliked each other so."

"I never disliked Elizabeth," Darcy replied.

Lydia laughed. "No, you did! Everyone in the whole neighborhood knew you'd said, on first sight, she wasn't handsome enough to tempt you."

Elizabeth flushed. "Enough Lydia."

Lydia laughed. "Such a joke! That you then married. But I was so happy to hear from Mama how you gave her and Kitty a house and some income to live upon."

"And then I sent Lord Lachglass after them," Elizabeth said.

Lydia rolled your eyes. "To blame yourself 'tis very much like blaming King Louie in France for the ogre coming back and shooting at my dear Dilman at Waterloo! You did not want it to happen."

Darcy frowned as well. "My people failed to protect them — we should have known Lachglass might do something of this sort, and—"

"Do not blame yourselves!" Lydia exclaimed. "Johnny," she turned to her husband. "Do tell them they are quite silly."

"The colonel has said I'm to lead the force that goes with you to retrieve Mrs. Bennet and Miss Kitty. Your mother is a... well intentioned woman."

Lydia elbowed him.

"She does not deserve to be used as a hostage," Captain Dilman said. "Insane man. An insane man to do such a thing. As my Lydia said, you have no fault for failing to predict the actions of a mad creature."

Darcy frowned. "If I'd only had a few men to stay in the house with them and installed better locks, and—"

"It was Mr. Wickham anyway," Lydia said with a frown. "I am most put out with him."

"Wickham!" Elizabeth exclaimed. "What does *he* have to do with the matter?"

"He sent me a letter. The sad man was drunk as a wheelbarrow in some brothel — poor man. Wrote he felt quite guilty, and that he'd already gambled half the money away. Mr. Blight gave him some twenty guineas to lead him to the cottage."

Darcy growled. "I ought to have killed Mr. Wickham when I could."

"Poor man, I heard from Denny that he has the pox now," Lydia said. "The old regiment was here in Brighton, a year ago, those who hadn't been discharged after the war. Glad he did not give it to me."

The group walked, escorted by the soldiers, to the house that Colonel Pike, General Fitzwilliam's friend and Captain Dilman's commanding officer, had rented on the outskirts of the seaport town.

"What is it like," Elizabeth asked Lydia as they walked, "to be back in Brighton?"

"Oh quite the same — pretty as ever. And exciting enough, though it is emptier than during the war. I was so gay, so young, and quite naïve then." She laughed. "I was sure as rain, no sure as cloudy days, that Mr. Wickham planned to marry me. Took at least a month and a half before I realized that was not his notion at all. Quite annoyed with him then, but I had nothing better in sight. I came back here immediately after he left me in the lodging house. He'd had enough of me, and left me in our rooms without warning, and with a note to Mrs. Younge that I would settle the accounts."

Lydia laughed, though Elizabeth saw nothing at all funny with the story.

"Mrs. Younge?" Darcy asked looking sharply at her. "About your height, brown hair and with a pretense of gentility and education. A friend of Wickham's?"

"Ah, *you* knew her too? She wasn't a kind one. Would sell her own daughter for a profit, but the constables laughed when she tried to have me thrown in the debtors' prison for the money Wickham owed her. They said it would be absurd and wrong to charge an abandoned woman in such a case, and that if she could not show any papers I had *signed* saying I would pay, they would not bother me at all. And they did not. So she just tossed me out, into the winter."

Elizabeth gasped, remembering her own cold time. "Why did you not come back? Papa was still alive that winter."

"I have a notion that was her idea when she tried to have me arrested for the debt — she knew my family was quality, and she had the notion I would send to Papa to pay my debts to leave prison if that happened. Likely thought I might be better off if I did that, which perhaps I might have been — but I was with child then, and I do not think Papa would have been happy to see me."

"He abandoned you with child!" Darcy exclaimed, clearly disgusted.

Lydia shrugged as though to say that such a man was George Wickham.

Elizabeth studied her sister's nonchalant expression. "Papa would not have thrown you entirely off, if you came to him repentant."

"Repentant." Lydia rolled her eyes. "I was certainly not *repentant*. Made my choices, and though I was a naïve fool, I'll not apologize for being lied to, and I'll not apologize for being imprudent — I wish I'd not been such a fool, but it is no sin to trust the wrong sort."

"Perhaps not…" Elizabeth said. "I made a mistake in who I trusted to employ me."

"I'll certainly make no apology for trying to have a jolly time," Lydia added. "Life is too short to worry about a little scandal."

"I do not agree with *that*," Darcy said dryly. "For it was a great scandal."

Lydia laughed. "You *do* suit Lizzy — seeing you two together. I worried for you, Lizzy, ever since I heard 'bout your marriage. La, I could barely remember you, Mr. Darcy, but never thought you were the sort of man Lizzy could like."

Darcy smiled and took Elizabeth's hand and kissed it smiling widely. "I am."

"I read that story you wrote, Lizzy — about how you fought off that horrid earl. Read it five times, aloud too, did I not?"

"She did," Captain Dilman confirmed.

"I know how terrible it can be to walk whilst it is freezing. I did not even think of going back to Papa — I had a notion I'd return to Harriet and Colonel Forster in Brighton. So when Mrs. Younge turned me out, just the clothes on my back, I walked straight here, in the middle of winter. I had good shoes and a good coat, but it was not a pleasant walk."

"More than fifty miles!" Elizabeth exclaimed. She looked rather shocked at Lydia. The warm wind blew over them, but she still shivered. "You did not."

"A farmer gave me a ride for some five miles of the way, and I found friends to sleep with all but one night. 'Tis easy to find friends when you are friendly yourself. There is many a poor person out there who if asked kindly, not standing upon your dignity, would give their last penny to feed a child."

Elizabeth tilted her head disbelievingly.

That was *not* her sense of how the world worked. She wondered, but was unwilling to ask the question, if these friends who Lydia said had helped her may have been men who received a friendly recompense.

It would be unkind to ask in any case. And whatever her past, Lydia *now* was married, and married to an officer of the British army.

"And then we met." Captain Dilman embraced Lydia. "I saw her when she came back to Brighton — I was still an ensign then, for two more months — and she was the prettiest girl I ever saw, wandering round, like a bedraggled cat who'd slept in her fur."

Lydia kissed her husband full on the mouth, in front of his soldiers. "He took me in, and ensured I was kept well — I never approached Harriet, or anyone from the regiment at that time. I was too shamed to. But I was also quite happy here. And then we decided to marry. And after that I miscarried Wickham's child, which I suppose was God's will — ah, but here we are, at the camp of the regiment."

There were lines of barracks housing for the soldiers, built around what had once been a farmhouse; it was all relatively empty, as this place had been constructed to hold a far larger force before the dismissal of soldiers followed close on the end of the war.

The colonel's house was a decent sized timber framed building, white and brown, with two floors, the second overhanging the first all around, and producing a nice covered porch the commanding officer of the regiment sat on while he watched his men parade in the drill grounds.

Colonel Pike was a short man with balding hair and a deep limp that made him almost drag his foot as he supported himself heavily with a cane.

Lydia's husband saluted the colonel while the men who had escorted them stood at attention, the buttons on their coats gleaming, and the white belts of their uniforms making a clear X.

Elizabeth had always rather wondered if that was the best design for an uniform, as it looked like an excellent target for the enemy to fire upon. However when she mentioned this while in Calais, General

Fitzwilliam's brother Fitz William laughed and said that musketry was so inaccurate in the general, that a man would be *safer* if aimed directly at.

Colonel Pike shook hands firmly with Darcy. "My old friend Fitzwilliam's cousin, eh? A fine man. Fine man. His regiment was in the square in front of ours at Waterloo. They took the beating of Marshal Ney's horsed horde far worse than we did, and they stood firm and would not break. It was inspiring to watch, in betwixt that cannon fire that sought to blow our heads off."

"Did you gain your wound at Waterloo?" Elizabeth asked after she had been introduced to him.

Colonel Pike blinked at her twice, and then laughed. "My leg? No, not at all — not even a battle wound. Fell off a horse wrong, some ten years ago, and the leg never healed right. Doesn't bother me much, except when the weather is bad — come, come — too nice a day to sit inside. Sit down here, Mrs. Darcy, Mr. Darcy, Mrs. Dilman, sit down."

All of Elizabeth's anxiety suddenly returned. What would happen tomorrow?

They sent a messenger to ride to Lord Lachglass's estate, some fifteen miles to the northeast, to tell that miserable excuse for a peer of the realm that Elizabeth would meet him tomorrow to talk about the return of her mother and sister, but not in his own house.

The conversation between Mr. Darcy and Colonel Pike ran round and round, and Elizabeth could focus on none of it. Her stomach ached and twisted. Tomorrow it would all be decided.

Darcy took her hand and squeezed it, and Lydia took her other hand.

Elizabeth could see from a tightness in Lydia's eyes that she worried too.

After fifteen minutes, Lydia stood up and pulled Elizabeth to her feet. "No sense waiting here, you must meet your niece! Come on, Lizzy, come on."

So they went over to a collection of houses where the married officers of the regiment had taken their rooms, and Lydia called out to a woman who watched her daughter, Lydia's and several other children toddle around the fields. They came over, with the woman holding the young girl, who looked to be two or three, in her arms.

She handed the darling little girl to Lydia, and the toddler babbled happily to her mother in that incomprehensible speech of very young children. Lydia smiled, laughed and listened. She knelt and put her child on the ground, holding her by the hands so she could stay upright. "Fanny, say hello to your Auntie Lizzie."

Lydia waved the girls hand for her.

Elizabeth's face softened as she introduced herself. "Hello, how do you do?"

Little Miss Dilman hid her face in the skirts of her mother.

Elizabeth laughed. "What a sweet girl, is she shy?"

"Nothing like me." Lydia insisted, "I'd introduce myself to any stranger, no matter how frightening they look — I'd introduce myself to you, Mr. Darcy, just for a lark, if I was challenged to."

"I believe you," Darcy smiled down at the girl who was now also his niece. "Such a pretty looking girl."

Fanny toddled towards Darcy at this, apparently less frightened of him, for some reason, than of Elizabeth. So Darcy picked the little girl into his arms, holding her far more lightly and easily, and he poked her nose and cheeks and made faces at her until she smiled and laughed.

It filled Elizabeth with something tender in her heart.

She desperately hoped she would, and soon, be able to present Mr. Darcy with his own child, with their child.

They walked back, with Darcy still carrying Lydia's child, to the house of Colonel Pike. Lydia explained that her and Captain Dilman lived quite modestly — they only had one room, in a house they shared with several other officers. The couple was putting aside the money so that once he had been in grade long enough, Captain Dilman would be able, with borrowing from some friends also, to purchase a major's commission.

Elizabeth felt odd to hear this, now that she was rich once more, and now very rich, instead of merely rich.

Elizabeth had wondered often after Papa died, and they had become poor, just how they had managed to happily spend so *much* while he lived. But now that she was rich once more, the past months in Paris had given her a sense of how that could happen.

It was easy to stop caring about the prices of matters, and so long as Mr. Darcy assured her that they were setting aside ample money for the dowries of any daughters she might have, and to purchase the commissions, law partnerships or livings of any sons after the first she might have, she could without any anxiety or second thought simply buy any book, or hat, or painting that caught her eye while making her morning visit to the Palais Royal to look at the crowd and take coffee.

When they returned to the colonel's house, Elizabeth noted how the stooped beggar with huge nose and scar across his neck sat in one of the alleyways between barracks buildings, extending his hand out desultorily, as if bored now by the action, any time one of the soldiers passed him by.

While they waited Elizabeth played with little Fanny, who eventually overcame her shyness of Auntie Lizzy. Darcy played with her too, and Elizabeth's heart swelled every time he made the child smile.

He would be such a good father.

"So what do you think of my husband?" Lydia said after they had been waiting nearly two hours for a return of the message sent to Lord Lachglass. Her voice was slightly angry. "A fine man is he not?"

"He seems so to me," Darcy said.

Lydia stared at him, judging, and then she nodded. "And you, Lizzy?"

"I like him. And he likes you, and you are happy, that is what is important... He is... more than I expected for you."

Lydia laughed. "I am fortunate, he was always the kindest — he married me when I was still full of Wickham's child, because he had come to love me, and he did not want my child to be born into the world illegitimate. Do you understand? That is the sort of man he is. That is my husband — then *Mama*." Lydia growled. "I nearly clawed her eyes out that day. When she came to visit us when we were in Newcastle, after Fanny was born. She saw how we lived, still then just one room, but even smaller. And we could barely afford that one room — there are so many costs for the mess that every officer is obligated to pay. I do not think it is at all fair to the poorer sort of officers; one of those ways that the quality sort try to make the lives of others unpleasant. Expecting everyone, whether they have family wealth or not, to contribute the same to the mess. It is like what Lord Lachglass has done."

"Not too like," Elizabeth replied.

"I nearly clawed Mama's eyes out when she said I should have married someone who had some connections and consequence, and who could help her. Or she even suggested, she even suggested—" Lydia growled. "She suggested I ought to have sold myself as the mistress of some rich man — I would never, never, ever do such an intimate thing. The conjugal embrace with a man who I did not like, and like for himself — do not look at me that way. I am no hypocrite, I think women should be as free before they marry as men are, and I do not condemn myself for the fun I had with Mr. Wickham, or others, or with my dear Johnny before the church sanctified us. Not at all. It is imprudent for women because children are a chance, and I fancy that is the real reason the church claims it wrong and evil. Trying to scare girls with hellfire from doing things that feel very good, but are imprudent. The purpose is to make life easier for the parents who pay the tithes to the vicar, not to help women avoid sin. It is my firm opinion that girls just want to enjoy themselves."

"Certainly not every girl," Elizabeth replied.

Lydia laughed. "Not Mary."

Elizabeth laughed too. "Mary is happy in her way — she sends me and Darcy a great many letters upon all the books and lectures she has explored since we gave her the money to attend them freely in London. I believe she wants me to know that she uses her time well."

"If *that* is her notion of using the time *well* — but as Mary is happy, I'll not think ill of her for it, though her notion of enjoyment and mine are decidedly different."

The messenger sent to Lord Lachglass returned on a sweating horse. A groom took the horse and led it to water as the messenger handed the letter to Mr. Darcy.

Darcy read the letter several times, and then a thin smile crossed his face. "He has agreed to meet us on his lands, out of sight of his house, in the middle of the game forest."

"Ah." Elizabeth said, "As we expected."

"He demands that you enter his power completely though, or else he will not release your mother or sister — he thinks tomorrow shall be a transfer of prisoners."

Elizabeth's stomach was flipping with fear. But she took in a deep breath. She had faced Lord Lachglass, and she had faced Mr. Blight once before. Tomorrow she would face them again.

Darcy gripped her hand fearfully, and though his face was stiff, she could see he was frightened too.

They did not say anything; there was nothing further for them to plan. Tomorrow would come, and what fate declared would happen, would happen.

Her heart beat heavy.

After some time Darcy stood to take a turn around the streets, and Elizabeth pulled her feet up onto the wicker chair she sat on and wrapped her arms around her legs. As Darcy walked down the street, the beggar with the bulbous nose came out to him, stooped, and he extended his hand out pitiably, pointing to his throat helplessly.

Darcy handed him something and then walked on.

The beggar looked at what Darcy had given him, and the dying light of the sun caught a glow of something that was not happiness on his face. He then shuffled away, staying stooped the entire way, and disappeared from Elizabeth's sight.

That night, in bed, the two of them clung tightly and passionately to each other. There was an intensity to how they came together that Elizabeth had never felt before, for she feared the morrow.

They made the time run with love, though they could not make it stop.

And it was only when the night was darkest, during the hour before dawn, that they fell fitfully to sleep in each other's arms.

Chapter Twenty-One

Lachglass was less than he had once been.

That was Darcy's first thought as their party came, rifles out and ready, to the location they had been ordered to meet Lachglass.

It was a clearing deep in Lachglass's own estate, where they were led by one of his gamekeepers, a nervous young man who kept insisting to them that he just did what he was told, and he had nothing to do with the master or Mr. Blight.

Lachglass could easily have picked men from amongst his gamekeepers hidden in the thick spring foliage, waiting to shoot. Of course, the men here were nervous soldiers who were very ready to shoot back. But they were exposed, and the trees and leaves behind and around him made Darcy's neck ache.

This was the perfect sort of land for an ambush.

Darcy had hunted enough to recognize three good spots around where hunting blinds were probably placed.

Darcy's heart pounded in fear with every step deeper into the estate. None of that showed on his face. He held Elizabeth's arm and almost gaily walked along, helping her over the occasional thick trunk fallen across the path. It was for Elizabeth that he was principally frightened, but as Darcy smiled and pointed out to Elizabeth a bird's nest nestled in the branches of a tree they walked past, he knew that he was frightened for himself as well.

So easy to turn from this quintessence of dust into dust.

At last they reached the clearing, heavy with the thick scent of grasses, damp earth and leaves. Lord Lachglass stood in the clearing with a half dozen pale and frightened looking men, badly outnumbered by the platoon of soldiers they had borrowed from Colonel Pike's regiment.

Mr. Blight stood next to Lachglass, his face pale, and his lips thinned as he saw the group of soldiers arrive. But he did not look particularly scared.

Lord Lachglass held the wavering tip of his gun on Mrs. Bennet. He held it in his left hand, as his right hand had been wrapped up with a huge bandage, and he held the pistol protectively against his side.

His other men looked between each other, and backed away from Lachglass with their hands held up as they saw the soldiers enter the clearing.

The rake's nose was twisted and flat. His hair seemed to have thinned. But that was not where the chief change was. There had always been a vicious brutal energy to Lachglass, but if you watched his

---

movements it was as if everything animal and vital in his soul had been replaced by something hollow that could disappear at the first moment.

That scared Darcy almost as much as the way Lachglass showed no concern at seeing the group of soldiers who had come with Darcy and Elizabeth.

This was not the face of a man who cared overmuch if he survived. Darcy tightened his grip on Elizabeth's arm.

"What... what do all these men do here? You, captain, you trespass upon my land." Lachglass waved dismissively at Captain Dilman, as if he expected the man to actually turn around. "I give no permission for your presence, I am an earl, and you are to leave."

He gestured his pistol at the soldiers, without ever actually pointing the weapon directly at any of them, before turning his weapon once more on Mrs. Bennet.

"You stand accused," Captain Dilman said in a ringing voice, "of kidnapping and other crimes. I am here to bring you to arrest, and to see you stand trial."

Lachglass sneered and shuffled around Mrs. Bennet, so that he now held his gun against the back of the trembling woman's head. "You have a warrant, I take it."

"A warrant signed by his honor, Mr. Crews, a magistrate in Brighton."

"No jurisdiction." Lachglass dismissively waved his wrapped up right hand. "Get away, and when *I* sign a warrant of arrest against myself you may come here."

"Nevertheless, you shall release your guests, or you shall be thrown in prison today."

Lachglass laughed, a high-pitched keening sound. The way his finger seemed to play in the trigger of the gun terrified Darcy. Was he about to see Mrs. Bennet's head splattered across the lawn due to an accidental misfire?

"This is all too tiresome. You know I cannot be prosecuted. As a peer of England I have a right for the first accusation of any crime, save murder, to be dismissed. Even were it true that I had abducted this woman," he kicked Mrs. Bennet hard in the back of her leg, and she moaned piteously, "I would not be punished for the crime due to my position and rank. Save us both the annoyance and get yourself away — But *you*."

Lachglass saw Miss Bennet, and he snarled.

His nostrils flared with hatred, his eyes went narrow, the cords in neck throbbed. He spat at her, the spittle landing in Mrs. Bennet's lap.

"At last," he laughed with mad gayness. "At last here to face *justice*. You are come at my invitation to SUFFER." He jerked his injured hand to the side, and his voice dropped, barely audible across the grassy clearing. "Oh, my little governess. How I will make you suffer."

Captain Dilman shouted, "Release these two women and surrender yourself, or I'll shoot you myself."

"Now, now, all of you point your guns away from me," Lachglass hissed, poking the barrel of his pistol into the back of the whimpering Mrs. Bennet's head for emphasis. "This weapon has a hair trigger. It has nearly gone off twice in the last minute already. Shoot me, and in my final jerk, I'm sure to pull it and splatter her brains with me."

Darcy exclaimed, "Be reasonable, Lachglass. You don't want to die."

"So tiresome. Life is become tiresome." He sighed, looking Byronic with his puffy pale face filled with ennui. "I care not very much. I am ugly now you see." He gestured with the bandaged hand at his nose, not moving the pistol in his other hand from Mrs. Bennet's head. "Your wife made me ugly."

Neither Darcy nor Elizabeth had anything to say to that.

"Haha!" the earl crowed victoriously. "Come to me, Elizabeth. Come closer. It will be one or the other. Your mother's life or yours. Will you be such a coward as to stand and watch me blow a hole in your mother's head? Will you? Will you!"

"Don't! Don't! Don't!" For the first time since they arrived Mrs. Bennet said something. "Me! Shoot me! Not her! Not my daughter! Let him shoot me!"

Elizabeth started walking towards the laughing Lachglass. Darcy grabbed her arm, but Elizabeth with a surprising strength wrenched herself away from his grasp. She spoke in a frighteningly calm voice. "We must get him to point anywhere but Mama."

"No… this is too dangerous."

Elizabeth walked slowly forward. Her eyes focused on the pistol that was stuck towards her mother's head. "Here I am," she shouted when she was thirty feet away from him.

How did Elizabeth sound so calm?

"Haha! Come closer! Closer so I can see your eyes as you die."

So saying, Lachglass pulled the gun from Mrs. Bennet's head, lowering his arms again to aim at Elizabeth.

A crack of a single rifle shot rang across the field, firing as Lachglass began to move.

The earl's head exploded into a blood blotch, with the entry wound right above his nose and dead center between his eyes.

His gun went off in his dying convulsion, as he'd promised, and it fired uselessly into the air above Elizabeth and Mrs. Bennet.

Kitty had been sitting behind him at such an angle that she was splattered with brains and blood. She began screaming.

Elizabeth ran up to her sister, ignoring Mr. Blight and the other men who worked for the deceased Lachglass. She held Kitty tight, and whispered some sort of consolation to her, and then after an instant she went to Mrs. Bennet and grabbed her, beginning to pull at the ropes binding her to the chair.

All of the earl's men, except Mr. Blight, threw their weapons to the side. But Mr. Blight began to aim his pistol at Elizabeth as he snarled angrily.

Three soldiers shot him dead as he moved, splattering his body with bloody holes.

Darcy ran up to Elizabeth, and he helped her with a hunting knife to saw the restraints off Mrs. Bennet and Kitty. The women embraced each other fiercely, and then Elizabeth turned and threw her arms around Darcy, squeezing him as tightly.

Oh, God. Oh, God. Oh, kind Jesu. They all were safe. It all was over. Oh, God.

She was so warm, and she smelled fragrant, and they squeezed each other till he could feel her bones.

The soldiers came up; they tied ropes around the hands of Lachglass's retainers, to take them before the courts for acting as accomplices to Lord Lachglass in his crimes. Captain Dilman stepped up to the corpse of the earl and poked him with his foot.

Dead. Very dead. The man was very, very dead.

Chapter Twenty-Two

One Week Before in Cambrai

General Fitzwilliam fitted the big broken plaster nose over his real nose, and he allowed his valet to work some actor's plaster into his skin, substantially darkening the color and giving him an ugly scar along his neck.

He watched carefully what the man did, as he would need to replicate it while in England. When he had planned this scheme with Darcy, they decided it would be best if he never spoke while in England, since his voice was recognizable.

General Fitzwilliam was sure he could *look* the part of another, he did not believe he could reliably disguise his voice in such a way that would fool anyone who knew him, and he would have many acquaintants in the army camp in Brighton.

"You will be well, Fitz?" he asked his brother as he quickly made his preparations to disappear.

"On the contrary," his brother replied, "I expect I shall be exceedingly unwell for the entire time."

General Fitzwilliam barked out a laugh.

The regimental surgeon sat across from his patient who bounced up and down on General Fitzwilliam's small bed. He said, "I'll take enough blood from him to *ensure* that he won't be well."

Fitz winced and flinched away from the surgeon. "I just need to look a little pale."

"It will be good for you. I am sure that there is *some* underlying illness you know nothing about which will be improved by the bloodletting. Everyone has *some* underlying illness, the only question is if they know about it or not."

"I'm going to expect a particularly good bottle of Scotch, Richard. For letting you set this lunatic at me." He laughed. "Never made a lick of sense to me how bloodletting could do any good. We generally want to *avoid* bleeding in the army. If I ever was in a serious bad way, I'd not let the doctor cut me. Suspect it is just their trick to keep the patient so ill that they need a regular visit."

"None of that suspicious nonsense." General Fitzwilliam turned away from the mirror, and he hunched so that there was a prominent looking hump in his back. "How do I look?"

"Nothing like the general, that is for damned sure," the surgeon said.

Fitz whistled. "Very, very fine disguise. I'd pass you on the street without knowing you."

"Well then, I'll be off for our rendezvous in Brighton. I have a message of my own for my cousin, but do you want me to give him any personal regards?"

Fitz laughed. "Damned glad again, *I* need not claim any relation to that man. I'd ask you to wish him a jolly Happy Christmas, and a fine New Year as well, but after *your* personal regards have been received, he'll hardly be in a proper state to appreciate those from anyone else. The pity."

General Fitzwilliam laughed and started whistling. "It will be such a fine day. I think some part of me has wanted to do this since I was seventeen and I saw him beat his poor horse to death because he fell off. It will be a good day — make sure you look as ill as possible, and groan, and do not let anyone who is not in the conspiracy examine your face closely, and—"

"Don't be a mother hen." Fitz grinned. "Ten days or so of nothing to do but lie in bed and pretend to be sick, and maybe read a novel." He worriedly glanced at the surgeon. "I will be well enough that I can read?"

The surgeon said in a serious voice, "I fear General Fitzwilliam even lacks the strength to keep the pages of a book raised. He certainly can sign no papers until the period of crisis is past."

"Deuce. Should have known this was a crap assignment. Well, General Fitzwilliam will order *you* to read to me."

"I have many duties," the surgeon replied with an almost malicious smirk. Of course it was General Fitzwilliam's opinion that all the best surgeons had a malicious streak. It was necessary to do the hacking parts of their job right.

"Don't ya worry. Don't ya worry," General Fitzwilliam's valet, Jacob said. "Much as I hate to let the old general—"

"I'm only thirty and five."

"—go off all alone into danger, I'll keep ya company. I'll even read to ya. Even one of those novels, and not the bible, though the bible would be good for ya soul."

"Especially," the surgeon inserted, "when you are so ill as to be quite on the verge of death, and with a contagious illness, so no one will be brave enough to bother General Fitzwilliam as he engages in deathly struggle with it. Major Williams, I'd recommend asking for him to read from the Bible to you."

"All in hand I see." General Fitzwilliam began whistling again, and he left the room. Ten minutes later he was on a horse to Calais, accompanied by an old veteran soldier who could be trusted in anything. From there he hopped on a packet boat owned by the Rothchilds whose captain owed him a favor.

*****

Two tied, blindfolded, and gagged gamekeepers in the employ of Lord Lachglass sat against the far rocky wall of the finely constructed hunting blind overlooking the field where Darcy and Elizabeth had come to parley. They both had large purpling bruises on their foreheads.

The location had been chosen by Lord Lachglass so he could put a pair of his most trusted men in this well-hidden hunting blind and have them shoot Elizabeth and Darcy if anything went wrong.

Both of the gamekeepers had that morning, long before General Fitzwilliam beat both of them over the head with a short truncheon, agreed they would do no such thing, and if the pair ran away, they would shoot *over* their heads, and then claim to their employer that they had both missed.

That was before they had seen the soldiers.

The pair in fact would not have dared to shoot at all, if they had had the opportunity.

The Scottish soldier who had months earlier pretended to the Bow Street Runners to be illiterate as Elizabeth escaped England, stood next to the general, keeping an eye on Fitzwilliam's back as he'd taken the shot. "Ye made a fine shot. Fine, fine shot I tell ye."

"I did." General Fitzwilliam wiped his handkerchief over his forehead. "Deuced closer than I wanted. But clever of Mrs. Darcy to get him to shift his aim point. But damn. A hell of a close matter. My cousin is a lucky man. She would have been a fine soldier if a man."

"A brave woman. That she is."

"That she is."

"A fine shot, sir," Fergus repeated as he quickly disassembled the rifle and without properly cleaning it packed the pieces away into long loaves of bread they'd carefully carved to let them fit the disassembled weapon in this morning. It was a trick they'd learned from the guerillas fighting the French in Spain. "A fine shot."

General Fitzwilliam let out another long breath, some of the tension going, though he still needed to escape the murder scene and safely return to Cambrai, and his half-brother and his duties. "One of my better efforts," he said, as the two of them hurried out of the hunting blind, walking through the denser parts of the forest. They went directly away from where the soldiers and the excitement was still audible. "Did I ever tell you of the times I hunted with Lord Lachglass? On this estate. We once shot at deer from this very hunting blind. Lachglass was an excellent shot,

160

but he preferred to wing the birds to killing them, so they'd suffer before they died. It was my first realization — something was rotten in his soul."

"A fine shot on your part, sir. Ye made a fine shot."

"I should have done this years ago. Years and years ago."

They reached the stream that General Fitzwilliam remembered from hunting on his uncle's estate so many years ago, and the two of them used a bar of soap they'd packed with them to wash off all the residue of the powder from the gunshot.

"How does my disguise look?"

"Perfect, General. Perfect."

Chapter Twenty-Three

A drizzle fell from the sky when Elizabeth, Darcy and the soldiers returned to Brighton that evening with Mrs. Bennet and Kitty. Jane and her husband, and Mary and the Gardiners had independently decided to come to Brighton after receiving the letters Elizabeth and Darcy had sent out describing what had happened and the portion of their plans that was not illegal.

Elizabeth's stomach still ached with the after echo of her fear, and she did not think she would ever forget the fear of those minutes, or the sense of terror she felt as Lord Lachglass's gun turned towards her.

Jane ran out of from under the porch where she stood with the rest of them as soon as she saw the group arrive, followed by Lydia, Mary and Mr. and Mrs. Gardiner.

Mr. Gardiner embraced his sister.

Mama had not entirely recovered from the shock she had suffered, and every few minutes she profusely thanked Mr. Darcy, and the soldiers, and everyone else. Elizabeth had the impression that she did not understand that it was not one of the soldiers who shot Lord Lachglass.

Kitty had recovered from her own shock more easily than Elizabeth ever would have expected her to, and after they had mostly cleaned the blood off her dress she had been fairly amiable and almost cheerful as they had walked back to the carriages. She talked a great deal with Captain Dilman, curious about how Lydia did, and about a brother-in-law she had not yet met.

Except... there was something in Kitty's eyes, something that was in all their eyes. It had been a desperate and frightening situation, and that they would all survive had been by no means a sure thing.

Everyone talked, and Colonel Pike asked what happened, and Captain Dilman gave his report, and they went into the drawing room, where the housekeeper provided them tea. Colonel Pike claimed to be a confirmed and permanent bachelor, though perhaps he was less confirmed than he pretended, as he glanced at Mary from the side as he said that.

They had been all talking while they waited.

Everyone talked; the Gardiners' fortunes had been improving of late, for while prices everywhere were still depressed, business matters were not so bad as they had been immediately after the end of the war. Darcy spoke to Jane's husband a great deal, who Elizabeth could tell he liked.

It was a crowded party that was happy for the most part.

After a while the rain stopped, and Elizabeth needed some air, so she stepped out with Darcy onto the porch. She learned back into his arms and he held her snugly and tight. He kissed the top of her hair, and once more, and then again. She relaxed deeper and deeper, the terror and bloodshed of this morning began to seem as a distant past, something gone, forever.

The sun was setting, turning the sky brilliant reds and oranges and crimson, and there was a rich smell of vegetal growth everywhere, and the white seabirds flew high in the sky, squawking and flapping their wings.

The stooped beggar with the scar on his neck shuffled along the road in front the colonel's house again, and he turned to look at them and he smiled. And Elizabeth and Darcy smiled back at General Fitzwilliam, and then in his disguise he shuffled away towards the ship that would take him back to France.

Elizabeth and Darcy kissed again, smiling at each, squeezing each other tight, and feeling how they were well and alive. And then they went back inside, to rejoin the rest of their family.

*****

General Fitzwilliam was snuck by the guard at the door to his rented house in Cambrai into his own room. The guard was partially in on the conspiracy, and his eyes silently asked a question that he had too much decorum to directly ask upon seeing his general. However General Fitzwilliam's grin showed him clearly that the result of his quest had been a success.

Of course no one outside of General Fitzwilliam, his brother and Fergus knew *precisely* what he had returned in secret to England to do. But everyone who knew Major Williams had been in the bed pretending to be both General Fitzwilliam and ill, could make fairly good guess. But all these men were military veterans who had seen General Fitzwilliam in his old days as a colonel lead them bravely under fire, with presence of mind and a sharp tactical skill.

General Fitzwilliam quietly padded his way into his room where his half-brother lay on the bed with a thin sheen of sweat standing over his forehead, staring up at the ceiling blank eyed.

He turned his head absently and moaned piteously upon hearing the entry into the room, and then when his eyes realized that it was his brother, Fitz jumped out of the bed and threw off the covers. "Thank Jove, thank the skies, and the grounds, and everything that you are *back*."

He wore a fine silk nightshirt of General Fitzwilliam's that General Fitzwilliam rather liked. The instant Major Fitz stood, he groaned in pleasure and stretched his arms high above his head. "Jove, I could run a mile."

"You seem surprisingly happy to see me, since this is the end of your vacation."

"Vacation! Leisure. The deuce! This was no vacation. Have you ever tried, when you were entirely healthy, to lie in one place for more than a week without moving? There was a close call when the Duke stopped in for one of his inspectionchas the first day you were out, and after that we decided I must always stay near the bed prepared to look the invalid. Vacation! This was the hardest most unpleasant duty you've ever given me."

The young officer paced back and forth stretching his legs and almost growling as he worked the kinks out of his body. "A run, on foot. And then a horse gallop for a ten-mile distance, at least. At least."

"I cannot win, I tell you to lie in bed and you complain, I tell my other men to exercise and drill and they complain. You all just will not be satisfied."

"Making a man lie in a bed for ten days without break is a damned fool way to reward a man. You might use it to torture those who you want to pretend you are pleased with, but who have secretly angered you." He turned and looked at General Fitzwilliam suspiciously. "Say... I haven't done anything?"

"I'm still in too good spirits to needle you by pretending you had." General Fitzwilliam with an annoyed grunt got the last of the plastered nose off his face. "Strange that I do not feel some remorse, or sense of tragedy, or guilt, or something of that sort. My mother's nephew. My cousin. The deuce of it is, I don't feel anything of that sort. Just a solid, cold satisfaction at delivering a fine shot."

Looking almost like himself in the mirror, General Fitzwilliam pulled a heavy glass bottle from his bag and handed it to Fitz. "For you, for keeping *me* in Cambrai these last weeks. A fine cognac from Darcy's stores, so you don't need to worry about my taste in alcohol."

Fitz laughed, and unstoppered the bottle. He took sniff of it and whistled. "Very fine. How were Mr. and Mrs. Darcy?"

"Happy, and embracing each other last I saw them. Surrounded by Mrs. Darcy's family who all arrived in Brighton in time to greet their return from my cousin's estate."

Fitz poured two shot glasses full and handed one to General Fitzwilliam. "To Mr. and Mrs. Darcy."

They clinked the glasses and General Fitzwilliam drank his down. He let the rich alcohol swirl around his tongue for several seconds to savor the taste before swallowing it. Fitz sipped his slowly.

General Fitzwilliam stretched out, and laughed. "I suppose I'll need to take my turn lying in the bed, before my miraculous recovery happens."

There was a knock on the door, and the surgeon's voice called out, "It's Mr. Holmes."

Fitz and General Fitzwilliam called out at the same time, "Enter."

The surgeon bowed his way into the room. "General Fitzwilliam, you look much better, but you really should not stand around *drinking* so soon."

"I'm not going to let you bleed *me*." General Fitzwilliam laughed.

"Very kind of you, Major Williams, to call on the General as soon as you returned from your trip to Paris."

Fitz shrugged. "I had business with him."

All three men laughed. The surgeon came forward and studied the bottle on the counter. "Oh, oh my. That's a very fine bottle. Very fine."

"No!" Fitz cried. "Not after how you've tortured me the past weeks."

"I only bled you twice."

"I'm healthy, entirely healthy."

General Fitzwilliam laughed and pulled another bottle from his bag. "Mr. Darcy was quite generous with the stores he laid in for himself in Paris; I have enough for you both."

"Well, in that case." Fitz laughed and poured a third glass for the surgeon and handed it to him.

Like Fitz, Mr. Holmes savored and sipped the liquid.

"So matters in this mysterious family matter of yours that necessitated this matter…" Mr. Holmes vaguely waved his hand as he spoke. He then held up his hand. "I of course do not want you to tell *me*."

"Matters went very well."

General Fitzwilliam looked at his reflection in the mirror one last time before taking off his clothes to crawl into bed. He looked harsh and wolf like.

Family was important. Perhaps the most important thing.

Afterward:

Any book anyone writes is partly inspired by other books that he has read. I think most of you know this.

There is no such thing as isolated and pure creativity; creativity is mostly putting together mixtures of ideas that come from elsewhere. Normally an author however will not be sure quite where many of the ideas that he uses come from. They are hidden by the way memory mixes everything together and time causes you to forget lots of things.

While the rest of the story has little similarity to it, the opening scene where Elizabeth rescues herself from Lord Lechery by bashing him over the head with a vase was inspired by the opening scene of Denise Domning's excellent *Almost Perfect*, where the heroine breaks a vase over the head of a earl to rescue her sister after her father lost a bet wagering for her to become his mistress.

They think the earl is dead at first and run off, but of course he is not.

I also think there was some influence from Beth Massey's *Goodly Creatures*, which I've recommended before in these little post essays. It was one of the first P&P fan fics I ever read, and its premise involved an earl who was Colonel Fitzwilliam's cousin raping Elizabeth.

The scenes set in Paris were inspired by my memory of Victor Hugo's description of Paris in 1817 at the start of the second section of *Les Misérables*, when Hugo told the story of Fantine's last day before she was abandoned pregnant by her lover. Unfortunately, as it turned out, rereading that scene did not give me any clear idea of what Paris would have been like to wander around in 1817, because the scene turned out to be basically Victor Hugo in his fifties listing out all of the pop culture trivia he could remember from the years when he was a teenager.

On which subject, Elizabeth's comment about hoping for some poet to write a story about the Notre Dame Cathedral was of course a reference to Victor Hugo's *Notre-Dame de Paris,* which is known to English audiences as *The Hunchback of Notre Dame*, and which has been on my reread list for three years.

It was published in 1831, and Elizabeth *was* very pleased to be able to read the story about the cathedral she had wished for, written by a great poet, even though he did write it in prose.

As the chapter in *Les Misérables* titled *Paris in 1817* was *not* a guide book to Paris in 1817, I looked up an actual guide book to Paris from roughly the time period. I based the scenes in France on a book written in 1828 titled *A Guide to France, Explaining Every Form and Expense from London to Paris,* by Francis Coghlan. It was the first of a series of guidebooks written by this nineteenth century Rick Steves over the next thirty years for a variety of strange locales including Central Europe, Southern Italy, and Manchester.

The bit about Manchester is something of a joke; he actually wrote a guide in 1838 to using the railroads between Birmingham, Manchester and Liverpool, which is not actually exoticizing the northern half of England. On the other hand a book many of you have probably at least seen the excellent BBC version of Gaskell's *North and South,* a book which *does* in fact exoticize the North.

As someone who has read substantial amounts of twenty-first century travel advice, reading Coghlan's nineteenth century travel guide gave me a reverse culture shock. The travel advice of that different country which is the past sounds so *similar.* There were lists of prices, descriptions of locations and how to get in them, and the standard advice: Be careful of pickpockets and don't show off your money, and things go faster and easier if you are able to get by with just a carry on (in Coghlan's time, a single carpet bag).

I had a similar reverse culture shock when I first learned to read French, and found that the comment section of French newspapers online was exactly like the comment section on English language newspapers, except in French. On which topic, I did a fair amount of my research for the scenes in France by reading Wikipedia and academic articles in French.

For some reason the French Wikipedia is often more detailed about things in France than the English language wiki. Strange. I had not ever really expected to get a practical use out of knowing French — and I could have found out most of what I did if I only read English, but it still was fun.

I have a few further notes about the research on this book, but I'm going to interrupt your now regularly scheduled description of how I wrote my most recent book, for your even more regularly scheduled request to donate money to fight extreme poverty. So please be part of those of us who fight for a better world.

When I started writing, a major reason I wanted to write novels was that I could ask people to join me in acting to make the world a better place at the end of my books. This is why even though I changed the way I write these fundraising appeals to make them less of a downer than the ones in my first books — an example of me responding, whether for good or ill, to negative reviews — you are never going to read a Timothy Underwood novel that *doesn't* say you can make the world a better place, and that doesn't remind you that there are people who are literally dying who you can literally keep from dying.

You should feel really good about yourself if you help people who live in places far away from you, who you will never meet nor know.

I beg you from the bottom of my soul, give to a valuable cause, and make the world a better place.

Please, if you have a good job or income, donate with me to some cause, even if it isn't extreme poverty in developing nations.

Providing medical care to people who are extremely poor is probably the way that you can make the biggest difference to people who are alive today.

I am only saying what follows to give an example of what one person does to make a difference:

Last year I donated 10% of the amount I spent on housing, clothes, food, etc. I excluded from this amount money "spent" on taxes and health insurance and dentists visits and the like. Groups I hang out with on the internet probably think this is too little money, since it is less than 10% of my gross or net income, while I suspect most people would find that a rather large amount of money to donate.

Everyone needs to decide for themselves what they can comfortably do to make the world a better place, and what will not hurt themselves and their families. But you should find an amount you are comfortable giving, and you should give that amount.

Most of the money I donated went to Doctors Without Borders, which as you probably already know is an effective and transparent organization that does an enormous amount of good in war torn and conflict ridden countries. It is a good choice if you are deciding what cause to support, but not the only good choice.

So now back to talking about things I learned as I wrote my book: The way that senior officers were arranged in the British army during the Napoleonic wars frankly seems bizarre and nonsensical to me. But they did win the war, so clearly it wasn't *too* malfunctional.

The first thing that I've found some authors are confused about is not weird: Brigadier General was not a regular rank in the British army during the Napoleonic period. Instead, on occasion, regimental colonels and lieutenant colonels would be given a provisional appointment to the position of brigadier general that only applied for the duration of the conflict, and only in the theater for which the appointment was made. The reason for this was to select the commander for groups of four battalions that would be stuck together to be given a single commander. The rank of major general was the lowest permanent general's rank in the army.

This is the part that is weird to me. The British army would promote all of its lieutenant colonels as a group to the rank of full colonel — a rank that was functionally meaningless, as it had no additional pay or responsibilities. And then they would a few years later promote all of the surviving colonels to the army rank of major general — this did not mean that these officers were employed commanding large units of troops, they very possibly weren't. In some cases they might not have any military employment, as in the case of an officer who Wellington sent home from the Peninsula, and who, despite never having any active military duty again, was promoted in the next round to the rank of lieutenant general from major general.

Every regiment had a colonel of the regiment, who handled administrative duties, and did basically nothing else. And regiments were organized into separate battalions, one of which might be in Spain at the same time the other was in India, and these two battalions basically had no connection, except having the same colonel of the regiment, and both had a separate lieutenant colonel commanding them.

I *think* France was actually a safe place to flee from British law at this time. An extradition treaty was signed between Britain and France in 1842, but as far as I could find from looking through several articles on the history of extradition, there was no treaty prior to 1842 between those two countries, though France had established extradition treaties at a much earlier date with most of its neighbors, and was in fact in the eighteenth century the country that did the most to develop the practice of extradition for common crimes.

Before I came up with the plot of this novel, I'd thought there was no extradition treaty, because while doing the research several years ago for the trial following the duel in Colonel Darcy (still one of my best books! You should read it, and don't you know want to know what the duel and the trial were about?) one of the court records from the Old Bailey I read was of the trial of a man who had killed someone in a duel and fled to France.

This man stayed in France for ten years, and he was only arrested and prosecuted for murder following his return.

Honestly, the planned plot of this novel might have been very different had I *not* had that bit from that trial wandering around in the back of my head, looking for more stories to connect to. I know that it was based on that story that I simply assumed Elizabeth would be safe from British prosecution if she fled to France and stayed there, and then after having the novel half written I panicked and started looking into extradition laws, when I suddenly wasn't sure if that was actually true.

What precipitated this panic was learning from Coghlan's guide that travelers should apply for a passport to France from the French embassy that offered them for a nominal fee. I also was reminded of something that I had half learned while reading *Les Misérables* many years ago, that internal travel in France at this time required the possession of a passport which would be checked in every city the traveler went to. Of course Valjean's passport specified that he was a criminal, so everyone who he met learned that immediately.

Obviously given the panic and the manner with which they left for France, Elizabeth and Darcy would not have collected a passport from the French embassy. So I needed to figure out what would happen next. I found two accounts while reading about French passports with stories of travelers who arrived in continental countries which required passports for internal travel where they had not known they needed to acquire a passport.

One story was about Mary and Percy Shelley being surprised that passports were demanded of them when they returned to Italy in 1816, since that had not been bothered about the previous time they had travelled through the area. The other was the story of a man who arrived in the Netherlands without a passport, and had some worry about being able to go on, but this was solved according to the man's journal with the help of fellow British travelers.

Neither account specifies *how* the problem of obtaining a passport was solved.

So for my novel I assumed they used a combination of respectable appearance and bribery.

I initially began to write the proposal scene with Darcy kneeling on the floor, but then I checked if that was already a tradition. A bit of googling showed me that A) most of the answers to that question found by Google were written by freelancers who write search engine optimized blog posts for fifty dollars a pop. That is if they are particularly lucky and well paid; B) it definitely was not the thing men did until some point in the nineteenth century. I then remembered, we are told what Darcy was doing when he proposed.

He did not kneel either time he proposed, so he didn't kneel in my story either.

On a similar point, everyone is shocked when I and my wife admit that *I* did not kneel when I proposed. But it was sweet and romantic, and quite perfect. So… uh. Men contemplating the popping of the question: Kneeling is not mandatory, fight against expectations. Be romantic in your own unique individual way. By copying Darcy.

As for future Pride and Prejudice variation plans, I am afraid I don't have any P&P stories right now ready to start writing on. This novel was a rough draft I had half finished already when I returned to Mr. Bennet's Daughter a few months ago, and now that I've finished it, I need to come up with more ideas. To be honest, it will probably be at least a half year before you see another book by me, I feel like I want to take a break from P&P and work on my own settings for a while.

Thank you to everyone who read this book, and I hope you enjoyed it. Leave a review if you think it is well worth reading (or if you think it is well worth avoiding). The reviews really do help people find and read the book.

Timothy Underwood
May 2019,
Budapest

About the Author

I am from California, but currently I am living in Budapest with my wife. I first discovered Pride and Prejudice on a long day of travel out of Mexico as a teenager. I recall being very impressed with myself for getting the jokes. I read a lot of nineteenth century literature that year, of which Austen and Charlotte Bronte, of course, were my favorites. It was years later that I discovered and repeatedly binge read Pride and Prejudice fanfiction.

Now I get to add to the pile of fanfiction able to binge – and I love it when I get messages from people telling me that they are binging on my books.

If you liked this book, leave a review. It is a way of helping other people find books they liked.

I can be reached at timothyunderwood.author@gmail.com.

Made in the USA
Monee, IL
29 June 2020